PRODIGALS

PRODIGALS

ALAN DEAN FOSTER

WFP
WORDFIRE PRESS

EBook ISBN: 978-1-68057-327-5
Trade Paperback ISBN: 978-1-68057-326-8
Dust Jacket Hardcover ISBN: 978-1-68057-328-2
Case Bind Hardcover ISBN: 978-1-68057-329-9
Library of Congress Control Number: 2022936262

Cover design and artwork by MiblArt
Kevin J. Anderson, Art Director
Published by
WordFire Press, LLC
PO Box 1840
Monument CO 80132

Kevin J. Anderson & Rebecca Moesta, Publishers
WordFire Press eBook Edition 2022
WordFire Press Trade Paperback Edition 2022
WordFire Press Hardcover Edition 2022
Printed in the USA

Join our WordFire Press Readers Group for
sneak previews, updates, new projects, and giveaways.
Sign up at wordfirepress.com

DEDICATION

For the folks at MiblArt, who did this marvelous cover while working out of...Lviv. In between occasionally having to take cover in their basement

So, let's not have any more artists complaining about having to work under "difficult" conditions

—I—

Morning, Dev."

"Good morning, Charlie." Slipping the brown leather strap off his shoulder, Devali Mukherjee let his satchel slide gently down onto his desk. Slender as he was, it slid off easily. Regular cardio sessions at the gym together with running in the city parks kept him trim and fit, if not muscular. Settling into his seat, he leaned back and contemplated infinity— alongside his much paler friend's currently fashionable unshaven visage. Dev frowned. Although it was not required by his job, he took particular pride in his neatness. That meant keeping his straight black hair cut short and his beard invisible. "Anything of interest this morning?"

His colleague took a breath before beginning. "Well, the Chinese are making irritated noises about some components of the last aid package we promised to Vietnam, suicide bombing at an international school in Lahore killed a security guard plus the two bombers, the Mapuche Resistance Front is still threatening to pull out of the peace talks we've been brokering in Santiago, and the Chinese-Taiwan talks seem to be making some progress even if the pace makes a snail race look like the Indy 500. Oh, and one more thing." Pulling down the hem of his white shirt so that it once more fully covered his belly he paused for effect, though considering the nature of the news it was unnecessary. "At 02:47 this morning, a giant alien spacecraft appeared over Panama."

Dev offered a thin smile as he methodically unpacked his laptop. "I know it is early, and it is Friday, but is that the best you can do?" It struck him that Charlie did not smile back.

"No, I can do better than that." His white-shirted colleague nodded at Dev's desk. "Turn on your computer. Go to any channel. Doesn't have to be all-news. Everybody's carrying the same feeds."

Dev hesitated, smiled afresh, then frowned. Straightening in the chair, he entered his initial security clearance for the day. Another screen appeared, featuring a fresh request. Upon receiving the second requisite security code, the monitor flashed to life. Most of it was currently occupied by a very famous female news anchor. She was speaking rapidly and sweating profusely. Muting the sound automatically brought up the equivalent text at the bottom of the screen. Occupying much of the tropical sky behind her was either a superimposed special effect from a big budget fantasy film or something the approximate length and width of New York's Central Park. A glistening charcoal gray that resembled rough cut marcasite, it hung suspended among the clouds, looking like a gigantic conglomeration of recently mined druzy that somehow was richly illuminated from within.

Dev stared at it, unaware that several billion other inhabitants of the planet were at that moment doing exactly the same thing. Among the several billion, those who were not panicking were mostly silent. He did not know that for certain, of course, but on remembrance it struck him that the fourth-floor complex where he worked had been unusually quiet when he had exited the elevator. He hadn't thought about it at the time because a little uncommon quietude did not galvanize the senses in the same way as, say, an exploding terrorist bomb accompanied by panicked shrieking. Now that he looked back on it, he realized that the usual stir of activity, the background susurration of idle chatter, had been entirely absent.

Rising, Dev moved to stand behind his friend. If it was an office gag, a clever prank, then it was also playing full time on Charlie's monitor. He looked around. Everyone else was similarly glued to their respective desk screens. No one was glancing in his direction and giggling. He was forced to concede the possibility, perhaps even the likelihood, that it was not a joke. That he, and everyone else in his immediate vicinity, was presently witness to Something Momentous.

"Have they made contact?" He found himself whispering without knowing why.

"According to all the reports that have been verified thus far, the visitors haven't done anything." Charlie's initial insouciance had given way to a deepening solemnity. "That's assuming there's anything definable as 'visitors' inside. Aside from what hints at internal illumination, there's nothing to indicate that the object is tenanted. There's already been a lot of speculation to the effect that it's nothing more than a mechanical drone, perhaps some sort of scientific probe. It was first picked up by a bunch of amateur as well as professional sky searchers when it materialized inside the orbit of Mars." Charlie glanced back at his colleague. "You know: those folks who spend hours looking for new comets and asteroids. It came straight toward Earth at a whacking great velocity, apparently sending everybody's air defense systems into spasms as soon as it got close enough for them to detect it. We've received one report claiming that in the ensuing confusion the Russians shot down one of their own satellites. Before anybody's systems could get into serious defense mode, it hit the brakes and stopped right where you see it." He gestured at the monitor. "There it sits, or hovers, rather. Not moving, not communicating, doing nothing except frightening the bejeezus out of folks."

Not sharing his coworker's fatalistic sense of humor, Dev was furiously conjuring his own opinion. "If it's an autonomous probe, it's doing its work peacefully."

"So far. Interesting choice of positioning. Why Panama?"

"With luck we may find out."

Charlie made a rude noise. "With luck we may not."

Dev eyed his friend disapprovingly. "The greatest encounter in the history of humankind, and you just want it to finish its work and go away? Aren't you the least bit curious about its purpose? Its ultimate intentions?"

"Yes," Charlie admitted. "But I'm more scared than I am curious."

Fifteen minutes or so passed, during which an assortment of pundits pontificated on screen and the alien object maintained its attitude of doing absolutely nothing. At the end of the highly uninformative quarter hour, two men appeared and approached the desk. Neither Dev nor Charlie recognized them. Proof that they were not native to the fourth floor was evident from their apparel. Instead of open-necked shirts of varying hue and sleeve length, they wore dark suits, white shirts, and dark ties. Their shoes were dark, their socks were dark, and their expressions were dark. All that was missing, Dev thought, were the dark glasses. Those probably resided in inside jacket pockets, waiting for the right moment to be extracted.

Stopping beside the desk, they looked both its owner and Dev up and down.

"Which one of you is Devali Mukherjee?" Before Dev could reply, Charlie spoke up.

"Who wants to know?"

By way of reply, the nearest of the two visitors removed a small wallet from an interior breast pocket and flipped it open. Charlie and Dev stared at it. When the wallet's owner felt they'd had sufficient time to assess the contents, he snapped it shut and returned it to its resting place. Dev responded.

"I'm Mukherjee. You couldn't tell by looking at us?"

"We don't work that way," the other visitor said. He took a step forward. "We need you to come with us, Mr. Mukherjee."

Someone released a couple of butterflies in Dev's stomach. "Am I under arrest or something? Do I need to call my lawyer?"

"You're not under arrest." The second speaker made an effort to smile. It didn't do much for the seriousness of his expression, Dev thought, but at least the man tried. "But we do need you to come with us."

Far less reticent than his colleague, both due to his slightly pugnacious nature and also the fact that he wasn't being asked to go anywhere, Charlie straightened in his chair and raised his voice.

"Why should he go with you anywhere? Because you flashed some Federal ID? Where are you taking him?" Attracted by the commotion, several other operatives tore their attention away from their monitors to look curiously in the direction of the confrontation.

Unhappy at the sudden attention, the first agent lowered his voice. "It's a matter of national security. That's all I can tell you. As for destination, we're going to the Pentagon."

Dev started slightly. "I'll guess: this involves the alien craft?"

"National security. I can't say anything more." The agent took a breath, sighed it out. "Truthfully, Mr. Mukherjee, the two of us don't know anything more. We're transport; that's all."

Dev nodded and stepped around the desk toward them. Charlie looked alarmed. "What is this? Dev, you don't have to go with these guys!"

"I know." He smiled reassuringly. "But I think I want to. I will call you and Mary tonight, to let you know that everything is okay."

"You'd better." Charlie looked on with concern as the three men started for the elevators, the two visitors flanking his friend. "If I don't hear from you, I'll...." He broke off.

What would he do?, Charlie wondered. Notify the media? He'd likely lose his position, or at least risk a demotion. He wasn't in Dev's place. Unlike Mukherjee, he had a wife and three kids. Dev wasn't married. As far as Charlie knew, he didn't even have a steady girlfriend. A myriad of thoughts whirlpooled in his head.

Did that lack of extant intimate relationships have anything to do, perhaps, with why the two agents had taken Dev and not him?

————

The ride from downtown DC should have been relaxing. The April weather was exquisite, cool as the sheets in a baby's crib. Strollers dressed in their spring best wandered the streets of the capital, though many betrayed a tendency to quickly glance skyward every so often. Despite the arrival that now completely dominated the news there were no signs of panic. Everyone knew of the alien visitant hovering in the sky above Central America, but no one knew anything about the ship or its possible contents. Under such circumstances, what else could the inhabitants of a major metropolitan area do but go about their business? At least, those that hadn't been semi-abducted by phlegmatic government agents.

From the rear, the Pentagon's neo-classical architecture was as utilitarian as the rest of the building. It was the absence of greenery, he told himself as the driver pulled up to the entrance, got out, and opened the door on his side. There was no topiary here at the back. Missing were the neatly trimmed lawn and hedges that softened the look of the main entrance. Neither of his escorts spoke as they flanked him on the way toward the colonnaded entrance.

Identification was flashed both as they entered and numerous times thereafter. Lying in wait, a silent electric transport cart whisked them deep into the building. The endless corridors were not new to Dev. He had been inside several times before, all on work-related matters. Though his escorts offered not a word, not a clue as to the reason behind his visit, Dev suspected that his current visitation was not social.

The cart halted before a doorway that was identified by a number and the name of some brave, otherwise long-forgotten warrior. Sliding off the cart, his escorts went with him as far as the portal. One presented his ID to the armed guard standing to the left of the entrance. Taking it, the soldier passed it over a readout, then handed it back. There was no beep, no flash of lights, but the door opened. A middle-aged woman clad in severe black relieved only by the carved topaz rose hanging from a gold chain around her neck regarded him expressionlessly. Reflecting an absence of vanity, her short hair was gray bordering on silver. Her stare was penetrating—killer grandma.

"You are Devali Mukherjee?"

"None other." He offered a broad smile. It was not reciprocated.

"Come with me."

He turned to bid his courteous but uninformative escorts goodbye, but they were already gone, having vanished into the bowels of the gigantic building as quietly as they had arrived. With a slight shrug he turned to follow the woman who had offered the perfunctory greeting.

They passed through an outer office occupied by half a dozen or so desks behind which solemn-faced functionaries worked intently at monitors and keyboards. Not one of them glanced up as he passed. Another doorway loomed ahead. That was hardly unexpected. That it was flanked by two more armed guards was unusual. His guide pushed through, stepped to one side, and indicated that he should enter.

The half dozen or so civilians in the conference room were chatting energetically with an equal number of uniformed men and women. Arguing vociferously, an Air Force colonel appeared about to come to blows with a Navy admiral. Two extremely well-dressed seniors were gesturing repeatedly at a tablet screen while talking so rapidly that Dev couldn't make sense of anything they were saying. Feeling increasingly alone and out of place, he stood there until a slim, tall, pleasant-faced gentleman with a beard the color of Carrara marble came over and took his hand.

"Mr. Mukherjee, yes?"

Dev gripped the proffered fingers. "Yes. You—you're Walter

Davidson, aren't you? Special Assistant for Science to the Office of the President?"

The man nodded. "Please come in. I'm very glad you were able to join us."

Dev looked back the way he had come. The door behind him had long since closed. "It seems I had more free time from work than I thought when I got up this morning."

Davidson's expression turned somber. "I'm afraid for the foreseeable future none of us is going to have much free time."

"I'm NASA's point man in Washington." Dev didn't try to emphasize his role. Not in this room. "You're the advisor to the president on scientific matters." He indicated the talkative assemblage. "We're here to discuss the alien visitor?"

"Not exactly." Davidson guided him toward an empty chair at the big conference table. "We're to try and decide what to do about it."

They were halfway through a preliminary briefing on the basics of First Contact when the Air Force colonel put down his phone. Dev had noticed the man deep in conversation with the Navy and Army representatives but was too engrossed in the general briefing to wonder about it.

"Excuse me. Everyone, quiet, please." Conversation around the table quickly ceased. "For those of you who haven't met me yet, I'm Colonel Jefferson Lackland." He looked directly over at Dev. "I've just been talking with your people at Houston. There's been some contact there."

Before Dev had a chance to react, a woman seated at the table responded.

"Chiasa Katou-Zimmer here, consultant. That was unexpected. Whoever they are, they don't waste time on formalities." The woman who spoke was of Asian heritage, but her accent was all California. Japanese American, Dev guessed. Short and slightly plump, she wore contacts that turned her eyes an unexpected violet. Though he could not see beneath the businesslike blouse and pants, a hint of bright color at both her wrists suggested the presence of unseen full sleeve tattoos. "Contact by organics, or by the artifact itself?"

Looking across at her, the officer didn't hesitate. "Organics. Aliens."

For a second time, Dev's considered response was preempted, this time by the man seated next to the forthright woman.

"Jakob Zimmer. Consultant. How do we know that?" Like the woman who had spoken, the man seated beside her hailed from somewhere south of sixty. He was the very image of a tenured university professor: laid-back demeanor, solid color bow tie, hand-knit sweater, high forehead, graying hair, and a slight supercilious curl of the lip suggesting that he was certain he was the smartest person in the room. Only the earring hanging from his left earlobe implied there might be more to him than the purely conventional.

"They've sent pictures," the colonel told him.

As with her predecessors in intercession, Dev didn't recognize Diana Pavesi when she spoke up. She was short, stout, and very blonde, with multiple ear piercings that were currently filled with an assortment of tiny silver animal icons. Black skirt and the chromatic flush of floral designs that enlivened her blouse completed his impression of someone good enough at their job to be able to ignore office convention. "Can we see them? When can we see them? What do they look like?"

"Humanoid?" Katou-Zimmer's query was openly hopeful. For such a stocky woman, Dev thought, the dynamic consultant had a voice so unexpectedly sweet it would have done a nightingale proud. It fell slightly. "Cephalopodan? Amorphous?"

"I have no idea." The colonel pocketed his phone. "NASA is not releasing any images yet. Not to anybody." He glanced at the CIA representative, who nodded in concurrence. "You'll have a chance to see for yourself tomorrow. The four of you and Gavin Reed other have been designated the official contact team. You're going to Houston. Tonight."

Katou-Zimmer frowned. "Doesn't give us much time to pack."

"You don't need to pack anything. Anything you want or need, just ask for it when you get to Houston and it'll be provided. Clothes, hygienic items, anything. As long as it doesn't violate protocol or security."

The gravity of the moment notwithstanding, the increasing solemnity in the room was beginning to weigh on Dev. "Money?" he ventured.

If the colonel recognized the humor, he still replied without smiling. "If you want. Anything. Although that's not likely to be of much use to you until—after."

"After what?" Jakob Zimmer demanded to know.

"After whatever ensues. Friendly relations, indifference, the end of the world as we know it: money might not be at the top of anyone's requests."

"It's already the end of the world as we know it." Pavesi said it so softly that only Dev overheard her.

"Any other questions?" It had been evident from the first that Colonel Lackland was not a man to waste time. Individual personality traits aside, the rush to action concerned Dev.

"Yes. There are people I'd like to …" He hesitated.

Lackland finished for him. "Say goodbye to? Explain what's going on? Not possible. You can't tell anyone where you're going or what you'll be doing. From the moment you leave this room anything you do or say will be considered an issue of national security and subject to all appropriate restrictions and penalties. When you get to Houston, you'll be met by people with whom you can broach matters of personal interest." There was a modicum of sympathy in his voice as he addressed Dev directly. "Once all of you arrive, Mr. Mukherjee can probably answer some of your general questions. He works for NASA and will know his way around the Center." Not knowing how else to respond, Dev nodded in confirmation of the obvious.

He was not the only one curious as to the reason for such haste. "What's the hurry?" Katou-Zimmer wondered aloud.

"Why can't we have a day to gather ourselves? To prepare, at least just a little."

"There is some preliminary research that, if we are given time to do it, might help in facilitating initiating formal contact," her husband declared. "Materials that might usefully be perused, even in haste."

"You can request they be given to you when you're on the plane that's waiting for you," Lackland told him. "Anything you want can be downloaded before you depart, or while you're in the air." The Colonel's gaze shifted to Katou-Zimmer. "As for the rush, it seems we're not the only ones the visitors are interested in talking to. They have made arrangements to meet contact teams elsewhere besides outside Houston."

"Where? Gavin Reed, consul—team member." Speaking for the first time, the fifth member of the contact group had a deep voice and spoke with a precision that had clearly been well-prac-ticed. College debater, Dev mused. Maybe an ex-lawyer. Not quite big enough or fast enough to be a professional football player, not tall enough to be a professional basketball player, and too smart to try and build a short career out of getting banged around by others less intelligent than himself. Lawyer, maybe, though that vocation didn't fit the need at hand. Whatever the visitors wanted it was unlikely to involve formal litigation. Dev decided that Gavin Reed, regardless of his actual vocation, looked wholly competent.

Lackland turned his attention to Reed. "Near Moscow. Also Brussels and Beijing."

The United States, Russia, the European Union, and China, Dev thought. The four great world powers. That was surely no coincidence. It suggested that the aliens had been studying human culture and society for a while. For how long? That was just one of a thousand questions he wanted to put to the visi-tors. He hoped he would have the opportunity to ask at least a couple of them. Meanwhile, he had one more query for the increasingly impatient Lackland, who by now was plainly eager to be rid of them, send them on their way, and be freed of the responsibility of preparing them for their upcoming endeavor.

"One last thing, Colonel. Why us?" He indicated his fellow civilians. "Why we five?"

Before Lackland could reply, the Army representative spoke up. "You've all been carefully vetted, at least as thoroughly as we could, given the intense time pressure. Being NASA's main man in Washington, the choice of you, Mr. Mukherjee, should be obvious. Ms. Pavesi has an eidetic memory, or as near as one can have these days, and is a long-term government employee. She will record everything you see, say, and do in the event the visitors do not allow electronic devices in their presence. Mr. Reed is an ex-SEAL who has spent time in more countries than any of us here will ever visit. He is a—military analyst. Dr. Jakob Zimmer is a linguist of world renown and his wife, Dr. Katou-Zimmer, an anthropologist whose reputation matches or exceeds that of her husband." He managed a slight smile. "I don't know these things for a certainty: I'm only restating the information that has been provided to me.

"One more thing," the Colonel added. "None of you three— Mr. Mukherjee, Mr. Reed, or Ms. Pavesi—are married or living in an ongoing relationship. None of you including the Zimmers have any ex-spouses or children. Other individuals besides the five of you, some with more impressive credentials, were considered for this enterprise. One reason many others were rejected was because it was decided that external personal entanglements might prove potentially detrimental to the work."

And because if we end up dying in the course of 'this enterprise,' Dev told himself, *there will be fewer if any to mourn our termination.* But he didn't voice his concern. Doing so would have accomplished nothing. It certainly wouldn't have swayed the opinion of any of the military or government functionaries in the room. He and his quartet of companions had been nominated, voted on, and suborned to positions of importance they could not resign. Not that he wanted to decline. But he would have liked the opportunity to say goodbye to a few friends, and to the stray cat he fed daily outside his building. He knew someone would take care of the cat. As for his friends, they would doubtless manage without him.

Before they departed, Lackland and the others in the room each came to shake the hands of the newly designated contact team. Frozen smiles were much in evidence as the representatives of both the military and the government wished the team members good luck. It was plain that each and every one of the well-wishers was greatly relieved that they were staying in Washington. In their case, Dev understood, a sense of self-preservation far outweighed any individual curiosity they might have regarding the appearance and motives of the visitors.

———

Given its luxurious interior, the plane had likely been hastily commandeered from a private individual or aircraft rental firm. There were real beds with full linen, and soft lighting, and a pair of attendants who silently and smilingly provided food, drink, and anything else requested. The five members of the newly anointed First Contact team were the only passengers. The pilots did not come back to introduce themselves or see how their passengers were doing.

Dev found himself sitting up in the seat next to his bed. Across from him, Gavin Reed was peering out one of the ports on his side of the aircraft. Turning, he leaned slightly to look across the aisle and out Dev's window. His size meant he did not have to lean far. He nodded, then gestured toward the nearest port.

"Have a look. It's Devali, right?"

"Everyone calls me Dev." Turning, he put his face close to the nearest window. Outside, beyond the blinking light on the tip of the starboard wing, could be seen two pairs of additional lights. Reed's voice reached him.

"F-22s. I've got a pair on my side as well. We're being well looked after." Rising from his seat, he began removing his clothes, undressing down to his underwear. Without having been summoned, a flight attendant appeared to hand him a precisely folded set of pajamas. In his size. "I'm going to get some sleep. Suggest you do so as well. No telling what tomorrow will bring. That's one thing I learned right away as a traveler. Eat and sleep when you can because you never know when the next opportunity to do either will materialize."

Dev accepted his own set of sleeping attire and, less ostentatiously, dressed himself for slumber. Finding himself unable to turn off his thoughts, he asked for and received a pair of books on the list that had been printed out and placed on his bed along with a trio of chocolates and an elegantly printed page of things not to do while on board. Scanning the book list, he saw that someone had done their research, however hurriedly. Settling down with one of the tomes, he adjusted the flexible light that arced over the bed and dove in. It was well into the late-night hours before the last words tripped off his consciousness and he was able to sleep.

———

Considering that the end of the world might be nigh, Dev was in a good mood the following early morning. Never one to sleep well on a plane, he'd managed to sideline both the excitement and the tension he was feeling long enough to grab a couple of hours of actual rest on the comparatively short flight to Houston. In fact, everyone on the team (he had by now come to think of it as a team) had succeeded in grabbing at least a modicum of shuteye, perhaps because they were all experienced travelers. It stood them in good stead as they were led to a pair of waiting black SUVs.

A major tourist destination, the Johnson Space Center was surrounded by every manner of accommodation from cheap motels to five-star resorts. Hoping to be ensconced in one of the latter, Dev was as surprised as any of them when the vehicles that had picked them up at Ellington Field instead drove straight to the Center. Turning off Ellington, they followed Fourth Street south until it dead-ended near JSC Building 7. At just after 4:00 AM, the area was deserted. Doubtless the absurdity of the hour had been deliberately chosen to mask their arrival as much as possible.

Gripping the handle of her carry-on bag, Pavesi came over to him. "You're the NASA guy. Where are we?"

More than a little disoriented himself, he finally pointed westward. "The Kraft Mission Control Center is over there, across the park."

Her frown was visible in the isolated light that scarcely illuminated nearby structures. "'Park?'"

"Yes. There are trees and trails, fountains and ponds. It's a place for employees to relax, have something to eat and, hopefully, brainstorm." His lips tightened as he surveyed their surroundings. He had some idea why they might be dropped off here before daybreak, but not why there would be no one to meet them.

Behind them, the pair of SUVs came to life. Their drivers and escorts offered neither explanation nor words of encouragement as they made the U-turn that would take them back up Fourth Street.

As soon as they were out of sight, a single figure appeared from within the nearest building. She was walking fast as she came toward them, in little mincing steps like a constipated ballet dancer.

"I'm Ariana Townsend. I'll be your host and intermediary while you're here." Her attention went immediately to Dev. "Dr. Devali Mukherjee?"

He extended a hand. "I don't think we've met."

"We haven't." She grinned meaningfully. "You know the Center. Impossible to know everyone. Especially if you operate in different orbits."

While acknowledging the hoary pun, he did not comment on it. "I'm in public relations and congressional advocacy."

"I know. I'm with Services."

"What kind of services?" Katou-Zimmer asked.

"Right now, making you comfortable. You still have some time to sleep before this afternoon."

"What's this afternoon?" Reed inquired.

She looked up at him, having to crane her neck to do so. "You meet the aliens. Everything's been arranged."

"That's fine, that is." Zimmer looked like a man who very badly wanted a cigarette. "We're supposed to be the contact team. Why haven't we been informed before now?"

"Because," Townsend replied patiently, "the place and time of the meeting were only finalized a couple of hours ago. Please come with me." Turning, she led them toward the park. They followed, the Zimmers murmuring between themselves, Pavesi and Reed silent, Dev wondering if they were going to be expected to sleep out in the open on benches.

Once within the park boundary, Townsend proceeded to lead them off the paved path they were on and out across an open swath of grass. Upon reaching a cluster of trees she removed a small, round disc from a pocket and spoke into it. In the middle of the grove, a medium-sized oak promptly tilted backward to reveal a set of steps leading down. Dev, who thought he knew every inch of the Space Center complex, was as impressed as the rest of his colleagues.

One short flight down, they found themselves in a small concrete-walled chamber devoid of ornamentation save for lights gleaming inside transparent fire- and bomb-proof boxes. The elevator before them was just big enough to hold everyone and their minimal luggage. As he entered, Dev noticed buttons on the control panel for four floors. Only the first and second were flattered with numbers, leaving him to wonder what might inhabit the lowermost, unnumbered levels.

Following a rapid descent, they exited to find themselves facing a desk behind which was seated a young man wearing the expression of the deeply earnest. He and Townsend exchanged words and something unseen, whereupon the large door behind him, driven by a dead-silent motor, opened to admit the arrivals to a T-junction. Taking the left one, their guide halted before a much smaller desk. The woman seated behind it rose to greet them, her smile Texas wide and apparently genuine. It was a relief after all the solemn expressions Dev had encountered over the course of the past twelve or so hours. She looked like a small-town ex-beauty queen.

"You can call me Daisy." Not, he noted, "My name is Daisy." Just, "You can call me."

"I'll be here until 8:00 AM Hopefully you'll all still be sleeping when Lily, my replacement, arrives." *To be followed by Rose, no doubt,* Dev thought dryly. She gestured down the corridor that stretched away behind her desk. "You'll find everything you need in your rooms. If there's anything else you require, use the intercom."

"Food?" Reed asked tersely. "Not now. Breakfast." *He really is a man of few words,* Dev mused.

"There are menus in your rooms. Order whatever you like, whenever you want. Or you can eat together later."

"Right now I'd settle for a shower," Pavesi told her.

"In your room."

Zimmer voiced a thought. "You said 'menus.' As in, printed menus?"

Their hostess nodded. "We try to keep the use of electronics down here to a minimum. Security."

Dev glanced over at Reed. "So no one can hack into your breakfast choices."

The taller man stared back at him. Then, realizing that they were going to have to work together, he proffered the most humorless smile Dev had ever seen.

"Funny. Yes, amusing."

Don't hurt yourself with hysterics, Dev thought. He decided that being on the same team as Gavin Reed might present some difficulties. On the other hand, if things were to devolve into hostilities, Reed would be the first man Dev would choose to hide behind.

His room was small but surprisingly plush. Concurring with

Pavesi's choice, he luxuriated in a long, hot shower. Delighted to see that tea was available alongside the expected coffee, he availed himself of a cup of Darjeeling first blush and settled in to watch an all-news channel. Apparently the restrictions on electronics did not extend to closed-circuit systems bringing in signals from well outside.

Understandably, the news remained dominated by talk of the alien visitors. Assorted pundits of widely variant qualifications engaged in all manner of speculation. As for the general public, reaction varied across the expected sociological spectrum, from delirious wide-eyed hopefuls anticipating the dawn of a golden age of human-alien cooperation to heavily weaponized survivalists in full-blown cackling I-told-you-so mode. There were so many shots of the alien craft from so many different perspectives that Dev quickly grew tired of them. Nothing was happening. Nothing would happen, apparently, until sometime much later in the day. As he set his empty cup aside and clicked off the TV, he wondered where contact was set to take place. In the park above them? Downtown Houston? He would find out soon enough.

As would the rest of humankind.

—II—

He woke to the sound of Champagne coming from concealed speakers. To be precise, Claude Champagne's *Symphonie Gaspésienne*. What was truly impressive was that Champagne was a largely unknown composer, that the piece was a favorite of Dev's, and that to the best of his knowledge he had never told anyone at the Johnson Center about his admiration for it and for the composer. But somebody knew.

What else did they know about him?

Enough, anyway, to anoint him 20 percent of the team responsible for attempting humankind's first contact with an alien species. *No, that isn't entirely accurate,* he corrected himself. To be precise, he was 20 percent the American team attempting first contact. If there was anyone in the U.S. intelligence community in a position to know what was happening outside Moscow, Beijing, or Brussels, they had yet to share that knowledge with him and his colleagues.

No time to ponder on what his counterparts on other continents might be doing, he told himself. Doubtless some of them were likewise wondering what the Americans were up to.

Sometime during the early morning, his room had been

entered while he slept, and a beige-colored jumpsuit had been laid out for him. It was accompanied by black half-boots that were soft on the inside, tough on the outside, and exactly his size. A patch with his name on it had been sewn onto the top of the jumpsuit just above the left breast pocket. Another representing NASA adorned the right shoulder. All shirt, pants, and shoe attachments were Velcro; there were no buttons, zippers, or laces anywhere. The pockets were empty.

Not long after he had concluded his morning ablutions, a soft chime came from the vicinity of his room's door. *Probably been watching us ever since we arrived,* he told himself. *While we were asleep. While we were in the bathroom.* He shrugged it off. Given the critical nature of the task immediately ahead, personal privacy was likely something that the members of the contact team had already forfeited.

The man waiting for him out in the hall offered a polite greeting, asked how he had slept, and made inoffensive but unenlightening small talk as he led Dev down the corridor. In the small dining area that was an adjunct to the nearby subterranean cafeteria he rejoined Pavesi and Reed. The Zimmers arrived a few minutes later. Dev's escort was replaced by someone new. The new man frowned at the couple as they filled their plates.

"You're late."

"We're old." Jakob Zimmer pulled out a molded plastic chair and took a seat.

Their new attendant was not so easily put off. "You're fifty-four. Your wife is fifty-two. That's not old."

"We have aspirations." Chiasa Katou-Zimmer began buttering an onion bagel.

Emerging from the compact cafeteria food preparation area, the chef doffed his toque, entered into dual duty mode, and informed them all politely but firmly, "You have twenty minutes. I'd advise less talking and more eating."

Pavesi pulled a face at Dev, who smiled slightly in return. This far south he didn't have to ask for hot sauce for his scrambled eggs. Following the chef-guard's advice he ate as quickly as he dared. The breakfast was perfectly adequate. But given the option, he would have chosen something else for a possible last meal. He missed his mother's pakoras. Hell, at that moment, he missed the mass-produced ones that could be found in the frozen ethnic foods section of his local DC market.

When the appointed time arrived, they were shepherded out of the cafeteria and down another series of corridors until the final one split into two outside a tunnel. A pair of electric carts waited there, each manned by a silent driver. As they climbed in and took seats, the ever-irrepressible Dev murmured to no one in particular, "We're going to Disney World."

Behind him, Gavin Reed responded in his gravely, irritatingly solemn tone, "It's my understanding that the aliens shoot comedians first."

Looking back at the bigger man, Dev was unable to tell if he was being serious or joking.

"I'm just trying to lighten the atmosphere."

The cart they were in started forward.

"Let's hope atmosphere doesn't become a problem." Reed sat back, crossed his arms, and looked away.

There were very few bends in the tunnel and very little conversation to accompany the journey. Only the Zimmers chatted between themselves. Following the reproach by Reed, Dev kept to himself. Pavesi likewise said nothing, but her eyes seemed to be taking the measure of every meter of tunnel.

When they came to a dead end, they found four people waiting for them. Each was dressed as if for a casual day's outing in the park: shorts, sandals, short sleeved shirts, the inevitable sunglasses. One of the young men wore a fake mariner's cap. No one shook hands with the contact team as they were led away from the tunnel and up a wide ramp. At the top, one of the women opened a locked door. Bright sunlight flooded in, and Dev had to shield his eyes. One of the escorts immediately handed him a pair of shades. As they were led out, Dev looked around in surprise at their surroundings. Pavesi commented on his reaction.

"I know where we are," he told her. "I'd come here on week-ends, sometimes, when I was working down here." Turning, he nodded back the way they had come. "Johnson Space Center over there." He pivoted toward several floating piers lined with boats that lay just ahead of them. "This is Bal Harbor Marina, on Clear Lake."

Pavesi chugged alongside as their four faux-day-tripper escorts led them forward: two in front, the other two behind. "What are we doing on a lake, do you think?"

"No idea." Again, he gestured forward. "But the lake opens up into Trinity Bay. Gulf of Mexico access from there."

The boat they boarded did not appear designed for open ocean travel. It hinted at reasonably spacious belowdecks and boasted a flying bridge, but it was no yacht.

"There are drinks and comfortable seating down below." The smiling young man who greeted them did not have to elaborate: the directive was obvious enough. Dev followed the Zimmers and Reed down the narrow stairs while Pavesi trailed behind.

As soon as the five of them were out of sight, the boat took off with a rising whine from its inboard electric motors. It took the new arrivals a couple of moments to acquire a semblance of sea legs. Since everyone else was apparently doing fine, Dev held off mentioning that he was prone to seasickness. Hopefully they wouldn't be on the water too long.

Having explored the refrigerator, he was letting some flavored sparkling water tickle his throat when Reed drew him over to a starboard side port.

"Have a look, everyone. We've got company."

Peering out, Dev saw that not one, but two fast Coast Guard response boats were paralleling their craft. Turning, he saw a third off the port side. *More military escorts,* he told himself. Just as their plane from Washington had been escorted. From their size he guessed ... he hoped ... that the water journey would not take long.

He was as relieved as he was correct. As the armed chaper-ones slowed and fell behind, their boat pulled up to a very unprepossessing wooden dock. Fashioned of cypress, it looked as if it had been there for some time and not knocked together for the occasion. There were people there to help them out. Unlike the quartet of minders who had accompanied the team from the Johnson Center, none of them wore fake weekend attire. Soldiers stood behind them, clad in full gear and shouldering weapons. A brace of Humvees were waiting where the dock kissed the land.

"Any idea where we are?" Pavesi was studying their surroundings intently.

Dev shook his head. "Not yet. Once you get out of the city, especially across the bay, everything looks alike."

The small convoy of vehicles bounced along a dirt track until it finally intersected a narrow, paved road. As they turned down it, Dev strained to look back behind them. His vision was good, and he was able to make out more soldiers, more Humvees, and what appeared to be lumps of white and orange speckling the width of the road. And a couple of tanks.

Roadblock. As they headed south, a sign came into view that identified their modest thoroughfare as Road 562. It sported a pair of recent bullet holes. A second sign supplied the distance to Smith Point.

Seated in the back, Reed leaned forward. "'Smith Point.' That the nearest town?"

"That's the only town, I think." Dev spoke without turning. "If I remember correctly, most of the land we're now traveling through is undeveloped or nature preserve."

"I would imagine," Pavesi said, "that there would be another roadblock south of here, sealing off the town. Unless contact is planned to take place in the town itself."

Something of a radical notion, Pavesi's idea was soon shot down as the convoy turned eastward onto a dirt track. The single smaller sign they encountered along the way announced, "Lake Surprise." *Either someone had a mordant sense of humor,* Dev mused, *or else it was simply a charming coincidence.*

As they exited their vehicle, he saw that the land surrounding the lake was only slightly higher than that body of water and equally flat. The expanse of marsh and grass that fronted the lake was broken only by occasional flare-ups of live oak and hickory, willow and ash, locust and hackberry. Small hawks patrolled the area, intent on rodent assassination. Walk eastward on the peninsula and a hiker would quickly end up in East Bay. Beyond that lay the thin strip of the Bolivar peninsula and beyond that, the Gulf.

It was dreary hot, desperately humid, and the earth underfoot exhibited a disconcerting tendency to squish underfoot. It was clear now why they had been provided with boots instead of ordinary footwear. As they were led toward the Teflon-flat, waveless expanse of Surprise Lake, the silence among the contact team and their escorts was broken only by the wet sucking sounds of boots being pulled from the muck. Despite the auditory incongruity, no one laughed. Dev had hoped for the encounter to take place on more solid ground. In case he had to run.

Raising his gaze from the GPS he held, one of the escorts halted and said simply. "Here. Stop."

Everyone complied. Except for the Zimmers, who kept up a constant murmuring between themselves, a kind of acoustic telegraph, no one said anything. Dev thought up several amusing observations to lighten the mood only to discard them one by one. It just wasn't the time. Humanity's first contact with an intelligent alien species demanded that levity be set aside. This was difficult for him, but he managed.

The appearance of the arriving alien contact craft made it easier.

In mass it was larger than the biggest terrestrial aircraft. Though the silvery, almost chrome-like exterior contrasted with the somewhat darker gray of the main ship, Dev doubted the lighter coloration was in any way indicative of its occupants' intentions. Pale blue, perhaps, might have signified something akin to optimism. Or candy-striping.

Or they might not, he told himself firmly. He was anthropomorphizing. In the litany of alien responses, bright colors might signify hostile intent. This was not the occasion in which to engage in cultural presuppositions.

In general appearance, the body of the alien craft resembled half an ovoid lying on its side with blisters of varying dimensions erupting from its curving flanks and top. Emitting a steady red glow, the flat underside was pebbled like a golf ball. Several long, narrow shapes extended from the more tapered end of the vessel, though whether they indicated its front or back Dev could not say. These also drew Reed's attention. He leaned in close and whispered.

"Those long, pointed protrusions?"

"I see them," Dev murmured back.

"Antennae? Scanning probes?" The big man hesitated. "Guns? Some other kind of weapon?"

"Maybe they're barbecue skewers." Seeing the look on Reed's face, Dev hastened to add, "I'm just pointing out that since we know nothing of their technology, it's futile as well as unwise to make hasty ungrounded assumptions. Maybe we'll find out when they land. If they serve any of the purposes that you mentioned, I suspect we will find out." He frowned at a sudden thought. "What are your people going to do if they are guns and their owners prove openly hostile? We're all unarmed here."

"Not entirely." Reed did not explain. What he did say was, "If I told you how much sophisticated ordnance is presently trained on the big ship hovering in near orbit, the smaller one that's coming down now, and this particular piece of Texas dirt that we're standing on, it might raise your heart rate to dangerous levels."

Dev swallowed. Looking around, all he could see besides the contact group, the waiting vehicles on the road behind them, and the descending alien vessel were trees, grass, birds, and bugs. Anything lethal that had been emplaced in the immediate vicinity was well camouflaged.

"This *particular* piece?" he mumbled.

A somber Reed nodded. "No relatives, remember? Everything is done for a reason. Everyone is chosen for a reason. A multiplicity of reasons."

Dev looked back at him. "You too? But even knowing that, you still volunteered, knowing that we might—that things might not end well?"

Reed pursed his lips and gave a little shrug. "I've been all over the world, Mukher … Dev. Dozens of countries, dozens of firefights. I've seen too much death to be frightened of the prospect. Respectful, yes: frightened, no. Of course, if I die here today, the military will lose a singular asset."

"There's something singular about you?" an expressionless Dev inquired.

A twitch that threatened to become an actual smile toyed with the corners of Reed's mouth. Or it might have been just a nervous tic. "As far as I know, I'm the only member of the US military who raps while playing the bagpipes. My heritage is kind of a soup."

"What are you two mumbling about?" Pavesi edged over to join them. As the shortest member of the group, and moderately overweight as well, she'd had a more difficult time than most slogging across the saturated soil. Dev felt for her.

Straightening, Reed raised a hand to shield his eyes from the sun as he returned his attention to the alien ship. "Nothing. Wondering what's going to happen, that's all."

Pavesi joined him and Dev in turning their gazes upward. "We'll know soon enough. Whatever it is."

Given the level of technology demonstrated by the visitors thus far, perhaps what followed should have been expected. Dev was nonetheless surprised when the alien craft made contact with the first grasses, settled into the sedge, and stopped before it could become immersed in muck. While the red glow from its underside vanished, the ship continued to hover just above the water level. A portal opened in the side. Or more properly, a portal-sized opening appeared in the hull. There was no movement, no raising of a door or sliding aside of a barrier. One moment the flank of the craft was solid; the next, an oval portion of it had vanished.

Two shapes emerged.

The one in front was the same height as Chiasa Katou-Zimmer: a little over five feet. What Dev could see of the pale, whitish body was broad and cylindrical with no visible segmentation save for the head. This hairless blob sat on a short flexible neck. Two oval orange eyes with bright golden slits for pupils were fixed forward. Two smaller, vestigial orbs above them suggested the presence of a more primitive pair of light-gathering organs. A single visually attractive piece of gold-hued material enclosed the body. Less engaging was the sight of small things moving about slowly beneath the fabric. He considered asking Pavesi for her opinion about this quease-inducing observation but decided there was not enough time for her to give a proper reply. Also, he wasn't sure he wanted to know.

Two tentacles emerged from each side of the body. Darker in hue than the rest of the alien flesh, they boasted multiple black bands whose greasy luster reminded Dev of licorice. The alien walked on these, the spatulate ends of the tentacles apparently far less fragile than they appeared. Differently shaped devices hung from its neck, jiggling slightly as it approached. There was no sign of anything resembling a recognizable weapon.

That was not the case with the second alien. Bipedal and massively built, it strode along behind the quasi-cephalopod with an easy, fluid gait. Over its leathery skin it wore a suit of black and dark green material. Concave and shaped something like a communications disc, the large, wide head showed ripples and folds in the skin. The two eyes were large, round, and yellow, with tiny black dots for pupils. Ears were large, leathery, and thin. A transparent dome of a helmet covered the head, but both three-fingered hands were exposed to the air. The presence of unprotected hands and other flesh suggested that the creature was not allergic to Earth's oxygen atmosphere but that it needed something more to breathe. Or maybe, Dev surmised, the helmet provided some kind of filtration. Perhaps the creature needed less oxygen and not more. Or possibly it needed to breathe some kind of supplementary gas. The pack on its back could have served that function and more.

Below the pack, a pair of prehensile tails flicked back and forth just above the ground. At the moment they were gripping a long, tapering length of some shiny material that was dotted with lights. The narrow end of this mechanism was pointed in the direction of the contact group. In *his* direction, Dev realized. Additionally, each alien hand held a smaller device, the ends of which were similarly aimed at the humans. *They might be sensing instruments*, he told himself. Taking bio-readings, sampling the atmosphere, collecting minute airborne particulate matter. But the feeling he got from the alien's posture and from the look of the three implements, however unsupported by actual evidence, did not incline him to think they were scientific apparatus. His considered opinion was that any one of the three was much more likely to be capable of decapitating, disintegrating, or dissolving the members of the contact team where they stood.

Katou-Zimmer was speculating aloud as she studied the aliens. "Not sexual or species dimorphism. They are far too different in structure."

"Completely distinct." Pavesi, the team's other biologist, was in immediate agreement. "No structural similarity whatsoever."

"As opposed to you," the alien commented, "who exhibit all the characteristics of a uniform species."

It was possible that this wholly comprehensible response, delivered in perfect American English, shocked the members of the contact team and their escorts at least as much as the initial appearance of the alien mothership had stunned the entire human population. It was left to the alien to break the ensuing stunned silence.

"I am called Vantolos. I have communicated. Have I not made myself understood?"

His mastery of complex linguistics rendered utterly superfluous, Jakob Zimmer still felt it incumbent on him to offer the first reply. That had been the intent from the time the team had been put together. It was not expected that it would proceed with quite such a degree of ease.

"I'm—my name is Jakob Zimmer. You must excuse our initial hesitation. No one anticipated that you would speak our language." He bobbed his head slightly. "I have to compliment you on your unexpected fluency."

All four tentacles curled up and around at the creature's sides. This allowed the central trunk to drop comfortably to the ground. Having done duty as legs, the quartet of flexible limbs now served as arms. Behind the speaker, the tall, thickset biped contributed not a word. The three intimidating instruments it held remained pointed (Dev could not bring himself to think "aimed") at the members of the contact team.

"Your language is a simple one, easy to analyze and learn. Also, communication is a specialty of mine." Dev wanted to inquire as to the nature of the large, possibly armed biped's specialty but held back. "I have been designated to communicate with your species here at this location."

Uncharacteristically, it was Pavesi who spoke out. "What about the other locations? Where your other ships have come down? The ones that have appeared near three of our other major cities?"

The body did not move at all, save for whatever unpleasant small things were in motion beneath the golden material, but the smooth skull turned to look at her. The wide, narrow, toothless mouth opening flexed.

"They are conducting studies. Upon the conclusion of their investigation of their surroundings, they will return to their respective vessels. The language we are presently speaking is your dominant language of exchange, as determined by our instrumentation in the course of our approach to your world. Adjuvant studies suggest that your tribe is the dominant one utilizing this language. So it was decided to conduct the thrust of our business with you, on behalf of your entire species."

Business? Dev's thoughts whirled. Was the alien's translation entirely perfect? "Business" was not a word, not a term, he expected to be used in the course of a first contact. There was a perfunctory ring to it that he didn't like. On the other hand, if the alien was telling the truth about the other three landing craft only making observations and not being involved in promulgating actual contact, the US government would be exceedingly pleased. The Pentagon, perhaps not so much.

Zimmer extended a hand. "Whatever the future may bring, I am empowered by my government … tribal though it may be … to welcome you to Earth, in the hope that both our speci—" noting the looming presence of the second alien, he quickly adjusted his greeting accordingly "—that all of us may continue forward in a spirit of learning, friendship, and cooperation."

The one who called itself Vantolos digested this before replying. "That depends." Next to him, Dev could see Reed tensing. The big man's right hand slipped slowly into a pocket. What lay concealed within? A communication device? A recorder? A grenade?

"'Depends'?" Pavesi beat Zimmer to the response. "Depends on what?"

Oval alien eyes squinted in her direction. "On whether or not you comply, swiftly and willingly, with our demands."

Okay, an increasingly uneasy Dev told himself: while the utilization by the alien Vantolos of the word "business" had been unexpected, following it with "demands" was downright unsettling. Assuming the exchange was being relayed back to Washington, Langley, Colorado, and other important strategic locations across the country, he could imagine the effects. How was the president reacting? Would he trigger a sequence of predetermined commands, would he be consulting with congressional and military leaders, or would he be preparing to make a hasty address to the nation? Were NORAD and others making ready to attack the alien mothership? But how could they do so with any remotely reasonable hope of success without any knowledge of the aliens' military capabilities? The demonstrable fact that the visitors possessed sufficient technology to power a huge ship between star systems suggested that whatever weaponry they controlled likely consisted of something more lethal than gunpowder and flaming arrows. The trio of worrying devices being held by the larger alien hinted as much.

Glancing to his right, he hoped that if it was a grenade Reed was fondling in his pants pocket, the big man would give the situation a good deal of thought before activating and releasing it.

Easy now, he told himself. Gavin Reed had been selected to the contact team because like the rest of them he was unlikely to do anything untoward. That meant he had the ability to observe and analyze before reacting. Sure enough, Reed's hand stayed in his pocket, along with whatever resided there.

"What kind of demands?" Pavesi finally inquired.

The slitted orange eyes focused on her while the two minor oculars located above appeared to brighten slightly. "We will present you with a list tomorrow at this same time and place. It is not extensive, nor are the quantities of material demanded excessive in volume. Similar requests will be made, at the equivalent local times and places, by our contact teams operating near your other major cities."

"I see." Pavesi mulled the alien's response, uncomfortable with its brusqueness. No hint of negotiation had been mentioned. She had to ask the necessary question. "What if we refuse to comply with your demands?"

A deep rushing sound came from the much bigger alien. As it spoke, or rather reacted audibly, the surface of the half-domed helmet it wore rippled like pond water around a tossed stone, suggesting that the material of the helmet was not as solid and inflexible as it appeared.

Vantolos's reply was cold. Dead cold. "Then we will raze all four of the primary cities which serve as capitals to the four tribes with whom we have made contact." So saying, the quartet of banded tentacles curved downward and pushed, raising the cylindrical body off the ground. With a spider-like pivot, the alien interlocutor turned and started back toward the ship waiting beside the shore of Lake Surprise, followed by its intimidating bipedal escort. It was not lost on Dev or any of his colleagues that both aliens turned their respective backs on the contact team, contemptuously indifferent to how Reed or any of them might choose to respond.

"Wait!" Pushing past Reed's outstretched arm, Zimmer took a couple of steps after the aliens. "We have questions! So many questions."

Twisting its neck, Vantolos looked back at him as its powerful tentacles continued to propel it away from the team and toward its ship. "There is no need for questions. We will state our demands tomorrow. You will abide by them or suffer consequences that are too horrible to contemplate. We have no time for your inconsequential queries."

It took only a few moments for the alien pair to re-enter their ship and the dissolving portal to close behind them, leaving a smooth metallic surface in its wake. A soft thrumming came from the craft and the red glow reappeared beneath its underside. As it began to rise, a brace of egrets unfurled flag-like white wings and bolted from the vicinity of its stern. The contact team watched as the craft accelerated skyward. In moments it had shrunk to a glint. Then it vanished completely, doubtless on its way to rendezvous with its mothership.

Zimmer coughed, turned, and began to exchange anxious murmurings with his wife. Pavesi was speaking into what looked like a phone on steroids. Reed's right hand, thankfully, had emerged from his pants pocket holding nothing. The big man was still shading his eyes and staring at the place where the alien craft had disappeared into the thin, sluggish clouds. Somewhere, a hawk cried out questioningly.

Digging the point of one boot into the soft muck underfoot, Dev considered the encounter that had just transpired and spoke for all of them.

"That," he murmured softly, "didn't go well."

—III—

S oft, indirect lighting illuminated the meeting room where everyone assembled that evening. No one remarked on the conditions, but Dev was privately thankful for the location. Never thinking it necessary, he had neglected to mention, on everything from his original application at Thomson Engineering to his subsequent NASA employment form, that he was mildly claustrophobic. Exhaustion from the hurried trip down from Washington had helped him to cope with the previous night's underground accommodations. Now fully awake and chronologically acclimated, he was relieved that the current gathering was being held above ground.

The fact that the windows were opaqued did not trouble him. It was spatial constriction that perturbed him, not darkness. The opacity was necessary so that everyone present could clearly view the images on the large monitors that hung on three sides of the room. A couple of these were presently dark. An active pair provided alternating views of major television channels: one monitor was dominated by American networks while the other featured a mix of European and Asian sources. Real-time translations crawled across the bottom of the screens displaying foreign broadcasts.

Of the remaining screens that were operational, one showed the president's office in the White House. The second feed came from the Pentagon. Both offices were crowded. The president dominated the first while General William McKendrick, the head of the Joint Chiefs of Staff, held court in the second. Conversation in both locations was vigorous and ongoing.

Dev felt rather out of place. His grandparents, who hailed from a small village in Andhra Pradesh, would have been rendered utterly speechless. Not so his mother and father. His father would have expanded with pride at the important position his offspring currently occupied and the fact that he was considered important enough to circulate among those in such positions of power. Always confident in her son's abilities, his mother would simply have smiled knowingly. *If only*, Dev thought, *the circumstances were different*.

The Zimmers were conversing softly with Diana Pavesi. Eyes half closed, Reed had willingly succumbed to the aural addiction provided by his wireless headphones. Dev wondered what the big man was experiencing. Or were the headphones a deliberate distraction and he was actually paying full attention to what was going on around him? Was he just enjoying some music? Or working out the details of how he was going to shoot everyone in the room if that particular command was passed down to him? Looking at his face, it was impossible to tell. He had his eyes almost shut, but his mind open.

Mitch Cottle could boast of a Texas heritage that greatly preceded that of NASA's presence in Houston. The fact that his extended family had history, land, and oil on its side had not prevented him from acceding to the urge to be part of the space program. As a senior administrator at the Johnson Center, he knew pretty much everything there was to know about the installation, how it functioned, and the backgrounds and specialties of its personnel. He did not know anything about aliens. It was supposed—it was hoped—that Dev and his four colleagues might somehow be able to divine a little about the visitors.

That opportunity had been largely denied to them due to the

abruptness of the aliens' initial contact. In contrast, the visitors' intentions had been more than adequately spelled out. They were going to make demands that if not fulfilled would result in destruction. It did not take an expert in linguistics, not even specialists like Pavesi and Katou-Zimmer, to parse such brusqueness. All that remained now, or at least for the immediate future, was to decide how to respond.

It was at that moment that the President of the United States faced directly into the Oval Office pickup and spoke to the grandson of subsistence farmers who hailed from a country halfway around the world. Staring back, Dev found himself thinking of ... a double latte, no whip, extra sugar.

"I see that Mr. Mukherjee is present," the president said.

All eyes in the Oval Office turned to Dev. All eyes in the office of the Joint Chiefs of Staff turned to him. All eyes in the Johnson Center meeting room turned to him. It got very quiet.

"Yes, Mr. President." Keeping it short, Dev had learned early on, meant less chance of saying something preternaturally stupid.

"I'm told you are something of a quick go-to, where possible alien contact is concerned."

Pavesi and the Zimmers were gazing expectantly at him. Reed, perhaps ominously, still had his eyes half closed and his headphones on. Dev cleared his throat.

"It's something I've always been interested in, Mr. President. I've made it kind of a sideline specialty in addition to my regular work for NASA."

The president nodded. "As opposed to you just working with politicians here in Washington while keeping things simple enough for them to pass along to their constituents when budget time comes around." There was nervous laughter from a few of the congressional representatives in the room. Hewing to his first principle, Dev just smiled and nodded. The president folded both hands on his desk and leaned forward slightly.

"I'll ask others and we'll come to a joint decision as to how we are going to proceed, Mr. Mukherjee, but I'm asking you first, here and now: what do you think our response should be to the aliens' ultimatum?"

Dev kept smiling while inside he was frantic. He remembered one story his father used to tell when Dev was younger. It involved his grandfather's affection for a particular cow. Eventually, the cow got sick. Grandfather had to decide whether to try and pay for professional veterinary care, bring in a much cheaper traditional healer, or have the animal put down. Three choices, each of which had its downside for a simple farmer. Now the President of the United States was asking that man's grandson, Devali Mukherjee, to give an opinion on a matter that might affect the future of the entire human species.

"Go ahead." Dev started slightly. Diana Pavesi was smiling at him and nodding as she murmured across the table.

"Yes. You are here to support me," he replied gratefully.

"No," Pavesi countered. "We're here to criticize you. But someone has to speak to the matter first. You've drawn the short straw."

"I'm sorry." It was General McKendrick. "Could you speak up a bit down there? We can't quite hear you clearly and I don't want to have to wait for enhanced playback."

"Sorry." Uncertain where to look, Dev took a deep breath and settled for staring at the screen that showed the Oval Office. "While everyone would rather have heard something from the aliens along the lines of 'we come in peace and extend the hand, or tentacle, of friendship to our galactic neighbors,' I think the key thing to take away from what was certainly an unexpectedly brief encounter is ..." Wanting to make certain he recalled the phrase correctly, he looked over at Pavesi.

"'It is not extensive nor are the quantities of material demanded excessive in volume,'" she quoted from the meeting.

"Yes, right." Dev was thankful for the confirmation supplied by his colleague's superb memory. "Whatever it is they want from us ..."

"And from the Russians, the Europeans, and the Chinese," Zimmer interjected.

"… it is not 'excessive in volume,'" Dev concluded.

"Of course," Katou-Zimmer put in, "we as yet haven't the vaguest idea what that means."

"Quite true," said her husband. "Despite their apparent mastery of our languages, we have no notion of what the visitors may or may not consider 'not excessive.'" He grunted softly. "We don't even have a proper reference for what they mean by 'volume.'"

"It seems we are to find out tomorrow." Dev recognized the speaker as Elena Pinski, science advisor to the president.

"Perhaps more to the point," said a Navy commander seated not far from General McKendrick, "is the nature of the material they are requesting."

"Not requesting," the general murmured. "Demanding"

Everyone went silent as the president spoke again. "Requesting, demanding—I don't give a damn about the semantics. Doesn't anyone have any idea what these—creatures might want?"

"It is impossible to speculate, Mr. President," Dev found himself saying. "We can only wait until they tell us."

The President of the United States leaned forward and said tightly, "I read the abstract of your dossier, Mr. Mukherjee. Along with those of your contact team colleagues. As I recall, one of your prime tasks is to speculate. Please do so now."

As he replied, Dev tried not to look away. "It is difficult to imagine what a powerful, space-traversing group of aliens representing at least two different species might need that would require them to stop at a world like ours. Simple metals could easily be obtained from an asteroid or moon. Therefore, we can assume that since they have come here, to an inhabited world with a semblance of a civilization—" a couple of the presidential advisors bridled visibly at that, but said nothing "—we have to ask ourselves if they need something we make."

"Maybe they're just lazy miners," Katou-Zimmer put in, "and would rather we do their digging and refining for them."

"That's possible," Dev admitted.

In the Oval Office, Science Advisor Pinski spoke up. "The situation might not be nearly as dire as it appears, Mr. President. If all they want is a quantity of refined steel or aluminum or copper or something like that, between ourselves and the other three political entities they have engaged with, satisfying their demand shouldn't be a problem. Their main ship is big. Huge, yes. But I think we're safe in assuming that it's not empty, that it contains living quarters for its crew as well as whatever drive or engine mechanism is necessary to propel it, as well as other perhaps unimaginable devices." She was nodding encouragingly to those around her. "If they can handle the transference, we can probably provide what they want."

"If what they want is material we have available in quantity, yes." Dev was not arguing with the presidential science advisor. He was discussing other possible scenarios. In other words, science. "What if what they want is tons of coltan? Or rare earths? Or plutonium. What's worse, what if what they want is something we don't have?"

At the Pentagon, an admiral spoke up. "Based on the recordings of your meeting with them, they don't seem inclined to take 'not available' for an answer. At least, this Vantolos being doesn't. Nor does its bodyguard, or backup species, or whatever that tall monster with the weapons was."

"We don't know that the biped in the back was wielding weapons. Also, referring to any of the visitors as a 'monster' is probably not helpful in constructing a basis for mutual understanding."

"Neither is threatening to raze four capital cities," McKendrick growled. "What if they do ask for something like plutonium?" His gaze flicked to his right, to another unseen visual pickup. "Ms. Pinski, can the world come up with a ton of plutonium?"

In the Oval Office, the science advisor shook her head slowly. "Not all the countries with nuclear facilities pooling their resources could supply a fraction of that. Certainly not on short notice. Even if it was available, there would be serious political ramifications to consider as well as issues involving packing and shipping."

"Let's assume these mons ... the visitors," the president said, "do want something we can't provide. Then what? Do we fight back? General McKendrick?"

The reply by the head of the Joint Chiefs was solemn but firm. "We already have every available weapon that might reasonably be expected to reach the alien mothership trained on it."

In the conference room at the Space Center, murmurs of dismay came from Dev and the Zimmers. Despite his indignation, Dev noticed that Reed did not respond in kind. He more or less expected that. What surprised him was that Pavesi remained equally composed at the general's announcement. What, he wondered, might be hiding inside that marvelous memory?

McKendrick continued. "I have been and remain in touch with General Marchand in Brussels, General Jian in Beijing, and Field Marshal Rybokov in Moscow. They have prepared likewise, in the event such a decision becomes inevitable. We have all agreed to act in concert should the necessity arise. I pray that it does not."

"We don't know what kind of weapons systems they have." Dev and his colleagues looked at the usually reticent Reed in surprise. "They've threatened to destroy entire cities. If they can do that, it's likely that they can deal with anything we can throw at them. They might have anti-missile devices. Or defensive shields we can't imagine."

Dev looked from Reed back to the main screen. "I have to object to any such course of action, Mr. President. Fighting back, even from a posture of defense, might only enrage the visitors. It could spur them to deal out even worse devastation. They might unleash enough firepower to destroy not just several cities but the entirety of human civilization."

It was dead quiet in all the rooms, from Houston to Washington—until Katou-Zimmer spoke up in her sharp, clipped tones.

"If they need something from us, from a structured civilization, then if they destroy us, they won't get it."

"Yes. Yes, that's likely true." Not only the science advisor but everyone in both the Oval Office and at the Pentagon looked at least mildly relieved.

"So we're back to the main question." The president's frustration was palpable. "Can we give them what they want so that they'll spit harmlessly on us but otherwise leave us in peace?"

"I imagine we will find out tomorrow, Mr. President," Dev responded, "when we have our second meeting. Until then, I suggest everyone get some sleep."

"Easy for you to say," the president muttered. "All right then. General McKendrick, you and your staff remain alert for any changes in the appearance of the alien craft. Wake me if your people see anything that looks threatening. Or I suppose I should say, more threatening than it already is." His attention shifted. "Mr. Mukherjee, should your rest be interrupted by any flashes of brilliance reflecting on what we should do, what we could do, the same holds true for you. Let me know immediately. The same goes for the rest of you in Houston. If anything should change here, if the Russians or the Chinese or our European friends come up with a sudden brainstorm between now and tomorrow afternoon, you will be informed." He paused. "That's all for now, I suppose. If wisdom doesn't arrive by tomorrow, we'll just have to play it by ear." He mustered a smile. "I've been doing that my whole life. I'd be just as happy not to have to do it tomorrow. Thank you all, and may God be with us." As he rose from behind his desk, so did everyone else in the Oval Office who had been seated. Both the monitor there and the one in the Pentagon went dark.

Dev found himself nodding slightly in accord. *But which god,* he mused. *Ours or the aliens'?*

———

Given that the end of the world might be nigh, Dev was astonished at how well he slept. Certainly, it had something to do with the complete darkness and silence provided by the subterranean room. Doubtless the fact that he was completely exhausted also contributed. Regardless, he found himself famished by the time he had dressed and walked to the compact underground cafeteria.

The Zimmers were already there, chattering away between bites of food. Headphones on, Reed ate quietly, methodically demolishing a couple of enormous plates of food that appeared to contain at least one of every item the cafeteria offered. Dev didn't blame him. If his own gastrointestinal system permitted, he intended to try and match the bigger man pancake for pancake. If this was to be a last meal, he intended to enjoy every last unnecessary carb and sugar.

"Good morning, Dev."

Pavesi had come up alongside him so quietly he had failed to notice her.

"Morning, Diana." At the end of the serving line, they took trays and silverware. The cafeteria was fully staffed even though the contact team were the only ones eating. "Did you dream of what the aliens might want? Because that might make the next exchange go a little easier."

Taking a pair of croissants from the bread on offer, she shook her head. "Afraid not. Actually, I don't dream. Haven't since I was a little girl. But when I woke up this morning, I was thinking of Gubbio."

He frowned as he shoveled hash browns onto his plate. "Sounds like a dessert."

She smiled as she grabbed a handful of butter packets. "It's a small town in north central Italy. My grandparents came from there. They're gone, of course, but I've been back a few times. It's a lovely place, a bit off the main tourist agenda."

"Did your grandparents all have photographic memories, like yours?" Bacon and scrambled eggs. Toast. Dev thought fondly of his mother's roti and dosas. With chutney.

She shook her head. "I can't remember."

He returned her grin. A little humor was a good thing. Anything that helped to mute the possibility of a forthcoming alien-generated apocalypse.

The Zimmers did not keep to themselves so much as shut out the rest of the team due to the technical nature of their conversation. Reed was immersed in both his food and his—to Dev anyway—incomprehensible music that thumped through his headphones.

So it was left to him and the genial Pavesi to engage in what passed at the table for ordinary breakfast banter. They spoke of their childhoods, their parents and grandparents. Dev expressed a wish to one day found his own research and development firm, with offices in DC and Bengaluru. Pavesi voiced thoughts of retiring early, perhaps early enough to get married and have a child.

"One only," she told him as she sipped her coffee. "So I can spoil her rotten."

"Does it have to be a 'her'?" Dev asked.

"Yes." For an instant, just for an instant, he saw something in her expression and a stiffening posture that had not been there before. It was as unexpected as it was unmistakable. "I've seen what men have done to this world. Mostly men, anyway. It will be a girl."

He wanted to go there, to dig a little deeper, but decided against it. Now was not the time. Not today. Maybe tomorrow, he told himself. If there was a tomorrow.

What he wanted to do most of all was call his parents. It was strange, he mused. When he had ample time, when he was under no pressure, there always seemed to be something else to do. Something not necessarily more important, but that always took precedence. When they did talk, his mother would often nag him about not being married while his father would deplore his lack of visits, even though they lived not all that far away from DC in Jacksonville. He would do his best to soothe them, murmuring pleasant familial clichés over the phone, while reassuring them that he would come visit at the first real opportunity, and that he did indeed intend to marry when he could find the right girl, and no, mama, you can't plan an arranged marriage for me just because it worked out for you and dad.

Now, unable to use his phone or tablet or so much as a carrier pigeon to communicate a single sentence to the outside world, that was all he wanted to do. Talk to his parents. About nothing in particular and everything in general, about little meaningless inconsequentialities, about the weather and the price of bread and …

Reed was staring at him. Chewing and staring. Dev liked Reed, as much as Reed would allow himself to be liked. That did not change the fact that he knew if he violated communications silence in any way, shape, or form, Reed would crush whatever device Dev was attempting to use to contact the outside world, and possibly also Dev himself.

Think about other things, he told himself as he absently spread raspberry preserves on a piece of toast. Think about what you're going to do with your time when this is over. Visit your parents, certainly. Take a week off, spend some quality time with them, go to the beach, build a sandcastle. Break your personal dietary regimen and indulge in a hamburger, as big and sloppy and greasy as possible. Plan a trip to the old country, scout office locations in Bengaluru. Try as he might, he found he couldn't think very long about any of those things. Imminent destruction by way of an alien invasion has a way of blocking out anything akin to a casual thought.

Like everyone else, he had been caught off-guard by the aliens' ability to converse in English. That was an area of contact where he had expected Jakob Zimmer to take the lead and the two biologists, Pavesi and Katou-Zimmer, to follow. Reed would look on and watch for trouble while he, Dev, assessed the overall situation in expectation of being asked for opinion and analysis. By addressing the contact team in English, and colloquial, brusque English at that, the alien called Vantolos had scrambled everyone's preconceived notions of how such contact might proceed. Now they and every other human on the planet were faced not with complex issues of understanding but with demands. Demands that had been delivered in a cold, unambiguous terrestrial language. What they consisted of no one yet knew.

He glanced up at the wall clock, whose hours were backed by images of different NASA spacecraft. How primitive the most advanced space-traversing efforts of humankind seemed now. Less than an infant fumbling with blocks.

Rising from his chair, Reed removed his headphones and returned to the real world. "Time, everyone. Finish up. Half an hour for bathroom time." One corner of his mouth curled slightly upwards. "Time for prayer and final thoughts, if that's your inclination. Like yesterday, we'll assemble in the reception area."

Final thoughts, Dev mused as he used a napkin to wipe red sweetness from his lips. He'd grown up listening to his mother ramble on and on about reincarnation, remembered being utterly bored by the interminable details, and wishing at the time that he were anywhere else but trapped in the same room with her. Now, as he made his way back to his room, he found himself recalling a good deal of what she had said. He still didn't believe any of it, of course. He was a scientist, a representative of science and reason, and knew there was no more proof of reincarnation than of any of the other afterlifes proposed by religions large and small. Besides, if the aliens' demands could not be met and they ended up methodically destroying the Earth, what could he reasonably come back as anyway? A cockroach? Better just to be dead.

Buck up, he told himself. Whether the implacable aliens requested plutonium, or rare earths, or pails of diamonds, it was possible that their demands could be satisfied. If that turned out to be the case, they might very well take what they needed and be on their way, leaving the Earth and its peoples unharmed and moderately, if uneasily, wiser concerning the presence of intelligent life in the galaxy. Why anticipate Armageddon at ten in the morning?

Feeling a bit better, if not exactly optimistic, he attended to the necessary ablutions, made sure his attire was in order, and left his windowless yet comfortable room. There was no need to lock the door. The few possessions he had managed to bring with him, including a little money and some credit cards, would be safe concealed beneath the grounds of the Space Center. Anyway, there were no locks on any of the doors.

The mood was solemn as the five members of the contact team were led out of the subterranean complex and to the underground transport rail system. Even the usually garrulous Zimmers were reduced to a few subdued murmurs. Reed had his headphones back in, listening to Shiva knew what. No, not Shiva, Dev hastily corrected himself. Wrong god to invoke on this particular morning.

Emerging into the cloud-diffused light and heat of the marina helped to raise everyone's spirits. As they walked to the boat waiting to take them across the bay, Dev marveled at the activity around them, at the sheer ordinariness of it. So what if a giant alien spacecraft had shifted its location from Panama and was now hovering over the Gulf of Mexico? So what if rampant speculation as to the aliens' intentions took the place of actual facts because no government seemed inclined to tell the public what was really going on? It was a nice enough morning and if one was lucky enough to have the day off from work, a day out on the water fishing or just cruising was certainly in order, even if the government had staked out a temporary no-go zone around the whole of South Point.

They didn't know, Dev appreciated. Thus far, the four regional continental governments had managed to keep knowledge of the alien ultimatum from the general public. As far as the terrestrial population knew, rudimentary first contact was ongoing. Having spent much time in Washington, Dev knew that the secret couldn't be kept forever. The hope of the four governments was that secrecy could be maintained until after the menacing aliens had departed. If not, there would be panic on a scale unseen and unimaginable in the modern era.

It was possible that Pavesi, at least, was having similar thoughts. It might go some way to explaining why, when their boat and its escort craft were halfway across the bay, she suddenly ran to the side, leaned over, and heaved her breakfast and everything else in her stomach into the bay. The water was green; her face was not. It was not seasickness that had suddenly afflicted her but nerves of a different kind.

Dev managed to keep his food down as they pulled up alongside the old wooden dock, scattering a flock of outraged waterfowl in the process. Then it was into the waiting Humvees and down the narrow road. The expressions on the faces of the soldiers escorting them were unchanged from yesterday. There were no signs of increased anxiousness, no suggestion of heightened nerves. The regular troops didn't know about the ultimatum either, he concluded. The government had managed to keep the number of those individuals who did to a minimum: the president and his immediate advisors, the Joint Chiefs of Staff and their assistants, and a marginal number of civilian advisors like himself and the rest of the contact team. Undoubtedly it was the same in the halls of the Kremlin, the EU, and the People's Republic. Dangerous knowledge had been restricted to the heads of government, the military, and those designated to make contact or analyze the results of it. Among them, still to his own surprise, was Devali Mukherjee, only son of immigrants from a poor part of a poor country.

The weight of responsibility only increased as the convoy began to slow. He wanted to throw up, like Pavesi, but could not. He could bear the thought of failure more than he could that of embarrassment.

Lake Surprise had a calming effect, both on his soul and his nerves. Egrets and herons patrolled its shallows. Disappearing into the trees off to the left of the shallow, stagnant body of fresh water he glimpsed a flash of pink as a lone scarlet ibis abandoned its morning fishing to seek shade from the rising sun.

They waited. The time the aliens had set for the meeting came and went, leaving everyone in the contact party as well as their escorts subject to heat, humidity, and uneasy thoughts. Dev was about to wonder aloud if they had misconstrued either the time or the location when Reed, sparing of voice but sharp of eye, let out a grunt and pointed upward to where the alien landing craft was descending. Except for the slight hum it generated, it was, as it had been the day before, eerily quiet.

Everyone readied themselves as it came to a stop. Like yesterday, it remained hovering a few centimeters above the saturated soil. Once again, a portion of its side appeared to dissolve and eject a ramp. On the tips of its four powerful tentacles, Vantolos came striding purposefully toward the waiting humans. This time it was accompanied by not one but two of the tall, helmet-wearing bipeds. Each carried the same three devices whose purpose was suspected but which remained unknown. Many implications could be drawn from the fact that today there were two of them. Vantolos might feel the need for more personal security. Or if actual combat were to break out …

Dev dismissed the possibility, or at least set it aside. He was both anxious and eager to hear the specifics of the alien demands. And also, more than a little bit nervous.

Vantolos halted a tentacle-length away, its two escorts drawn up behind it. It did not pause to exchange greetings.

"As previously indicated, we are here to present our demands. You will listen. If you have questions deemed relevant, they may be answered, or not. Then we will return to our vessel. You will be given adequate time to comply with the demands. If you fail to do so, the alternative has already been iterated."

Curling downward, the tip of one banded tentacle pressed into the side of the golden material that enclosed the alien body. The fabric contorted. When it uncoiled and returned to its previous state, a small instrument lay coiled within the alien's pythonic limb. Straightening it, Vantolos pointed it in the direction of the contact team. One of the soldiers tensed, relaxing only when Katou-Zimmer put a hand on his arm and followed it with a slight warning shake of her head.

Using the instrument, Vantolos began to draw symbols and words in the air between itself and the contact team. The lines and curlicues, the three-dimensional shapes and geometric images, glowed brightly enough to be seen clearly even in the morning light. The members of the contact team studied them intently.

"These are the essentials we require." Just as it had declaimed, the alien had not offered so much as a good morning but had instead launched directly into the series of demands. "Finding appropriate translations was time-consuming, even allowing for the primitiveness of your basic chemistry. It is often so where scientific terminology is concerned."

Dev found himself looking from the suspended words and images to the team's two biologists, Pavesi and Katou-Zimmer. Although the words hovering in the humid air appeared to be English, he could not be certain of their meaning. His education had included more physics than chemistry.

Of one thing he felt reasonably certain: none of the ethereal expressions referred even obliquely to rare earths or radioactives. Or for that matter, to gold or diamonds or some similar product of the earth. While his knowledge of organic chemistry was limited, he could recognize the diagram of an organic molecule when he saw it.

His confusion was shared by his colleagues. Pavesi in particular had the strangest expression on her face. Sidling over to her, he whispered his interest without taking his eyes off the alien Vantolos and the shimmering imagery the alien continued to scribe in the air.

"What is it? What are they asking for?" When she didn't reply he raised his voice slightly. "What are they demanding? Do you comprehend any of it?"

She finally woke from her contemplation to look over at him. "That's just it. I'm pretty sure I recognize all of it. Not most of it: all of it." Raising her left hand and pointing, she traced over the hovering symbols. "It has outlined and visually defined a pair of glucose polymers." Her pointing finger moved. "That one there, that's amylose, a linear molecule. The one beside it is amylopectin, which is branched. Together they form a starch. A particular starch."

Dev wasn't sure he'd heard correctly. "'Starch'? The alien demand is for—starch?"

"Not just any starch." She looked over at him, her understanding of what Vantolos was designating leaving her no less bemused than her colleague. "A starch that constitutes about three-quarters of the kernel weight in maize. Apparently they want—excuse me, 'demand'—several tons of it."

Not fissile material then, a bewildered Dev realized. Not rare minerals or gemstones. Not cadavers or live human slaves.

The aliens were demanding ... corn.

—IV—

And not just corn, Dev learned when he finally regained his mental equilibrium. A large quantity of pentosans, which an equally dumbfounded Pavesi finally explained were polymers based on xylose and arabinose. The full chemical schematic of the second material the aliens stipulated was more complex, but Pavesi assured him it boiled down to—wheat bran.

There was more, all of it consisting of simple basic foodstuffs. All plant proteins, he was assured. Nothing derived from animals.

The imperious alien invaders were needy vegans.

No matter what the apparent reality, he reminded himself, *don't jump to conclusions.* There might be more to the alien demands. There *must* be more. The longer he thought about it, the less sense it made. Sentient beings who could build a craft capable of making an interstellar journey in less than a lifetime and likely a good deal faster than that surely were capable of designing and manufacturing the means to synthesize food! And why ask for terrestrial food? Did corn and wheat and sorghum and the rest of what the visitors were requesting grow on their homeworlds?

Equivalent plant evolution? It all gave new meaning to the phrase "seeding the galaxy."

Unable to resist and imprudently dismissing any possible repercussions, he posed the query to Vantolos. How much harm could there be in asking about corn? As soon as he began to speak, everyone's gaze turned to him. Reed looked particularly irritated. But Dev refused to be put off.

As it developed, Vantolos took no offense and replied to the question without hesitation.

"Of course we have the means to synthesize our own nutrients. What kind of primordials do you take us for?" The Zimmers looked uncomfortable, and Reed went from irritated to tense, but the single comment constituted the extent of the alien's belligerence. "In order for our synthesizing mechanisms to work, they require suitable feedstock. This can take the form of numerous carbon-based materials. Did you think the only thing we researched before making contact with your kind were your languages? The need to obtain organic feedstock is the sole reason for our visitation here. There is nothing else we require from you. In truth, you have nothing else to offer us. Your technology is so unsophisticated as to be beyond comment, and your global social arrangements are laughable."

Though the response to Dev's guileless question had been withering, it did not keep a curious Pavesi from asking one of her own. "Of course we couldn't begin to compare our technology with yours. That's self-evident."

The tentacle clutching the air writer writhed. "It is good that you recognize that, and important that you remember it."

"Even so," Pavesi continued, "you have come a long way, regardless of your point of origin. Might it be possible that, on further examination, there could be other items we could offer that might prove useful to you?"

For the first time, one of the tall, helmeted beings standing behind Vantolos leaned forward. Its mouth flexed. Vantolos's cylindrical trunk twisted slightly as it appeared to be listening. *There must*, Dev reflected, *be some sort of membrane in the helmet that allowed for sound to pass.* When the bodyguard, or whatever it was, straightened, Vantolos's trunk resumed its former posture.

"It is interesting that you are offering to engage in— commerce? It may be, as you say, that your world has more to offer than organic feedstock. I will see to it that our pre-contact surveys are fully re-analyzed. If anything is found that could prove helpful to us, and easier to obtain from you than by exerting ourselves in additional extraplanetary efforts, such an exchange might be pragmatic."

"What could you offer us in return?" Dev asked. The look Jakob Zimmer cast his way could have been interpreted as either praise or shock.

As always, Vantolos did not hesitate. "Some small aspects of our technology that would be suitable for adaptation by your simple minds might be provided. In fact, two of your fellow tribes have already put forth such a proposal. Theirs will be considered alongside yours."

The shock that ran through every member of the contact team was palpable, none more so than that which afflicted Pavesi and Reed. The alien had as much as said that its counterparts elsewhere were considering the trading of advanced technology with at least the Russians or the Chinese—or possibly both. Excusing herself, Pavesi turned and walked away from the summit. Dev could see her working her communications instrumentation. What he could see of her expression was grim.

He could empathize with her position. He would not have wanted to be the one to inform her superiors, much less the entire government, that the aliens were in the process of trading some "small aspects" of their very advanced technology to countries with whom the United States did not presently exist in a state of boundless friendship. In lieu of specifics from Vantolos, such technology could be anything. A cure for advanced diseases. A cheap and easy means for generating energy. A better and cleaner way to produce the plastics that were part of everyday living. A better *substitute* for plastics.

And of course, weapons.

"What happens," Katou-Zimmer asked, "if more than one of our 'tribes' can supply you with what you want? Will you exchange with all of us? Or only one?"

Vantolos was growing impatient. "You need not concern yourself with such trivial matters. We and only we will make that decision, which will be based not on what you desire but on what we deem the easiest and quickest for us. You will be notified of our additional requests, if any, tomorrow at this same time and location."

With that, it put down its fourth tentacle, adding its stability and strength to the other three, pivoted crab-like, and started back toward the landing craft. Its two tall attendants followed close behind.

The members of the human contact team immediately fell into intense discussion. Only Dev continued to watch the aliens as they walked all the way back to their ship. So even though it was recorded by multiple instruments nearby, he was the only one to see one of the big, armed (*Still didn't know for certain if those stick-like objects were weapons,* he reminded himself) bipeds turn to look back in his direction. Knowing nothing of alien expressions, he had no basis on which to interpret what he was seeing. But he found it significant that for the first time, one of the aliens had looked back. Why?

He did not have time to ponder the glance more deeply because Reed was soliciting his opinion on what had just transpired. Once again, everyone was looking at him.

"Why ask me? I'm not a specialist like the rest of you."

"That's why we're asking you." Zimmer's mouth formed an engaging little smile. "In our own observations we are knowledgeable, but also somewhat constricted by our more focused fields of interest. What did you think all that meant? What did you think was happening, there at the end?"

"Yes." Zimmer's wife further prompted Dev. "You asked the question."

"Well ..." Dev considered. "It seems plain enough that they're willing to trade."

"Yes, yes." If the impatient Zimmer had been holding a pipe, he would have waved it. "But is it as straightforward as it seems? Is there some other meaning, some other rationale behind the offer that we are not seeing?" He mumbled something to his wife, who shook her head by way of reply.

"I don't think so." Dev struggled to utilize the broad-based, non-specific knowledge that his colleagues did not possess. "I think they really are willing to trade. My question would be: why?"

Reed's voice rumbled up from his chest. "You heard it. There are maybe some things we can provide that'd be easier to get from us rather than them having to work to obtain them."

Dev nodded in agreement. "Exactly. And Vantolos didn't hesitate when Diana made the offer. Almost as if it was waiting for it."

Pavesi was still off by herself, semi-frantic on two phones at once. It was left to Katou-Zimmer to ask, "What are you saying, Dev?"

He looked back at her, then over at the others. "Maybe this isn't some kind of invasion at all. Maybe it's a trade mission." Turning, he gestured at the shore of the lake where the alien shuttle craft had been hovering moments ago. "Maybe all the pugnaciousness Vantolos expresses is nothing but a negotiating ploy to get a better deal. And mentioning that their other contact teams are also negotiating with the Russians and everyone else is nothing but a similar ploy." He thought a moment. "Or maybe what we've been hearing as belligerence is just their normal manner of speech. They may have learned our languages, but that doesn't mean they've mastered the inflections and tonalities."

"That's a lot of maybes." Reed looked dubious. "'Maybe' you're wrong, and a misstep in interpretation of what's actually going on could have serious repercussions. Like the loss of a major metropolitan area."

Dev nodded slowly. "Possible. Though despite the evidence in the form of their ship, we don't actually know what, if anything, they're capable of. If this visit is some version of alien commerce and their vessel isn't a warship of some kind, maybe all their threats are just that. Nothing but bluff to secure the best covenant."

The big man considered. "Are you willing to risk, say, Washington or Brussels on that?"

"It's not up to me." Turning away from Reed, Dev gazed out at the calm water of the bay. He thought of his father, who always seemed to know how to make the right decisions, even if they only involved a few dollars. "Like the rest of you, I'm just here to offer my opinion. It falls on the shoulders and minds of others to make those kinds of decisions, thank Rama."

"I would like to know," Zimmer murmured, "if the same proposal has been put in exactly the same fashion by other alien negotiators to our counterparts in Moscow, Beijing, and Brussels." He favored Dev with a fatherly smile. "If so, that would indeed suggest a kind of bargaining is in progress. The implications are—interesting."

"Yes," agreed his wife. "First demands, then threats, followed by an offer to trade technology for—what?"

"It doesn't matter," her husband insisted. "As Dev implies, if you can make demands, why subsequently resort to bargaining? Why not simply continue to issue demands?"

Pavesi looked thoughtful. "Perhaps that's how they are. Maybe it's their culture. To swing wildly between threats and offers of cooperation."

"Great," muttered Reed. "We've been invaded by all-powerful manic depressives."

"I don't know." Dev was shaking his head. "Something just doesn't feel right. About all of this."

Reed admonished him. "Feelings don't enter into it."

Turning back from the lake, Dev met his stare squarely. "Half the reason I'm here is to give voice to feelings." He gestured at the Zimmers. "I don't have your academic qualifications, or—" and he indicated first Reed, then Pavesi "—your status within the government. I'm an in-between, professionally as well as ethnically."

Zimmer's response was somber. "Your opinion carries as much weight here as that of any of us. Perhaps more. You are the only one of us with anything resembling expertise in the matter of first interspecies contact."

The vote of confidence was uplifting, but Dev wasn't buying it. "I've done some reading in an area that's far more speculative than fact-based, that's all. It's all guesswork." He looked over at the big man as the five of them and their escort started back toward the waiting vehicles. "All we can do is offer our best guesses as to what the aliens really are like, and what they truly want."

"You mean," said Pavesi, "besides corn and wheat?" It was meant to lighten an atmosphere that had grown increasingly solemn.

"No," Zimmer declared firmly. "I don't think we have to guess about possible other things. Vantolos promised to inform us tomorrow."

Tomorrow, Dev thought as he climbed into a waiting Humvee. How many tomorrows did they have to look forward to? Was the alien presence really about nothing more than grains?

He pondered the question all the way back to the old wooden dock and on the fast transit back to the marina. Around the shuttle boat and its subdued military escort, pleasure seekers out for a day's relaxation plied the bay in small watercraft. Humanity's amazing ability to ignore the improbable, no matter how threatening, was verified by boaters' and water-skiers' ability to engage in ongoing recreation while only rarely glancing at the speck above the clouds that was the alien mothership.

There was a click as the hatch leading to the deck was opened. Reed led the way upward, out into the diffuse sunshine of the humid south Texas afternoon.

"I wonder what it will be? What else the aliens might want?" Conscious of the swirl of cheerful day-trippers at the marina, Katou-Zimmer kept her voice low. As much as was possible, their armed escorts blended into the crowd. "Bushels of diamonds?"

Dev looked dubious. "Diamonds are cheap. Easy to manufacture. All you need is heat and pressure. No, I have a feeling that just like their unexpected need for organic feedstock, they'll ask for something totally unexpected."

"More importantly," said Reed, "what will they put forth in exchange? What kind of incredibly advanced technology will they condescend to offer us?"

"I can't imagine," Dev replied, "but the whole business puts me in mind of a story my grandfather used to tell. One day, back in India, he was offered the chance to buy an old but functioning Ambassador sedan for several thousands of rupees. In his whole life, my grandfather had never owned a car. So he bought it. It ran fine—for two weeks. Needless to say, he never saw either the seller or his money again." He eyed Reed evenly.

"What if we trade for technology that fails in two weeks? Or two years? Would we have any idea how to fix it? My grandfather didn't know anything about cars and eventually sold the Ambassador for parts."

"A fair point," Reed conceded as they approached the innocuous entrance to the Space Center's underground transport system. "Almost as important as wondering if they'll trade something different, and more dangerous, to the Russians or the Chinese."

"Our overseas friends know no more about alien technology and how to keep it functioning than we do," Zimmer pointed out.

Pavesi had been relatively quiet up until then. "One more thing, as long as we're taking about 'old cars.'" She paused. "They can crash and burn just as lethally as new ones. Especially if the owner has little or no understanding of how they work. We could receive in trade a device that controls the weather. That would be truly wonderful—as long as we are capable of controlling the device. The same holds true for anything that could be used as a weapon. Even modern weapons can backfire or blow up and kill their user. I had an old colleague of mine who was preparing to deliver—let's call it a 'gift package.' It went off prematurely. He lost two fingers. Imagine the consequences if the same thing happened with an alien device of unknown potential."

Katou-Zimmer turned philosophical. "Well noted, Diana. Or to put it another possible way, we should most assuredly beware of aliens bearing gifts. Even if they come with extensive instruction sheets."

————

The president, his council, and the Joint Chiefs of Staff, together with their respective adjutants and advisors, were all waiting to debrief the contact team via video upon their return from the second meeting with the aliens. In contrast to the first such encounter, when Dev had been more than a little overawed and enthused by his audience of political and military movers and shakers, the second time around he found himself oddly indifferent to the proceedings. Significant as they were, he found his thoughts drifting, away from the president, the generals and admirals, and their intent, well-meaning, but somehow distant queries.

Even as he listened to the anxious questions that were being asked and to the calm, carefully considered replies of his fellow team members, he was thinking about that last, fleeting, almost furtive glance from one of the tall alien bodyguards.

In the course of the two contact encounters, neither had spoken a word to the humans. One had said something to the principal alien, the tentacled Vantolos. Or maybe he (they would all be "he" in Dev's mind until gender clarification was provided) hadn't said anything. Maybe the armed biped had simply blown air into one of Vantolos's hearing organs. There was so much they didn't know about the gruff, commanding visitors. Given the abrupt nature of the two meetings that had transpired thus far, all they had to go on were endless analyses of the audio-video recordings.

Was the asperity intentional? Designed to intimidate, to restrict questioning and conversation while delivering demands? It was impossible to avoid the thought even as he knew that, like his colleagues, he risked imposing humanoid cultural norms on creatures that were utterly non-human. Perhaps in the ethos of tentacled interlocutors, brusqueness denoted courtesy and understanding whereas extended casual conversation was a sign of contempt and indifference.

But then there was that one backward glance....

During the course of conversation, the two massive bipeds had ignored the humans. Were they simply not curious about a newly met species? Or were they under orders, or commands, or some other unknown directive to ignore anything that was not an obvious threat to themselves or Vantolos? If such was the case, then why the look back, and at the very last moment?

Rising from the bed on which he had been watching television with the sound off, Dev walked to the compact bathroom to brush his teeth. He was obsessing over a glance. That attention to oftentimes obscure detail had been a characteristic of his since childhood. It had also garnered him several promotions, when he had found holes in arguments or, more importantly, in proposed budgetary material. Yet this time his fixation seemed misplaced, almost frivolous. There likely was nothing of significance to the alien's backward glimpse. Maybe it was doing nothing more than relieving pressure on its neck. Still, Dev could not shake it from his memory.

Possibly, he told himself, *because the two bodyguards were bisymmetrical bipeds.* Like humans, they had two arms, two legs, two eyes, hands with fingers (albeit two fewer on each) and walked upright. In appearance and in movement they were far more like humans than was the cephalopodan Vantolos. Yet Vantolos was plainly in charge. Were the bipeds Vantolos's comrades, equal partners in the unexpected stopover on a small planet? Or did they occupy lesser positions in the hierarchy of visitors? For that matter, were they and Vantolos' kind the only two species on the mothership? Might there be more, whose importance superseded that of Vantolos's people but who preferred to remain out of sight, pulling diplomatic and martial strings from the safety of their vessel?

His ignorance overwhelmed him. Because there was far more to it than just personal curiosity. His own fate, that of his family and friends, indeed that of the entire human species, might well depend on how efficiently he and his colleagues interacted with the aliens. He would have to be careful what questions he asked. While he badly wanted answers to so very, very many, he could not risk antagonizing Vantolos or his thus far silent attendants. There was too much at stake.

As he started brushing his teeth, the battery-powered brush humming softly, he stared back at himself in the mirror. What he saw there did not rouse him with confidence. Was there more danger in possibly asking the wrong questions—or in not asking the right ones? He and his colleagues knew so little. If they held back from inquiring, he told himself, they would learn nothing more. Such as the reason for the tall biped's single backward glance. Only one way to really find out.

At the next meeting, should the opportunity arise, Dev resolved to ask it.

———

Vantolos refused every suggestion that they might change the meeting place. Informed that the corn and wheat and other materials he had requested might be more quickly and easily delivered via a main container port such as New Orleans, or better still, St. Louis, the alien insisted it all be brought to the site where the previous encounters had taken place. The poor undersecretary of agriculture who had been charged with fulfilling the aliens' demands was greatly relieved when he was informed that the tons of requested grain did not have to be trucked down the narrow road that bisected the peninsula but could instead be delivered via ship onto scoop-like receptacles just offshore.

Having arrived in a single cargo vessel especially designed and equipped to transport grain, the sea-going vessel anchored off Lake Surprise while several aliens saw to the transfer of its cargo. Through binoculars, Dev and his colleagues could see at least two representatives of Vantolos's kind supervising the transfer operation. Under their direction, members of the body-guard species operated a variety of smooth, almost featureless machinery in conjunction with a swarm of automatons. Resembling neither alien species, these robotic workers were little more than efficient amalgamations of internal lights and busy limbs.

Dev was about to pose his why-did-you-look-back question to one of Vantolos's two personal bodyguards when it struck him that not only did he not know which of them had made the glance, he did not even know if the two present at today's encounter were the same pair who had accompanied Vantolos previously. They knew that the alien speaker was Vantolos because he identified himself as such. But as far as the tall bipeds were concerned, they remained essentially visually interchangeable. It might be easy to find out. Or it might initiate the apocalypse.

Nothing ventured, nothing gained, Dev told himself with an air of fatality. Lifting an arm, while aware that the gesture itself might constitute some inexcusable breach of alien protocol, he pointed at the slightly taller of the two bodyguards and addressed it directly.

"Did you look back at us yesterday, just before boarding your vessel? If that was you, I was wondering why you did so?"

From height and behind a transparent dome, the alien peered down at him. Its companion shifted his stance. Reed's expression tightened, Pavesi looked surprised, and Katou-Zimmer made a slight choking sound. But a wide smile broke out on her husband's face, and he nodded encouragingly at Dev, his neatly trimmed beard bobbing slightly.

The bodyguard did not reply. Vantolos did.

"If Oktonc did as you say, then it was only out of curiosity. Did you think your kind the only sapients afflicted with inquisitiveness?" Vantolos did not turn to look at the individual under discussion, but a tentacle rose to point backward in the taller bodyguard's direction. Dev was exceedingly pleased with himself for having identified the alien correctly as Vantolos continued.

"Unlike the Olone, my people, the Kaijank are less inclined to pursue interests that do not directly involve day-to-day survival. But they are not entirely lacking in curiosity. What I find interesting is that an individual of your primitive kind would take sufficient notice of such a small thing to find it worthy of comment."

For the first time, Dev realized, they now had English-equivalent names for both alien species. Emboldened, he pressed on. "Curiosity has always been an acute component of my personal makeup." He indicated the being who had been identified as Oktonc, who instead of gazing into the distance was now staring directly back at him. While the attention was a bit unsettling, Dev forced himself to ignore it. "It was the first time one of your bodygua—one of the Kaijank had shown any interest in us outside of formal proceedings."

"Keep it going, son." From nearby, an approving Jakob Zimmer whispered to him.

Dev needed no urging. At any moment, Vantolos might decide to terminate the exchange and return to his vessel. "I just wondered why neither of the Kaijank had taken the time to do something like that before."

Beneath Vantolos's golden garment, small shapes curled and writhed energetically. "As I said, while the Kaijank are not driven by inquisitiveness like the Olone, neither are they entirely immune to its call." Rising from the ground, a tentacle tip curled up and back to point at the pair of tall attendants. "Oktonc and Uleasc have their assigned tasks, as I have mine. Theirs is to watch for treachery or surprise among those with whom we exchange pleasantries. If he indeed looked back at you subsequent to our last meeting and just before re-entering our vessel, it was likely because he felt confident that all had gone well and would continue to do so until the moment of our departure. If he had felt otherwise, he would have favored you with more than just a glance."

Filing the implied threat for future analysis, Dev looked up at the big Kaijank. Alien and human regarded one another quietly for a moment. Then Oktonc looked away, toward the road where military vehicles stood waiting for the return of the contact team. Nothing was implied by his shifting glance, nothing had changed. Was it possible, Dev wondered, that the Kaijank had no understanding of what Vantolos had been saying? Did they, inside their domes, even have access to translation facilities? He hoped so. Ignorance had a tendency to lead to misunderstanding.

Vantolos did not appear concerned. "The extent of your curiosity is surprising and does you credit." He looked from Dev to Pavesi. "Do you feel likewise? Are you also driven to know?"

Pavesi nodded eagerly. Then, realizing that while the Olone had a fine grasp of common English, he might know nothing of human expressions, she added, "My profession requires me to learn as much as possible, in as many fields that are relevant to my profession as possible."

"An understandable response." Vantolos's torso turned slightly to enable him to regard the rest of the contact team. "I presume you all feel similarly?" The Zimmers added their own enthusiasm to that of Dev and Pavesi, while Reed managed a slight mumble in the affirmative.

The Olone paused a long moment, as if listening to sounds out of range of their hearing.

A moment later he declaimed in a tone that was devoid of his usual contempt and aggression, "Would it then please you, and perhaps also quicken the delivery of the items we have demanded, if you were to briefly visit our ship?"

Taken aback, Pavesi murmured, "I'll have to check with my

superiors." Reed immediately agreed with her position. The Zimmers readily concurred.

As for Dev, he almost forgot to say "yes," so excited was he by the prospect. For someone who had seen so many of his dreams fulfilled merely by having been appointed to the contact team, the offer to see *inside* the alien ship exceeded his wildest hopes.

He feared that Pavesi might have botched the offer when she looked up from her communicator and asked, "Can we make visual and audio recordings of what we see?" To Dev's relief, Vantolos was not fazed by the request.

"Certainly. You may make records of whatever you like."

So, the aliens had nothing they wanted to hide, Dev reflected. Maybe they were convinced that such recordings would prove useless to the uncomprehending apes making them. Or perhaps Vantolos and his superiors, assuming he had any, were in truth responding with an honest and open offer: a gesture of kindness coupled with condescension in response to the humans' ready compliance with their demands.

"What time could we arrange to do this?" Katou-Zimmer gazed expectantly at Vantolos. "We don't need much time to prepare and we ..."

The Olone cut her off. "Now. Soon everything we require will be loaded and we will depart."

"Will you return some day?" Katou-Zimmer asked quickly. "We have hardly had a chance to ask you any questions, and ..."

The alien interlocutor turned to her. "Come with me now or not at all."

Reed voiced the thought Dev and the others preferred to avoid. "How do we know this offer isn't some kind of trick? How do we know you won't just leave with us, so you can use us for ...?" He left the rest unsaid.

Vantolos replied anyway.

"'Use you'? Use you for what?" This time two tentacles rose to semaphore outlines in the air while the enigmatic shapes beneath his garment accelerated their twisting and wriggling. "What possible use could we have for a handful of primitives such as yourselves? You would require constant supervision to ensure you did not damage yourselves by attempting to interact with our ship. You would need your own food, facilities, atmosphere."

"You're breathing our atmosphere," the ever-observant Pavesi pointed out.

The alien swung to face her. "Your ignorance is profound. Yes, I can breathe the air of your world." One tentacle gestured behind him. "The Kaijank and others cannot."

"There are others? Other species on your ship?" a startled Dev inquired. Vantolos ignored him.

"You assume much. I can promise that if you come with me now, you will see many wonders, the sight of which will remain with you forever. Your 'recordings' will awe your species and give them much to ponder. Then you will be returned to this location. We have neither the interest nor reason to retain you on board our ship." He paused. "I give you one of your minutes to make up your minds." Dev found that the alien was again looking directly at him. "We will see how deep your curiosity truly runs."

"Not even enough time to check in with Washington." Reed was shaking his head slowly. "Any of you going?"

"We would never forgive ourselves if we decline," murmured Jakob Zimmer. Taking his wife's hand in his, he smiled down at her. She patted the back of his hand with one of her own and turned, resolute, to face the alien.

"Such a thing has been a dream of mine since I was eleven years old." Dev took a step to his right, to stand beside Zimmer. "If it's the end of things for me, what better way than to end with the fulfillment of a dream?"

"I *have* to go." Pavesi advanced toward the aliens and halted just out of tentacle reach.

A doleful Reed was still shaking his head. "Get gone or get fired. No wonder the department picked people for this team who didn't have family." With a sigh, he moved up to join his colleagues.

"I am impressed. Come now and be amazed." Dropping all four tentacles to the ground, Vantolos turned and started back toward the small ship. In a tight bunch, the five humans followed.

Dev noted that the pair of Kaijank brought up the rear. Not behind Vantolos this time. Behind him and his colleagues. In the distance he could hear the first stirrings of confusion, fear, and anxiety rising from among the waiting, watching military and civilian escort. A glance back showed one of the technical team starting toward the slowly withdrawing knot of humans and aliens. Two soldiers rushed forward to grab the man and hold him back. Without orders they were paralyzed. They had no appropriate orders because no one had seen, could have foreseen, a scenario where the contact team would suddenly decide, without requesting permission and plainly not under duress, to head for the alien craft in the company of its contact team. Doubtless a number of those in charge of the convoy were on their phones frantically inquiring what they should do. By the time anyone in a position of authority heard their requests, came to a decision, and conveyed it, the contact team would be rising skyward.

Dev almost felt sorry for them. Over the past couple of days, he had come to know many of them personally, even if there had not been sufficient time to form real friendships. He wondered what his own colleagues in Washington and at the Johnson Center must be thinking as they watched him march willingly toward the alien vessel. Just as they must be wondering what he was thinking.

A rush of thoughts and emotions threatened to overwhelm him. Was Vantolos telling the truth when he promised to return them? Pavesi already had her recorder out and working. Neither the interlocutor nor the two Kaijank gave the slightest indication that they were interested in impeding her effort. That much of Vantolos's assurance held true—so far.

Tilting back his head, Dev gazed skyward. Somewhere up there the great gray bulk of the alien mothership hovered in Earth orbit, taking on loads of terrestrial foodstuffs, woods, metals, and the other substances the aliens had requested. Soon he and his colleagues would board it. Would actually step aboard an alien spacecraft. For how long? An hour? Two? Vantolos had promised they would see wonders. How long would it take for all of them to be amazed and astonished beyond measure? His heart was pounding. A great, if brief, adventure lay before them.

Directly ahead, a circular portal resolved itself in the side of the smaller ship and a ramp extended. The Zimmers led the way, followed by Pavesi and Dev, with Reed a final reluctant boarder. As he stepped onto the ramp, Dev thought the material underfoot more closely resembled his grandmother's ceramic dinner plates than anything else. Then the portal closed behind them as Vantolos led them deeper into the ship.

—V—

Expecting surfaces hard and shining, Dev and his companions were surprised to discover that the interior walls of the alien vessel looked almost soft. Since no one moved to stop him, Dev reached out to run his hand along one sweeping, nearly translucent curve. Replete with concealed conduits, bulges, and concavities whose purpose was unknown, the small section of corridor felt like warm glass beneath his fingertips. He jerked his fingers away when a series of tiny but intensely bright lights ran away from his touch, quickly fading into the depths of the wall.

A fork appeared in the arched corridor down which they were walking. Vantolos continued to lead the visitors onward while the Kaijank turned down the other passageway. Plainly, now that they were aboard their own craft, the aliens felt that the bodyguards' presence was no longer necessary to ensure the interlocutor's safety.

A few steps on found them in a domed chamber. Just above the floor, a single row of what resembled oversized egg cups were embedded in the curving wall. At the far end, a pair of aliens sat in cups that had warped to fit their bodies. *Yet another new species*, Dev marveled. Compared to Vantolos they were small; beside the Kaijank they would have been positively diminutive. Lights and ovoid screens drifted in the air in front of and beside them. Like the Kaijank they were bipeds, but they had no need of the bodyguards' bulky suits or helmets. When one turned to its left to manipulate several colorful hovering images without touching them, Dev saw that it possessed huge, round eyes with proportionately large pupils. These gave the equally round faces a lemur-like appearance. Round ears protruded from each side of the bald, dark-skinned skull and he thought he could see thick lips framing a small mouth. Coupled with the loose red and yellow clothing they wore and the supple movements of their short arms and fingers, they looked like oversized rubber toys. He allowed himself a smile. It seemed that not every sentient Out There was as alien in appearance as the Olone or as intimidating as the Kaijank.

Noticing the direction of his stare, Vantolos said simply, "Those are A'jeii. Very competent folk."

In addition to the new species, the chamber was populated by a smattering of automatons of varying size. Some boasted tentacles, others manipulative digits more akin to humanoid fingers, while the majority displayed no limbs at all. Most were gray, but a couple boasted a distinctive golden patina. All were inscribed with incomprehensible symbols. They whizzed to and fro, intent on tasks guided either by programming or artificial intelligence. They ignored the new arrivals, the two small aliens up front, and each other with silent equanimity.

Vantolos directed the contact team to half a dozen nearby empty egg cups. "Sit. Or repose in whatever fashion your inflexible limbs find amenable."

An uncertain Pavesi eyed the cup in front of her. The interior was deep-set, jet-black, and far too small to accommodate the magnitude of her fundament. "I don't think that's made for me."

"Me either." Reed spoke out of need, not gallantry.

"*Sit,*" Vantolos repeated. "The apparatus will adjust as necessary. Observe." So saying he rotated on his four tentacles and slumped backward. Deforming like putty, the cup shape immediately twisted itself into a form suitable to accept the Olone's cylindrical trunk, protruding head, and sprawling limbs.

Exhibiting no hesitation, Katou-Zimmer pivoted and sat down. What reformed to welcome her was a reasonable approximation of a comfortable, padded, lounge chair. Her companions quickly copied her example. Dev found the soft but firm and slightly enfolding material very accommodating.

From his location he could see that the two small aliens forward had redoubled their activity. The light in the chamber dimmed slightly. Leaning forward, he looked to where Vantolos reposed, his anaconda-like appendages relaxed around him.

"When do we lift off?"

"'Lift off'?" Olonean eyes peered back at him. One tentacle rose from its position of rest to point at the floor. The tip proceeded to transcribe a series of small, tight movements in seemingly empty air. In response, the floor suddenly vanished— or appeared to.

Pavesi gasped, Reed uttered a startled curse, and Dev felt suddenly queasy. In contrast, the two elders among them, the Zimmers, simply clasped hands and stared, their expressions beatific.

To all intents and purposes, the floor at their feet had simply dissolved. Dev found himself gazing down at the Texas coast. As if someone had wielded a narrow paintbrush, white storm streaks spread across lower Louisiana and on into Mississippi. Thin as individual hairs, a few white lines in the water sketched the trails of huge oil tankers. Most of what he could see of the land was green, the result of good spring rains across the breadth of the American south. It was beautiful, spectacular, awe-inspiring. His world, his home.

The floor, or more appropriately, deck, had of course not melted away. It had simply been rendered breathtakingly transparent. Vantolos moved his tentacle tip again. In an upward arc this time, as if directing the beam of a flashlight. The solidity that was the deck returned even as the ceiling turned into a giant port. While darkness dominated the fringes, the center was filled with a massive, looming shape that was coming toward them. No, he corrected himself. They were rising toward it: the alien mothership. As he and his companions stared, an opening appeared in the side facing them. Far larger than the one they had used to enter the shuttle craft, it was more than expansive enough to accommodate the entirety of the craft they were now aboard.

"Soon," Vantolos told them, "you will encounter technology beyond all your imaginings. For an hour or so of your time you will be made to feel small and insignificant, but you will return to your people with tales and images of wonder. Be respectful, observe, and learn."

"What about the unloading of the organic and other materials we've provided to you?" Feisty as ever, Katou-Zimmer was not about to submit to casual alien admonitions.

Vantolos uttered a short, low-pitched whistle. "What a foolish thing to wonder. The materials are transferred from another of our smaller subsidiary craft to the main ship. With all the wonders that are available for you to witness, that is your first thought?"

"All right then," her husband countered. "What about the food synthesizing equipment that will turn our organics into your nutriments? Can we see that?"

"Certainly." The Olone could be contemptuous one moment, magnanimous the next. "A much more thoughtful request."

They were on the verge of being drawn up into the belly of the gigantic main vessel when Reed voiced a question that had certainly occurred to his colleagues but which they were resolutely disinclined to ask. Given his rank, status, and instructions, he had no choice but to do so.

"Can we see your weapons systems?"

Dev held his breath while Pavesi adopted a stony expression. The Zimmers looked disapproving. To everyone's great relief, and not inconsiderable surprise, their tentacled host replied without hesitation or apparent offense.

"I could show them to you, but without an adequately

mature technical background they would mean nothing. Your best people could study whatever images you recorded and learn nothing. Besides, you have already seen some of our weapons."

Dev remembered. "The long devices the Kaijank carried with them."

Slitted eyes turned in his direction as Vantolos eased himself out of his shape-shifting pod. They must have arrived and docked, Dev decided. There had been no sense of slowing or stopping, no feeling of making contact with the larger vessel. Just as there had been no movement or motion when they had lifted off. Somewhat to his surprise there was no sensation of weightlessness, which suggested some version of the long-imagined artificial gravity so prevalent in his youthful reading. Fictional technology made real, he mused.

"You are observant," the Olone told him. "It is to be commended." As the speaker stood on all four tentacles, his attention shifted back to Reed. "There is no reason to try to hide anything, including motivation, because you cannot fathom what you will see. Your intentions are primitive and obvious. You hope to observe and image technology that your own people can reverse engineer. Please realize that you are incapable of doing so. Accepting this fact will make your brief visit here much more enjoyable for you personally."

Ambling across the gray floor he approached the rear wall through which they had entered the corridor. Once again, a portion of the barrier appeared to dissolve at his touch. Slipping out of their respective pods, Dev and the others followed. A glance behind them showed the pods shimmying back into their original cup shapes. It struck him that ever since entering the alien craft he had not seen a single switch, button, or contact plate. Similarly, the A'jeii pilots, or conductors, had touched nothing, operating any controls and manipulating their multiplicity of hovering screens and readouts with movements of their overlarge oculars. Or maybe, he told himself, the aliens had achieved true mind-to-instrumentation connectivity. I think, therefore you do, he marveled silently.

They walked back up the corridor until they reached the point where they had originally entered the shuttle craft. A portal appeared in the same place as before, and Vantolos led them out into a corridor that was much larger than the one on the shuttle. It was busy with a breathtaking array of automatons, as were branching side corridors that led teasingly to unknown destinations.

For what seemed like a long time they walked in one direction. Occasionally the corridor would twist or bend like a dropped rope. The design of both the mothership and the shuttle reflected an aversion to straight lines. To a greater or lesser extent, everything around Dev and his companions was curved or bowed. He could only wonder at the construction techniques that permitted such flowing lines. Though he looked hard, he could not see a single bolt, rivet, weld, or seam. It was as if the interior of the ship, or at least of the corridor down which Vantolos was leading them, had been poured rather than assembled.

Without warning, the corridor opened into a vaulted chamber whose highest point rose some three stories above them. The by-now-familiar flurry of automatons was active here as well, but in contrast to the paucity of live crew on board the shuttle, Dev saw a number of Olone and A'jeii active at positions scattered around the open area. The entire center half of the forward section was transparent, showing the darkness of space and, in an unexpected reminder of home, the familiar disc of the moon. Among all the automatons, Olone, and A'jeii, Dev saw only a single Kaijank.

Flaunting lines of pulsing red and orange light across their otherwise dun-colored bodies, a pair of automatons approached. Devoid of feet, they hovered less than an inch above the deck. Assorted and presumably specialized limbs moved over and around the visitors, examining without touching. When they had finished, the devices retreated in opposite directions.

"Central control." Vantolos gestured with a tentacle. "While the ship is perfectly capable of self-operation, it is useful to have certain functions supervised by organics. When visiting a world, for example. As you can see, any type of manipulative digit or ocular functions effectively. Flexibility is a hallmark of any sufficiently advanced technology."

No less intent than Katou-Zimmer, Pavesi pointed out the blatant omission. "I only see one representative of the Kaijank."

Mysterious, flagrantly organic ripples increased beneath Vantolos's tunic. "The scarceness to which you refer has nothing to do with digital inadequacy. The Kaijank prefer to relinquish the routine operations of the ship to my kind and to the A'jeii." Observing that Reed had his communicator out and was making sweeping recordings of the central control interior, the Olone gestured diffidently. "Make all the pretty images you wish. They will provide fodder for your technologists to admire, if not duplicate. I am certain that …"

He broke off abruptly. Racing toward them along a raised, curving walkway was an A'jeii clad in a brilliant one-piece tunic or jumpsuit fashioned from some pale lime-hued material. When the light in the control center hit the fabric just right, it gleamed like green chrome. Though for all Dev knew, the short biped's attitude and expression might be indicative of anything from amusement to indifference, his initial reaction was that the alien appeared agitated. Halting just short of their tentacled guide, the A'jeii raised an arm and began thrusting it repeatedly at the Olone.

Certainly seems indicative of agitation. Dev tried his best not to imprint human attributes onto the alien.

"What's going on?" In the absence of any knowledge whatsoever of the words that were being exchanged by the two aliens, Jakob Zimmer was working hard to follow the conversation by studying gestures and reactions. With some hesitation he finally felt compelled to ask, "Is something the matter?"

Turning his body in the linguist's direction, Vantolos replied (rather hastily, Dev thought), "No, no, everything is fine. I am absorbing some minor new information that ..."

Shocking everyone, the much smaller A'jeii in the brilliantine ensemble took a step forward and with the three stiffened fingers of its right hand jabbed the Olone directly in the center of his cylindrical torso. Vantolos's pupils contracted, and a strained whistle emerged from his interior. Dev noted that at the same time, the moving shapes beneath his tunic fled from his ventral side around to his back. The A'jeii continued jabbering rapidly while gesturing repeatedly. Having expended itself on the now silent Olone, it turned to face the cluster of fascinated but bewildered humans. When it spoke, its voice was unexpectedly sonorous for such a small being.

"*Gish mar anodol ni ...*" The alien paused, then began again. Throughout it all, Vantolos stood off to one side. With all four tentacles remaining on the deck to support the body, the Olone had begun bobbing up and down like an agitated crab.

"Excuse me, I sorry." Not nearly as fluent as Vantolos, the A'jeii struggled with the unfamiliar alien speech. "I not trained in contact like undercooked untidiness over there." A hand gestured at the Olone. Ever one to note details, Dev saw that instead of the curving lines that streaked a human palm, the A'jeii's was marked by concentric circles.

"Vantolos," a wary Zimmer inquired of their guide, "who is this speaking to us? And are you *certain* nothing is wrong?"

Collecting himself, the Olone raised one tentacle and gestured. "That is Syrenii. You would call her the ship's 'Captain.'"

Reed's brow furrowed. "So then, you're not in charge here?"

"I?" Two tentacles rose from the floor to dance in the air. "I am Vantolos, the interlocutor. Contact specialist. You are speaking of the one in charge."

Not even a fellow Olone, Dev reflected. *An A'jeii.* Come to think of it, it had been two A'jeii who had piloted, or directed, the shuttle that had brought them to the mothership. Was he beginning to identify signs of a hierarchy within the alien ship's crew?

Or was it just coincidence? Of one thing he was certain: he scarcely had enough information on which to base such a conclusion.

"A 'she.'" Katou-Zimmer looked pleased to have one aspect of alien biology confirmed. "That infers sexual reproduction."

"For the A'jeii, anyway," Jakob remarked. "Unless ontogenesis is involved." Husband and wife fell to discussing reproductive possibilities and how that might affect the aliens' perception of humankind.

Like everything the Zimmers discussed, the ongoing dialogue was captivating, but more pressing concerns occupied Dev's thoughts. He followed up on Jakob Zimmer's query.

"I may be completely wrong," he said to the A'jeii captain, "but you seem to me to be somewhat—distressed. Does it have anything to do with our presence here?"

"Yes … no … difficult to explain. No, not difficult. Awkward." Turning away from the taller human, Syrenii once again launched into what Dev could not help but perceive as an ongoing haranguing of Vantolos. What made the exchange even more significant in Dev's mind was the fact that the Olone offered nothing in response: not a verbal riposte, not so much as an argumentative wave of one tentacle.

He and his colleagues were left trying to make some sense of what was happening. No explanation came from Syrenii who, upon concluding her diatribe, rebuke, information dump, or whatever it was, turned and hurried back toward the front of the control center. It was left to Vantolos to explain. The Olone looked to Zimmer, then back to Dev.

"While unsophisticated and abrupt, your fractional assumptions were correct. There is a slight and unforeseen awkwardness. As a corollary, I find myself personally discomfited."

Reed's voice was low and wary. "What kind of awkwardness?"

Vantolos looked over at him, eyes in a tight squint, one tentacle waving aimlessly back and forth in front of the cylindrical body. "Circumstances have arisen that required our immediate departure from your system. An emergency, you would say. I am sorry." Pivoting on his tentacles, he turned to go.

Go where? Dev refused to give in to the sudden panic he felt. They were in the control center or bridge or lookout station or whatever it was of an alien spacecraft and the creature who was their sole sustained contact was about to leave them. Leave them standing, with no one else to talk to, among a small flotilla of busy alien automatons, a host of diminutive and uncaring A'jeii actively engaged in tasks of their own, and one lone and disinterested Kaijank.

No one was surprised when it was Reed who did the unthinkable. Stepping forward, he reached out and grabbed the interlocutor by one shoulder. Or as it was positioned at the moment, hip. Reacting to the tug from human fingers, Vantolos turned. Dev tensed, expecting a bellow of outrage from the Olone. The Zimmers looked at once nervous and intrigued. Pavesi hardly moved.

No threat eventuated. No bellow of indignation was forthcoming. From the Olone there issued not a roar, not a shout, not even a sharp whistle of protest. Instead, Vantolos' exposed skin turned from white to a pale shade of yellow. Black lines matching those that striped his limbs appeared on his upper body and face. In the absence of any verbal response from the alien, Reed spoke firmly.

"You can't leave us like this. What are you talking about?"

"Yes." Surprising himself, Dev moved forward until he was standing alongside the much bigger Reed. A single automaton boasting one flexible limb paused to contemplate the confrontation, then moved on. "You said 'required.' Not 'require.' Does that mean we have already left Earth orbit?"

A shudder passed through the Olone's body. Shrugging off Reed's grip, the contact master scuttled sideways until he was standing beside the curving wall. Reaching out, one tentacle tip traced a circle on the nearest soft, responsive surface. A section some two meters in diameter immediately turned transparent. As it did so, Pavesi let out a gasp.

The ringed world whose orbit they were crossing was immediately familiar. As they stared, it shrank in less than a second to a tiny point of light before vanishing altogether. Astonishingly, there was no feeling of acceleration, no vibration, no sense of motion whatsoever.

Dropping into a crouch, Reed clenched both hands into fists. For an instant, Dev feared he was going to attack the Olone. What kind of defensive response that might elicit from Vantolos, not to mention the scurrying flurry of automatons or the increasingly active A'jeii, Dev could not imagine. Thankfully, his fears were not realized: Reed held himself in check.

The respect he had developed for his fellow contact team members now rose to even greater heights. Pavesi's expression was grim, but that was her only visible reaction. Staring at the star-filled image that had replaced the section of wall, the Zimmers were resigned but calm. Taking a step toward their alien counterpart, Katou-Zimmer spoke quietly but with the characteristic firmness that belied her physical stature.

"This is not acceptable. You must return us to our home. To our world."

The black stripes that now crossed Vantolos's face had doubled in number. Was their appearance a sign of anger? Embarrassment?

"I am afraid that is not possible." A tentacle tip gestured at the circle of superstructure the Olone had rendered transparent. "As you can see, we have already left your system far behind."

Reed had straightened but continued flexing his fingers as if he wanted to strangle someone. Dev had no doubt as to who that might be, though the process would be complicated by the fact that Vantolos had no neck.

"Turn around." His tone was low, threatening. "Turn this ship around and go back."

Slitted eyes shifted to regard the largest human. "That is not possible. I forgive you your ignorance. We have left your world: we cannot go back."

Pavesi fought to control her emotions. "Why not? I mean, we

don't expect you, or the A'jeii, or whoever is in charge of this ship to suddenly throw it in reverse, but can't you settle on a wide arc and come back around to our sun? Or are there technological reasons preventing us from returning?"

"Not technological, no," Vantolos conceded. "The reasons are —other."

"You're saying you can't take us home, but it's not a matter of technology?" Standing near Reed, Dev fed off the big man's quiet strength. "Then what *are* the reasons?" He took a step toward the Olone. "If nothing else, we deserve to know what's behind your refusal!"

An automaton the size of a large refrigerator and not entirely dissimilar in shape paused beside Vantolos. The two exchanged words before the mechanical moved off, intent on tasks elsewhere.

"You deserve *nothing*. You are here because you were here when we had to leave. You are entitled to nothing. Despite that, you will be well treated." A pair of tentacles described curt patterns in the air. "You could just as easily be ejected out the nearest access port, you know. You would do better to reflect on the fact that we are willing to allow you to remain alive and cease your pointless questions. Nothing you can say or do will alter the reality in which you presently find yourselves."

He indicated the departed automaton. "Situationals have been modified to accommodate you. Come with me. Or not, as you prefer." Pivoting, he started back toward the corridor that had led them to the control center.

They had no choice. One by one, they followed: holding back their anger and bewilderment, adrift in thought, swamped by emotion. Last in line, Dev glanced back at the control center. None of the automatons were following them, either physically or with their oculars. From the time they had arrived in the company of their Olonean minder, the single Kaijank had been oblivious to the humans' presence. Aside from a few quick glances, so had the far more numerous A'jeii and the pair of other Olones. Though their continued presence on board surely must be unanticipated it did not seem to have unduly upset the aliens, Dev thought. Was what he and his companions were presently suffering a common occurrence? Did the A'jeii and Olone commonly invite representatives of other species on board their vessel only to make an excuse for absconding with them? Or were they presently the unwitting witnesses to some truly unforeseen and unexplained circumstance? One that might sooner or later end with them being regarded as a nuisance that needed to be chucked out the nearest port? The latter was a possible fate at which Vantolos had already hinted. Better not to dwell on such possibilities.

There was nothing they could do about it in any case. There was nothing they could do about anything.

They were lost. To their world and possibly to themselves.

The quarters to which Vantolos directed them were in stark contrast to the ominous tone the Olone had taken in the control room. Pavesi peered warily into the first compartment, made accessible by their guide sliding a tentacle tip across an apparently solid gray barrier. Dev and the others crowded behind her for a better look. At least, he thought as he scanned the interior, initial appearances did not suggest anything so disheartening as a barred prison cell.

Within the characteristic curving walls, an assortment of cuplike pods of varying size and shape protruded from the walls and floor. Each was lined with the same black, rubber-like material that had padded the shape-shifting seats on the shuttle craft. There was nothing resembling a button, a knob, a dial, or a lever anywhere in the room.

"How are we supposed to live in this?" Reed looked in vain for anything resembling a chair, a bed, or hygienic facilities. "What's the purpose of all these bulges and extensions? They just look like variants of the seats we arrived on."

Vantolos had started back up the corridor in the direction of the control room. As he progressed, he dragged one tentacle tip along the near wall. At identical intervals, four more portals appeared. Then he was gone. Something shoebox-size zipped silently along the deck toward the mystified humans to study them for a moment before rushing silently past. Several lights glowed within its arched ventral side.

Pavesi looked at her colleagues. "What now?"

"I think," Jakob Zimmer mused, "that these are meant to be our living quarters, one for each of us. The body-adapting 'chairs' on which we arrived molded themselves to our individual shapes." He gestured at the interior of the room they were scrutinizing. "The pods on the shuttle vessel that Gavin referred to were of uniform size and only changed when we sat in them." He indicated the chamber. "These here are all of differing size and dimension. They may have different functions from those on the shuttle. We should each of us experiment with the ones in our respective rooms and then assemble to share what we learn." He smiled at his wife. "We will also have to explain to Vantolos why Chiasa and I only require one such habitation."

"If they *are* habitations." Pavesi was not yet convinced. "Maybe they're all ejection ports, like Vantolos hinted." Her expression was grim. "Maybe some of them are for freeze-drying fresh food. Or cooking it."

Pessimist though he was, Reed did not agree with her this time. "If they're unhappy with our presence, why have us eject ourselves? Or cook ourselves?"

"Cultural imperatives?" Katou-Zimmer's suggestion was not well received.

Dev took a deep breath and started to step into the chamber. "Well, we won't learn anything standing out here wondering why we shouldn't be in there. I'll go first."

A hand came down on his shoulder. "Why you?"

Dev looked up at Reed. "I feel that it is part of my job description." The big man grudgingly removed his hand.

Nothing happened when Dev entered the room. But when he turned to wave encouragingly at his colleagues, the portal through which he had entered vanished, leaving a solid wall in its place. It took him several increasingly anxious attempts, dragging one finger across the incongruously soft material, to make the portal reappear. Concerned faces gazed back at him.

"Okay," he murmured. "Easy open, easy close. Just run a finger across the right spot. Some practice required."

Zimmer nodded encouragingly. "Well done, Devali." He turned his attention to Pavesi and Reed. "We should all go begin our own explorations, in our own rooms." With his wife beside him, he started up the corridor.

Left to his own devices, Dev closed the 'door' to his chamber and moved to the largest of the cup-pods. Set on the floor near one wall, it was larger than the one that had transformed into a seat on the shuttle. Cautiously, he leaned into it and gently began running a finger around the black interior.

A minute or so of this tactile experimentation produced a soft popping sound. Like a rubbery balloon, the pod expanded in all directions, forcing a startled Dev to jump back. When the pod had finished expanding, he found himself staring at …

A bed. An ordinary, human-sized bed. There was a single thin covering of shockingly bright red. Approaching tentatively, he sat down on the edge. It gave slightly beneath his weight, supportive yet comforting.

How had it known to conform to a human need? If Vantolos had done likewise, had drawn a tentacle tip across the pod's interior, would the device have transformed into a completely different kind of structure? A suitable resting place for a multi-limbed Olone? Or would it have morphed into something else entirely?

Shaking his head in wonderment he rose from the platform and began repeating the finger-stroking gesture with the rest of the pods in the chamber, stimulating them one at time as he worked his way across the room. One pod turned promptly into a hemispherical table or desk, another into a legless but high-backed chair. More surprising still, another pod transformed into a shower. The temperature of the water that emerged from the perforated upper portion was exactly as he would have set it. There was a pod-container full of edibles; some familiar, some quite alien, all of it appealing to his palate. A finger swipe against the bare wall created a circular port through which nothing could be seen but blackness shot through with thin streaks of silver.

When one pod transmuted into a seat that could be nothing other than a toilet, Dev no longer held any doubts concerning the supremacy of the alien technology. How the pods had known to conform to the needs of a species never before encountered he could not imagine. The results were far more than supremely advanced and not quite magic.

When later the five of them gathered in the Zimmers' cabin to discuss what they had learned, the remarkable readiness of the pods in their cabins to transform into human conveniences was the first subject brought up by an admiring but bemused Katou-Zimmer.

"How can such inanimate devices know all the details not only of our body types, but our biological requirements? And the shower: who could imagine such luxury on a starship? One cannot help but wonder, does a being like Vantolos also cleanse his body with jets of warm water?" She shook her head in wonder.

"And if he does not employ such personal bathing methods," added her husband, "do the pods in his living quarters provide whatever alternative cleansing system is required? Simply by sensing that he is an Olone? I have often mused on what truly advanced technology could achieve, but this is the first time I have been compelled to contemplate technology that is species perceptive."

"The pods—or the room itself—comprehends ordinary English speech, too." They all looked at Dev. He was honestly bemused at their expressions. "You mean none of you have tried controlling your habitat by just talking? Without using the finger stroke?"

Pavesi stared at him. "How do you know it responds appropriately to speech? You've tried this?"

"I asked it for fried fish. With french fries. And rolls and butter. One of the wall pods produced all of it. Probably synthe-sized from the organics we and everyone else on Earth provided."

Zimmer was disapproving. "Not a very healthy diet on which to commence an involuntary interstellar journey, my friend."

"What difference does it make?" Reed had slid into melan-choly. "We're all gonna die on this ship, anyway. Or on some alien world if that's where they intend taking us. We're never, none of us, going to see Earth again." Hands folded, he sat on the edge of a pod chair and stared at the space between his feet. "I'm never gonna see my cousin's girl play soccer again."

Pavesi looked surprised. "We're not supposed to have any close relatives."

He looked over at her. "Distant niece doesn't qualify. Didn't show up when I applied so I figured I was in the clear. Doesn't matter now. What, you gonna notify the Pentagon?"

She didn't back down from his sarcasm. "I was just surprised, that's all. I didn't mean anything by it."

He returned his gaze to the floor. "I know. I know you didn't."

It was quiet in the room for a moment, until Katou-Zimmer, her attention on Dev, spoke up anew. "You just ordered food and it was provided?" Rising from where she was sitting, she walked over to where several pods hung on the far wall. "Which one?" Dev pointed out the appropriate pod.

"Green salad." She was careful to enunciate clearly as she addressed the pod. "Romaine lettuce, tomatoes, kale, sprouts, sliced cucumber. Oil and vinegar dressing."

A brief pause and then the black interior of the pod disap-peared. It was replaced with an intense yellow glow that slowly shaded to green. When this faded away, a bowl of some pale blue material sat in the opening. Even at a distance, greens and red tomatoes could be seen clearly.

Taking the bowl, Katou-Zimmer hesitated, then addressed the pod again. "Utensils? A fork?"

"Different pod." Dev pointed. Moving to stand in front of the indicated device, Katou-Zimmer repeated her request. The fork that materialized in the opening was fashioned of an unknown material that seemed to be a bizarre meld of plastic and wood. Picking it up, the biologist sampled the salad.

"This is beyond technology," she murmured, crunching away. "I can go as far as understanding how an alien synthesizing structure might analyze our digestive system and supply nutrients accordingly, but—salad dressing? A fork? Without ever having been presented with an example to work from?"

Her husband turned contemplative. "The aliens quickly learned our language. They knew what kind and variety of organics to demand from us. We do not know what else about us they studied and learned." Reaching out, he plucked a small tomato from the slope of her salad and popped it into his mouth, chewing thoughtfully. "A bit tasteless, but otherwise indisputably tomato. All synthesized and delivered on demand via a request couched in plain English."

"You say tomato," Reed grumbled, "I say I want to go *home*."

"You heard Vantolos." Like a bad odor, depression was spreading from Reed to Pavesi. "No way. No chance. And no explanation."

It was a conundrum Dev had pondered as intensely as the rest of them. Unlike them, his pondering had generated an idea. "That's what Vantolos told us, yes. Maybe another member of the crew would respond differently." His gaze met each of theirs in turn. "No harm in asking."

"Vantolos might not like us questioning his responses," Katou-Zimmer pointed out.

Reed rose from the edge of his pod chair. "Who gives a damn what the squid thinks?"

Her husband gestured forcefully in Reed's direction. "We might do well to avoid giving voice to casual insults. For all we know we may be under constant surveillance. It's possible that ..."

Reed's voice overwhelmed that of the older man. "I don't

give a damn if they hear me! What're they going to do—chuck us overboard? Or outboard? We're going to die anyway. Until then or until they otherwise somehow shut us down, we might as well explore everything resembling an option that we've got." Eyeing Dev, he nodded once. "What did you have in mind? Asking the captain, that little Syrenii creature?"

"Not exactly, no." Moving to the west wall, Dev traced a circle on its surface. Immediately, an image of the void outside appeared. "Since the ship itself has proven so responsive to our needs and requests, I was thinking of asking *it*. Or at least querying a pod." He smiled hopefully. "One pod responds to requests for food, another to requests for fluids. Maybe one will respond to queries for information."

Zimmer's cheeks bunched up as he smiled. "That, my young friend, is a brilliant idea! The pods provide sleeping facilities, hygienic services, and nourishment. Why not answers to questions?"

Suddenly hopeful, Pavesi was nodding agreement. "All it can do is ignore us." She straightened. "And if our inquiries are reported to the control center, to Syrenii or Vantolos or even the Kaijank, I'm with Gavin." She nodded in Reed's direction. "We're already doomed, sooner or later. Let's see what we can find out about options Vantolos may not have mentioned."

"Or deliberately chose not to mention," Reed added.

It grew quiet in the cabin. It took only a moment once silence had descended for Dev to realize that they were all expecting him to give voice to what could very well prove to be life or death questions.

—VI—

Thrust into the spotlight, Dev felt he could reasonably defer to someone better qualified to pose the critical inquiries. That he did not was due more to his own innate curiosity than to any fear of saying something that might prove damaging to their present situation. He *wanted* to ask questions. Besides, as Pavesi had obliquely implied, and Reed more directly, how much more hopeless could their current state become?

Facing the wall in which were embedded the smaller, food-providing pods, he asked straightforwardly, "Ship, how did you know what kind of foods to synthesize for myself and my companions?"

There was no reply. Essaying a variant of the query, Zimmer was rewarded with the same silence. They all tried, each employing variations of the same inquiry. Their compartments could provide beds, chairs, food, showers, and more, but it appeared that it could not, or would not, reply to a question verbally. Pavesi spread her hands and looked resigned.

"That's that, then. We're to be kept alive but ignorant." She started toward the portal. Or rather, the section of deceptively solid wall that could produce a portal in response to an applicable touch. "I don't know about the rest of you, but I'm exhausted. I'm going back to my cabin and try to get some sleep."

Zimmer nodded in approval. "I always think better after a meal and some sleep. Perhaps one of us will awaken to a brilliant idea."

"Or maybe we'll find out this is all a dream." Muttering to himself, a disappointed Reed followed Pavesi out the doorway she generated.

As her husband was preparing their bed, Katou-Zimmer walked up to Dev and put a hand on his arm. As she did with everyone else, the diminutive scientist had to tilt her neck back in order to meet his gaze.

"Don't feel bad. It was a good idea, worth trying."

He was only slightly consoled. "So many questions. We've got so many questions, and no way to get answers."

She gave his arm a maternal squeeze. "Jakob is usually right about such things. We've been under a great deal of pressure and all need to rest. Get some sleep, Dev, and we'll get together later and see if anyone has any good ideas on what our next step should be. Assuming we can find a way to access such options."

He nodded, turned, and had to use his hand to re-create the doorway. The opening lingered a moment behind him, letting him see back into the Zimmers' compartment. Sleep, Chiasa had advised him. How could he sleep? How could any of them? Pavesi he could understand. Their ongoing ordeal had completely worn her out. Reed's anger would eventually drive him to lie down and seek surcease in his headphones. The Zimmers—he was confident that the Zimmers could sleep anywhere, under any circumstances.

He was halfway to his own cabin when he decided that waiting for inspiration to strike was a poor waste of time. With every hour, with every minute, they were doubtless journeying farther and farther from home, from Earth. If the aural receptors in their living quarters would not respond to their queries, perhaps there was another way. As had been discussed, a potentially dangerous way. He felt it was incumbent on him to try. If he did not, then Reed probably would, and Reed was just stressed enough to go beyond questioning and do something that might get them all killed.

In contrast, if he made the attempt, he might only get himself killed.

———

He found Vantolos forward, just inside the entrance to the control center. At least, Dev assumed it was forward. There was no way, currently, to tell on what part of the alien vessel it was located. Remembering the numerous images he had seen of it while back on Earth (such a strange thought to have: "back on Earth"), he knew the ship was huge. Yet he and his colleagues had entered and been exposed to only a small section. Was the area that housed the crew more extensive but as yet unseen? Were there vast areas devoted to the propulsion system and related engineering? Or was the bulk of the ship's capacity devoted to carrying cargo such as the organics and other materials that the aliens had demanded and received? More questions he would have to ask.

It certainly seemed that he would have plenty of time available in which to do so.

Considering the dimensions of the ship, at least when viewed from below, the extent of the control center was hardly excessive. There was ample room for perhaps thirty or forty individuals to function simultaneously. As on his previous visit, most were A'jeii, though this time there were several Kaijank present instead of one, and two more Olone in addition to Vantolos. Dev felt a small surge of pride as he approached the tentacled interlocutor. He was good with details, and he felt confident he had memorized the distinctive pattern of the banding on the Olone's limbs as well as the slight mottling of his exposed skin. The small shapes underneath his tunic (a pale chromatic blue fabric having replaced the earlier gold, Dev noted) were moving about at a slow, deliberate pace.

Seeing the human approaching, Vantolos broke off the conversation he was having with a Kaijank. As near as Dev could tell, the big biped was currently unarmed. It was the first time he had observed a member of its species not in possession of a possible weapon of some kind. As the Kaijank turned and departed, a furious Vantolos turned to confront Dev. Balancing precisely on two tentacles, it waved the other pair forcefully in the human's direction.

"What are you doing here? You were told to remain in the living quarters that had been assigned to you! What are you doing here! Your living quarters are capable of supplying all your needs!"

Dev held his ground. In his own quiet way he was as frustrated as Gavin Reed.

"Not true. We need answers to questions, and our living quarters seem unwilling or unable to provide that."

One tentacle dropped to the deck to change the Olone's posture from bipedal to tripodal while the other continued to wave in Dev's direction. "Any questions you may have will be answered if and when we find it appropriate and reasonable to do so. Until then, you were ordered to remain in your quarters!"

"Actually," Dev countered tersely, "we were told to *go* to our quarters. Nothing was said about having to 'remain' in them." He waved at the busy control center. "Nobody said we had to stay there. So in the absence of any specified prohibition, I thought I'd take a walk. And ask questions."

Vantolos's pupils contracted slightly. "You believe yourself to be clever by speaking in such a manner. I can tell. How clever would you believe yourself to be if you were to startle a Kaijank in another corridor, one uninformed about your presence here, only to then find yourself shot down. You could not explain yourself. You would not have time. Neither balanced, thoughtful communication nor patience is a quality for which the Kaijank are noted. They tend to be reactive rather than contemplative."

Dev considered. "In other words, shoot first and ask questions later?"

The single waving tentacle dipped sharply, an emphatic gesture for sure. "A theoretical situation in which you or any of your companions could so easily be on the receiving end."

"But I'm not in 'another corridor,'" Dev pointed out. "I'm here, at the control center, talking to you."

"A conversation uninvited and now to be terminated." Rising, the tentacle tip jabbed back down the corridor from which Dev had emerged. The Olone's voice rose. "Go back to your quarters! Now! Or suffer the consequences!"

"What consequences?" a new voice inquired.

Intent on the Olone, Dev had not noticed the arrival of this newcomer. For that matter, neither had Vantolos. This might have had something to do with the A'jeii's wee stature. Dev was at once fascinated and a bit startled by the A'jeii's unexpected interjection. Its comment provided the first proof that the Olones, and Vantolos in particular, were not the only aliens capable of or familiar with human speech. Heedless of the undescribed consequences to which Vantolos had alluded, and additionally any that might be mentioned by the A'jeii, Dev leaped at this new opportunity.

"Your colleague Vantolos insists that I and my companions must remain sequestered in our living quarters or suffer unknown 'consequences.'"

As the A'jeii slowly digested this, Dev decided that, while fluent, speaking in alien English was more difficult for the smaller alien than it was for the Olone. If the tentacled species was more nimble when it came to exchanging pleasantries in alien speech, that would go a long way toward explaining why Vantolos had been chosen as the ship's primary contact individual for Earth.

This did not keep the A'jeii from unleashing a torrent of short, clipped, incomprehensible speech in the Olone's direction. Vantolos responded by protesting, or so Dev thought, with words in the same language the A'jeii was using as well as much gesticulating of his own flexible limbs. This neither slowed nor intimidated the A'jeii. When the short biped had finished yammering at the Olone, it turned to look up at Dev.

"I am Tilenyii, the—I am something akin to what you would call a supervisor. I am responsible for much that happens with this journeying now as well as in the future. I regret both this Olone's manners—they can be an acerbic folk—and his verbal treatment of you and the rest of your kind. But their volubility has its uses." The A'jeii paused. "I am sixth kin to the captain, Syrenii, who you met earlier. We are—what you might think of as distant sisters. We regret your presence here almost as much as you do yourselves. It was not planned. It was not intended. It was an accident."

"Then," Dev murmured hopefully, "rectify the accident. Take us home."

"Unfortunately," Tilenyii replied, "that is not possible. In that, Vantolos has been truthful. We cannot go back. We were compelled to leave your beautiful but confused world in a great hurry. A problem developed that demanded our immediate and rapid departure. So much so that there was not even time to return you to the surface of your world."

Dev tried another track. "If you have a problem that involves Earth, maybe I and my companions can help you. We are a diverse bunch commanding many specialties and …"

The A'jeii made an intricate gesture with her left hand, the three fingertips all pressing against one another. "Would that you could. Help us with our problem. But I doubt it."

With nothing to lose, Dev pressed on. "Try us. Tell me, and I will lay your problem before my companions."

"As you wish." Vantolos put a tentacle tip on the A'jeii's left shoulder. Irritated, she eased away from the physical contact. "This ship …"

"A fine ship," Dev essayed. "Vast and impressive."

"Indeed it is," the supervisor readily agreed. "Unfortunately, it is not ours. Or rather, it is ours, but not long ago was not."

That wasn't the response Dev was expecting. Not that he'd had anything specific in mind, but even so …

"I don't understand."

"In the matter of proprietorship," Vantolos began, "there are some ongoing questions as to …"

Tilenyii cut him off. "No need to equivocate, Olone. It wastes time." She returned her big-eyed gaze to the bemused human. "This vessel. We stole it."

Dev blinked. "I'm sorry—what?"

"We seized it. From its prior owners." The human's continuing silence appeared to puzzle her. "Appropriated it without permission. We, everyone on board—the A'jeii, the Olone, and the Kaijank—are vested in the acquisition of well-regarded property by means demanding the least effort on our part. Am I not making myself comprehended?"

Dev stammered a reply. "Yes—no—I think yes."

His thoughts were awhirl. So then, humankind's first, shining, significant contact with intelligent alien sentients had been with—if he was indeed understanding the A'jeii supervisor correctly—a multispecies pack of thieves. He wondered how that revelation would go down at the United Nations.

Would *have* gone down, he corrected himself. Now, with Tilenyii's unabashed admission, he saw more clearly than ever why he and his companions were not going to go home again. Earth's first alien visitation had been for purposes of acquiring property without compensation. Just as the aliens had acquired this ship. There was no reason for Tilenyii and Syrenii and Vantolos and their companions to revisit the site of their deceitfulness.

"Let me take a guess," he murmured. "If I understand everything correctly, there's really only one obvious reason why you had to leave my world on such short notice. It is because the rightful owners of this ship are after you."

"I do not believe a mastery of prescience is required to draw that conclusion." The A'jeii had a sense of humor, Dev realized, and it was as dry as desert sand.

"You're running," was all he could think of to say.

"As fast and as far as this most excellent ship's drive will take us," the supervisor admitted readily. "The owners are noted for their persistence. They will not rest until they have reclaimed their property." Another succinct yet elaborate hand gesture described arcs in the air between A'jeii and human. "Which means that we cannot rest, either. Not until we have succeeded in removing ourselves from their attention. Doing so will require much fretful traveling, some of it to regions little known and scarcely explored." Unexpectedly, a small hand reached toward Dev. Two fingers drew a line down the front of his torso, halting at his waistline.

"We are not evil, those of us who are presently crewing this craft. At worst, we might be regarded as less than sociable." She glanced sideways. "Certainly that applies to the Olone. But you see now why we could not linger in the vicinity of your world, your system. Not even to return you to your surface."

Dev nodded understandingly, assuming that if the aliens could so easily master human speech, they must also have acquired at least some minimal understanding of human gestures.

"Would you—would you really have destroyed some of our cities if we had not complied with your demands?"

"Destroyed your …?" Tilenyii hesitated only briefly. "Oh, that. Certainly not. Do you think us uncivilized?" She looked over again at the plainly irritated Vantolos. "Words make powerful weapons, especially when utilized by an overbearing Olone. But they cause no real damage, end no actual lives. Besides," and her attention returned to Dev, "we don't know if this ship mounts any serious armaments. It is possible, but perhaps unlikely. Insofar as we have been able to determine, it is a large and valuable but essentially straightforward transport vessel. The only weapons we ourselves possess are similar to those few you saw carried by the Kaijank who accompanied Vantolos on his visits to your surface."

Dev was reeling. Not only were their captors thieves but …

"You were bluffing. All your demands, all your threats, were nothing but—bluff."

Tilenyii's mouth twisted slightly, though whether the impetus behind it was a smile, a frown, or something else, Dev could not tell. Confirming what Dev had already decided, the dry A'jeii sense of humor came to the fore.

"The meaning of the term you utilize is understood."

Dev had come fearing hostility while hoping to secure answers to some questions. In that, he had been more successful than he could have imagined. The result, however, left him baffled and confused. One thing was certain, however. Tilenyii was right. The humans could not help their captors with their "problem."

"While running," the supervisor explained, "we found your world with a type of scan that—it does not matter. You wouldn't understand. Enough to say that we found you and your world, rich with the organics and other raw materials we needed in order to be able to continue our flight. We would have stayed longer and demanded more, but the same technology that enabled us to find you also alerted us to the approach of those whose vessel we have appropriated. With no time to linger lest we be found and trapped, we had to depart in haste." Tilenyii's eyes were large and limpid, but her voice was steel.

"This is what led to your present misfortune. We did not intend it, but we could not avoid it. Until some final decision is made regarding your fate and your future, consider yourselves guests. You may roam freely about the ship. You do not know enough to damage anything." The A'jeiian supervisor paused before adding, "You may even continue to ask questions."

Dev had one. "You stole this ship. Yet you seem to have no trouble flying it."

"'Flying'?" It took Tilenyii a moment to understand. "The ship, like any interstellar vessel, essentially 'flies' itself. Myself, Captain Syrenii, the rest of the A'jeii and the Olone and even the Kaijank, are merely passengers."

Dev frowned. "But the control center—I saw several dozen of

your kind as well as others active at what appeared to be control consoles and such."

"Effective backup requires efficient input. The ship is not wholly independent of its passengers. It requires some direction. We provide that. The A'jeii are very adept at such things." As an afterthought she added, "As on occasion are the Olone."

"And the Kaijank?" Dev wondered.

"Their physical presence and appearance is naturally intimidating. A very useful element when bluffing another species and such." A small, barely audible buzz sounded from the vicinity of her waistband. "I am being asked to supply some of that input of which I just spoke. While you will not be returning to your world of birth, you have before you an opportunity to see and learn such things as your primitive species can only have imagined. Some sentients would consider that a fair tradeoff. Explore the ship. Ask your questions. Survive." She turned and walked briskly away, trailed by a somewhat chastened Vantolos.

Feeling exceedingly lost, emotionally empty, and not a little stupid, Dev watched them go. Then he remembered not only where he was, but who he was. His companions needed to be told. He wondered if they would believe him.

If not, he mused as he turned back down the corridor, they could always ask their own questions.

————

Pavesi couldn't stop laughing. Dev couldn't tell if the tears running down her face were of amusement or pain. A somber Reed growled at her.

"What are you cackling at? What's so funny?"

She struggled to catch her breath. "The whole situation. From its very beginning to now. We go from quaking in fear over a possible invasion to finding out that there never was any threat of an invasion, or even of a hostile visitation. Rush-hour commuting on the Metro turns out to be more dangerous than a giant alien mothership hovering over Washington. Not to mention that our captors—yes, I said it, captors—are the alien equivalent of the inhabitants of a Potemkin village!" She shook her head at the incongruity of it all.

"I have to agree." Katou-Zimmer was sitting on the edge of the bed in the Zimmers' cabin, where everyone had once again gathered. "For decades a majority of humans imagined that a first contact with an advanced alien species would show them to be either ruthless invaders or benign superbeings." Seated nearby, her husband muttered something ironic in either Hebrew or Arabic: Dev couldn't be sure. "Instead," his petite but combative spouse concluded, "we get the interstellar equivalent of a pack of neighborhood car thieves."

"At least they've admitted what they are." Arms crossed in front of him, Dev shifted his back against the far wall. "Or at least, one of them did. It was Tilenyii, the crew supervisor."

Reed took a long, deep breath. "Based on everything you've told us, Dev, the A'jeii seem more open to discussion than the Olone. The Kaijank don't seem inclined to talk much at all, even among themselves."

"Muscle." Wiping at her eyes, Pavesi turned thoughtful. "Just like Dev said. The Kaijank are the aliens' muscle. Big bodies, strong backs, designated weapons carriers. They're at a disadvantage conversation-wise because they're either not oxygen-breathers or they need a different atmospheric blend." She eyed her companions. "I say any further negotiations we have about getting home, we talk directly with the A'jeii."

Dev pondered possible ramifications. "I do not think Vantolos will like that. He seems to take his position as official interlocutor pretty seriously."

"Like we should care what the squid feels." Though he had ideas of his own, Reed had developed a growing appreciation for Dev's point of view. "I'd caucus with the Devil himself if it would get me back to Virginia."

"Devils live in the next solar system over," Pavesi joked. Nobody laughed.

"Tilenyii says they cannot take us home," Dev reiterated,

"because they're running from this ship's rightful owners. Although we did not get into the specifics of their situation, I take it to mean that they cannot retrace their course."

"Makes no sense." Pavesi was clearly puzzled. "Space is, you know—big. They could easily circle around back to Earth and avoid any pursuit."

"We don't know that." Jakob Zimmer had an irritating habit of throwing cold water on one proposal after another. Or throwing logic at it. "We have no idea how their technology works, and we know nothing of stellar navigation."

"Maybe," his wife chipped in, "they *could* take us back to Earth, but they just don't want to."

Reed frowned at her. "If they could but just won't, why not?"

"Why yes?" she countered. "They have nothing to gain by returning us to Earth. They arrived there, they got what they wanted from our world, and they left. In a hurry." Her gaze met each of theirs in turn as she continued to speak calmly. "Frankly, I'm more than a little surprised they haven't shoved us out the nearest port already. We breathe their air, eat their food, and ask embarrassing questions. So why bother to keep us alive? We're no good to them, no good for anything."

Dev pondered his senior colleague's observation. "Maybe," he finally said, "we potentially are of some use to them."

Everyone turned to look at him. "For what?" Reed said.

"I don't know. But I do think that Chiasa is on to something. They have kept us alive, even provided us with living quarters, when they just as easily could have dumped us in a Saturnian orbit on the way out of our system. They must have a reason for not doing that. And I don't think it has anything to do with, say, an Olone's altruistic nature." Pushing away from the wall, he headed for the apparently solid space where a doorway could be made to appear.

"Where are you going?" Reed asked him.

"To ask some more questions. Want to come with me? Or do you have objections, Gavin?"

The big man waved a noncommittal hand. "No, no. Just

wondering. Go ask your questions. I look forward to hearing any new information when you come back." He rose from his pod chair. "Me? I'm gonna take another shower. Then I'm going to experiment with each and every pod in my quarters until I know everything they can do. If you *don't* come back," he shrugged, "we'll at least know not to press the subject."

Dev ventured a thin smile. "I have always tried to make myself useful."

———

He was retracing the steps that led to the control center when he reached the junction of corridors and on impulse decided to take the one leading off to the right instead of continuing straight on. In the course of making his way deeper into the vast ship he passed only a pair of A'jeii. The smallest and most numerous of the three sentient species on board exhibited an affinity for traveling in pairs, though whether this was for reasons of security, a reflection of specialized demands, a sexual relationship, or something else, he had no way of knowing. The problem with inquiring about such things was that while he badly wanted answers, he likewise did not want to be insensitive. Or worse, overstep serious boundaries regulating individual propriety. Since he had no notion of where such boundaries might lie or what they might consist of, he deemed it prudent to err on the side of caution.

In the course of his ramble, he encountered neither Olone nor Kaijank. Except for the pair of A'jeii, his only encounters were with a steady two-way flow of automatons. These were as varied in design and construction as they were in shape, color, and presumably function. Irrespective of size, speed, or number of limbs, those coming toward him invariably swerved to avoid the striding biped. All were as eerily silent as if they had been implants in the surrounding walls. In the absence of beeps, hums, whistles, creaks, groans, or any other noise, their vigorous mobility was more than a little unsettling.

Heedless of possible ramifications, he determined to try and stop one just to see if he could do so. The subject he chose for this experiment in human-cybernetic spatial relations was scarcely as tall as Chiasa Katou-Zimmer. Its smooth, cylindrical body came toward him on a wide metallic base that hovered a couple of centimeters above the deck. In keeping with the motive power of its fellow automatons, its propulsion system was dead silent. Facial features consisted solely of a pair of protruding vitreous hemispheres that broke the otherwise smooth uppermost portion of the bronze-hued body. There was no sign of synthetic nose, mouth, or ears.

As it approached, the automaton veered left to go around Dev. He quickly shifted his own stance so as to get in front of it. Sidling sideways, it attempted to avoid him by going in the other direction. Once again, he hurried to block its path. This noiseless dance continued for another several minutes, in the course of which the other automatons utilizing the corridor wholly ignored the mismatched couple.

Finally, the mechanical stopped, hovering in place. It did not back up nor did it turn to go back the way it had come. As to its destination and whatever intended function Dev had interrupted, it gave no clue. They remained like that for what seemed hours but was probably less than ten minutes. Determined to end the standoff on terms he would dictate, Dev held his ground. He had no idea what he would do if the automaton suddenly decided to simply continue forward. He did not know how heavy it was nor how much motive power it could muster. Even if it eventually did nothing more than push him backward and out of the way, he would have learned something.

It did neither. Instead, a sound issued from within the gleaming body. Gibberish.

"What? I don't understand," Dev said.

"Ah. The dominant language of the last inhabited world. Do you perhaps understand me now?"

The mechanical's accent was oddly familiar. It took Dev a

moment to identify its origin. It sounded, he told himself in amazement, exactly like …

Him.

American English with inherited Delhi overtones. Not as thick an accent as that which afflicted his parents' speech but definitely not Washington-New York. The relevant system on the alien vessel that was in charge of understanding and interpretation had evidently taken its linguistic cue from sounds collected in the course of surface contact with the human species. As he had been the principal talker in the course of such conversations, it had proceeded on the assumption that his accent was the most useful one to imitate. He felt oddly flattered. Standing his ground in a corridor on a starship far from Earth while conversing with an alien mechanical, the last thing he expected was to hear a synthesized voice that sounded much like himself.

"Yes, I can understand you now, thank you very much."

"You are most welcome." The cylindrical automaton replied with becoming, if disconcerting, politesse. "Will you please move to one side so that I may pass?"

"Sure," Dev told it, "after you have answered a couple of my questions."

"General information is not a specialty of mine. Nor is communicating directly with non-crew."

"Don't worry if you can't answer," Dev replied reassuringly.

"I was not worried," the automaton stated flatly. "I do not 'worry.' You refuse to move?"

Dev held his position. Just because he was not conversing with an intimidating Kaijank did not mean that the mechanical was incapable of causing harm. All science incorporated some degree of risk, he told himself.

"I'll move after you have answered, as best you can, some of my questions."

The automaton remained motionless. Paying the odd pair no mind, other mechanicals continued to whizz by in both directions.

"I will try to answer your questions," it finally declared.

"Please be quick or I will be delayed in performing my intended functions."

"I won't keep you long." Dev spoke as if addressing any passerby on any street. The reality was somewhat different. "First question: where are we going? What is our current intended destination?"

"Another inhabited world. If the instructions and charting are accurate, Mozehn, to be precise."

Dev nodded as if this actually meant something. "I see. And what will the crew be doing when we arrive at Moo-zahn?"

"Mozehn," the mechanical corrected him. "I believe the intention is to remain in that system in the hope that the legal owners of this vessel will abandon their pursuit."

A reasonable and understandable stratagem, Dev mused. "What about us? Myself and my friends, who have been removed from our world?"

"I have no idea." The alien mechanical replied without guile. "I am not privy to such deliberations. Since this vessel and all aboard are to remain in that system for an indeterminate time, I can make the assumption that you and your friends are to remain in that system for an indeterminate time. Please pardon me, but I am compelled to fulfill my intended functions."

The metalized cable that whipped forward wrapped gently but irresistibly around a startled Dev's waist. Lifting him off the floor, it swung leftward and set him down with equal ease. As the cable retracted the automaton resumed its original route, scooting silently past Dev and up the corridor. Slightly shaken by the abruptness of the act, he realized that the device had lifted him as easily as he would have a feather. Thankfully, this had been executed with the utmost gentleness. Except for a slight skin burn around his waist, he was unharmed. This time. He made a mental note to think twice next time before barring the progress of one of the vessel's diligent mechanicals. The next one might not react so considerately.

—VII—

can make the assumption that you and your friends are to remain in that system for an indeterminate time.'" Gnawing on an excellent synthesized stalk of imitation celery, Katou-Zimmer regarded the others in the room after repeating what Dev had told them. "We can draw two suppositions from that. Either things remain as they are with us staying on board this vessel—or else our dour, slightly anxious hosts decide to dump us on this new world, this 'Mozehn.'" A loud crunch permeated the ensuing silence as she bit off another inch of celery. "If the latter, one would hope it at least has a breathable atmosphere."

"That's all the mechanical said about it?" Pavesi's tone and expression mixed curiosity with anxiety. "Nothing about whether there's food to be had, or potable water? Are they just going to dump us there to be rid of us?"

Jakob Zimmer made calming motions in her direction. "Let's not jump to conclusions, especially unpleasant ones. It may be that the first option is in order. That our captor/hosts are simply looking for a place to 'hide out' for a while. Somewhere off the beaten interstellar track where they hope the rightful owners of this craft will not be able to find them. Assuming that prospect to be the correct one, there is no reason for them to 'dump' us there, or anywhere else. It's not as if we're using up all their food and water." He turned his attention to Dev. "Given the size of this ship, at least insofar as what we were able to see of it from Earth's surface, doesn't it strike you that it was designed—or is capable of holding a far larger crew contingent than what we have encountered thus far?"

Finding himself once again on the speculative spot, Dev paused a moment before replying. "It is true we can count the number of A'jeii, Olone, and Kaijank we have seen and that the total is not large. That doesn't mean there not more beavering away elsewhere on the ship. But given the high number of mechanicals we have encountered in proportion to the number of aliens, I think your guess is a reasonable one, Jakob. It matches up with what Tilenyii told us about how such starships are run: that they are guided and driven by devices much more than they are by organics. I have no idea what the bulk of this vessel's unseen volume is designed for. Maybe it has something to do with the ship's means of propulsion. Maybe it is empty space intended to hold cargo. Maybe it is some kind of interstellar cruise ship and was taken between passenger loadings, *narak*, who knows?"

"Why didn't you ask it?" Reed wanted to know. "The mechanical who replied to your questions?"

Growing testy, Dev glared at the bigger man. "I cannot imagine why I didn't ask everything that needed to be asked. Maybe because it wrapped me up in a metal tentacle and moved me to one side like I was a piece of cotton, when it could just as easily have cut me in half."

"Easy now." If Zimmer had had access to a smoke-worthy pipe, he would have been puffing on it energetically. "We're all under a lot of stress. There's so much we don't know and that we have yet to come to terms with in our new lives."

"If we're allowed to have new lives," Reed muttered. He was angry, but at Fate, not Devali Mukherjee. "We're at the mercy of a pack of alien midgets plus a bunch of bald thugs and a handful of gabby squid. Prospects aren't good."

"All of whom might very well be observing and listening to us this very moment," a terse Pavesi pointed out. Reed started to reply, absorbed what she had said, and went quiet. Earlier, he had been on the verge of violence. Now he was simply worn out and tending to the fatalistic.

"It doesn't matter." Katou-Zimmer gave a shrug, corroborating Reed's reaction without partaking of it emotionally. "There's nothing we can do except rely on the benevolent nature of our hosts."

"The benevolence of a bunch of starship thieves." A seated Reed had his head inclined forward and was rubbing the back of his neck with one hand. "Why does that continue to mitigate my optimism?"

"You never know." Dev tried to cheer them all. "We may be able to make ourselves useful, somehow. Ensure that we are continued to be treated well. Earn our keep."

"Sure." Looking up, Reed ventured a wan smile. "We could offer ourselves up as slaves."

Jakob Zimmer let out a mildly derisive snort. "I seriously doubt that advanced interstellar civilizations practice something as archaic as slavery."

"Why not?" Reed shot him a look. "They apparently have no problem practicing larceny."

"In such a marketplace," Dev said, "we would likely have some novelty value."

Reed swung his gaze from the older man to the younger. "That's not funny."

Dev found himself nodding slowly. "You are right. It is not."

"It would appear, then," Zimmer continued, "that our approaching options come down to captivity or abandonment. I would wish for a healthier choice."

"Doesn't matter," Reed reiterated. "It's up to the A'jeii and their collaborators what happens to us. We have nothing to do with it."

Dev rose suddenly from where he had been sitting. "I'm going to talk to the captain."

"To Syrenii?" Pavesi gaped at him. "What good will that do? They've probably already decided what they're going to do with us once we reach this Mozehn."

"If that is the case, then it won't matter what I say." Dev headed for the portal portion of the far wall.

"What if you say something offensive?" Katou-Zimmer warned him.

Dev looked back at her. "Then maybe I *will* get pitched out the nearest airlock. In that event, the rest of you will learn something from my encounter."

Pavesi walked over to put a hand on his arm. "This is very brave of you, Dev."

He shook his head irritably. "Bravery has nothing to do with it. I just cannot stand not knowing things. Such as what our captors' intentions are toward us."

She smiled and stepped back. "In that you're not alone. It's why we've all ended up here."

———

Syrenii was on the mid-walkway of the tri-level control center, so far forward that she appeared to be standing in empty space surrounded by a cottony mess of firmament. Blurred and distorted, the enveloping cosmic image looked nothing like what could be viewed through a telescope. Even as he strode deliberately toward the captain, or whatever the leader of a gang of alien ship thieves chose to call herself, Dev wondered what their immediate spatial surroundings might have looked like if the vessel on which they were traveling slowed down enough to return to normal space. Viewing such visions via detailed images taken by telescopes orbiting the Earth was awe-inspiring enough. Finding oneself among the actuality might prove overwhelming.

Still, he hoped for the opportunity. As Pavesi had so succinctly commented, curiosity was why they had all ended up in their present situation. Whether such inquisitiveness would kill Dev instead of the proverbial cat remained to be seen.

Striding down the narrow walkway that seemed suspended in the midst of a small portion of the cosmos was not easy. There were no railings and anyone suffering from acrophobia likely could not have managed it. Fortunately, heights had never troubled Dev. His natural scientific detachment further divorced him from any irrational fear of falling into the nearest distorted nebula underfoot.

As he approached the instrumentation cluster where Syrenii was conversing energetically with two other A'jeii, Dev noted that not just the walkway he was on but all those in the control center were more than broad enough for a pair of A'jeii to pass one another without crowding. Come to think of it, he told himself, the few passages he had explored within the ship were sufficiently wide and high enough to suggest that whoever its owners were, they likely ran larger than the A'jeii and Olone, though perhaps not the bigger, huskier Kaijank.

All three of the aliens paused to regard him as he halted. None drew a weapon to blast the insolent primitive from their presence. He had the feeling that they were expectant rather than angry. Had the pugnacious Vantolos been present, Dev suspected he would already be under verbal assault.

Instead, one of the A'jeii said coolly, "What do you want, human? Why are you not in your living quarters?"

Dev drew himself up, though if the A'jeii were not intimidated by the Kaijank, he doubted they would regard him as much of a threat.

"You studied my kind long enough to learn our language, to learn about our resources, long enough to figure out the best way to threaten us to get what you needed. So you must be aware that we are not the kind of species to simply sit around and do nothing while others determine our future."

"That is a statement, not a request," observed the second A'jeii. "What do you *want*?"

"To know what you're going to do with us once we reach this

Mozehn. To know what *fate* you have in mind for us. As fellow sentient beings we deserve that much."

"You deserve nothing." Syrenii was nothing if not blunt. "Not even the living quarters that have been provided to you. Not the atmosphere that you breathe. Be grateful that you *have* a future."

As Dev looked on, silent and expectant, something came over the captain. A tinge of regret, perhaps, or a soupçon of compassion. Or maybe just impatience. Raising a small hand, she pointed to the third, uppermost level of the control center. "Tilenyii is there, as is Vantolos. I have no time to spare for you, but the supervisor likes to converse, and the Olone lives to make noise. Go and assail them with your concerns. Perhaps they will deign to respond." Turning away, she resumed the discussion she had been having with her two associates.

Thus scorned, but not wholly dismissed, Dev did as he was told. Finding his way to the third level of the control center, he came up on the A'jeii supervisor and Olone interlocutor before they could avoid him. This time he was determined to get some answers or die trying. That the latter was more likely than the former did not dissuade him. Truth be told, he felt he could not return to his companions without some kind of useful information. He was one of those exceptional people who feared embarrassment more than injury.

Neither alien ran from him nor attempted to avoid his approach. Confirming what Syrenii had told him, Tilenyii looked up at him curiously. Standing on all four tentacles, Vantolos looked almost relaxed. Or as relaxed as Dev could remember seeing him.

"I just spoke to the captain ..." he began. Vantolos cut him off.

"You mean to say that the captain just spoke to you. I know Syrenii too well to believe that she allowed you to engage her in extended conversation of your choice."

The supervisor turned her attention to the Olone. "Let the creature say what it has come to say. You can berate it later."

Oversized eyes turned to Dev. Their owner's expression was almost welcoming. A shame, he thought, that behind them lay the possibility of an early demise for himself and his companions.

"My friends and I are grateful that you have allowed for us some kind of a future. If it is not to be on our own world, then what are we to think? We are traveling to this place you call Mozehn. What happens there? What happens to *us* there?"

Vantolos let out a wheeze as he lifted and waved one tentacle. "What a self-centered species you primitive bipeds are. Always thinking of yourselves."

"Gently, Vantolos." In an unexpected display of courtesy, Tilenyii employed the language of their captive so that Dev would be able to understand the entirety of the discussion. "The urge toward self-preservation is common to all sentients and not a cause for criticism."

Vantolos continued his tentacle-waving but added nothing verbally. Yet again Dev noted how the truculent Olone deferred to the much smaller A'jeii.

"I cannot say what will happen to you." As the supervisor looked up, Dev noticed for the first time a thin nictating membrane that in the absence of a thick eyelid occasionally flicked rapidly down to moisten and protect the large eyes. "Do not feel isolated in this because I cannot say what will happen to *us*. We go to Mozehn for two reasons. First, because it is a place unlikely to be visited by those who come after us. Second, because it can provide certain substances that your world could not."

Dev frowned. "So you're going there to hide out and extract natural resources?"

"We collect nothing," Vantolos snapped. "Just as was done at your world, the inhabitants of Mozehn will provide them to us. On demand."

"We hope." Tilenyii spoke while waving one small hand over what looked like a plain, flat piece of plastic that projected a flurry of intersecting images in the air above her fingers. "The

Mozehna level of technology is slightly more advanced than your own. Socially, they are far more advanced, having emerged from tribalism to govern via a normal planetary government. This will make it much easier for them to supply what we desire. It also makes them more dangerous, as they can react to us with a single sentient voice."

"It doesn't matter." Shifting backward, Vantolos waved two tentacles in the air, one of which came close to striking an alarmed Dev. "We will intimidate them as we intimidated your kind!" he half-shouted at the startled human.

"We hope," the supervisor said for the second time. "It may be that the Mozehna will not be as easily fooled as were the inhabitants of the more isolated Earth. For one thing, they have had prior contact with both my kind and the Olone." The stare she now leveled at Dev left the human feeling distinctly uncomfortable. "It is of some importance to note that they know nothing of the people of Earth."

Dev swallowed. "I'm not sure I understand. Why is that of some interest?"

As she spoke, Tilenyii continued to manipulate the small device in her left hand. "The situation posed by your presence here offers some interesting possibilities. The Mozehna know the A'jeii, the Kaijank, and even the Olone. But they know nothing of your kind." Large, bright eyes were locked on Dev's own. "You have seen how intimidating the Kaijank can be, but in reality, they shy away from violence."

Vantolos was aghast. "You should not be telling such things! Such knowledge is for the crew alone!"

Tilenyii looked over at the Olone. "That difficulty can be rectified. Perhaps our humans would prefer to be crew rather than 'guests'?"

"Wait—what?" Surely, Dev thought, there was some confusion in what Tilenyii was saying. Something misplaced in the supervisor's understanding of English. Or maybe Dev was losing his mind.

She proceeded to elucidate. "It was noticed from the

commencement of discussions with your kind that humans are natural negotiators. The A'jeii are not." She looked sideways at the hypnotically gesturing Vantolos. "The Olone are not. They are belligerent and argumentative, but when that fails they do not know quite how to respond." A small hand gestured. "Vantolos here is the most self-possessed of his kind I have ever met."

Dev pondered that assertion. If Vantolos was "self-possessed," the rest of his species must dwell in a state of perpetual stroppiness.

"Do you understand what I am saying?" The supervisor was waiting for Dev's response.

"I—think so." Proceeding on their way to their assigned tasks, a pair of ample automatons whirred past behind him, distracting him momentarily. "You're offering my friends and me a chance to join your group. Particularly if we help you in your negotiating with other species."

Tilenyii gestured again. Vantolos found this slightly insulting but said nothing. Such decisions were not his to make. "Yes, that is correct. As an alien kind possessed of potential unknown to the Mozehna, they will be naturally wary of you and your capabilities. You do not have to do anything except stand with the Kaijank, observe, and act confidently. You do not even have to carry a weapon. The very fact that you say nothing and appear before them unarmed will compel the Mozehna to wonder about your covert undeclared abilities."

"So, you want us to provide an implied threat. So you can steal from them," Dev concluded.

"So that we can survive. At least until we can sell or trade this vessel."

Dev was nodding slowly. "Setting aside for the moment the fact that you are asking us to go against our own system of morality, what happens to us if and when you do sell or trade this ship?"

"If you elect to join with us and assist us, you will receive individual shares as a consequence of the sale."

"That will not help us get home," Dev pointed out.

"No, it will not." As befitting its small stature, the A'jeii's voice was soft and low, forcing Dev to listen intently to make certain he heard all of the supervisor's words. "But it will make the remainder of your natural lives much more comfortable. And with the technologies that will become available to you, those natural lives themselves can be extended."

Dev realized there was no way he could simply dismiss the proposal out of hand. For one thing, whichever direction their future took ought to be decided in a group decision arrived at by him together with his colleagues. Tilenyii was offering him and his companions a chance to live a decent, if morally suspect, life in an advanced, multispecies interstellar society. He had to confess that such a prospect had its allure. But that was how *he* felt. It was the reaction of someone who had always dreamed of contact with and learning about other intelligent species. While he didn't feel that his silent presence or that of his companions could in any way intimidate an alien species, the A'jeii apparently felt otherwise.

He didn't know how the aging Zimmers would react to such a proposal, he doubted that Pavesi would look forward to it, and based on what he had come to know of the security specialist it was entirely likely that Reed would have no interest in such a scenario whatsoever.

On the other hand, he told himself, what other choices did they have? Abandonment on some hostile alien world? A one-way ticket out the nearest airlock—without a suit? Considering that the A'jeii and their allies could already have implemented that last course of action, Dev knew he ought to be grateful. Whether any of his companions would feel the same remained to be seen.

"I am interested." *At least stall for time.* "As for my companions, I cannot speak for them. I will convey your offer and we'll give you our reply."

"Excellent. It is settled, then. I personally look forward to a positive response from you and your companions. I can tell you that the captain will also."

Vantolos was less sanguine. Small crawling shapes rippled beneath his tunic. "You overestimate the abilities of these bipeds to conduct successful bargaining. You have not dealt with them in such situations. I have."

"We have the recordings that were made in the course of all such relevant exchanges on their world," Tilenyii reminded the Olone. "Their content leads me to disagree with your assessment."

A tentacle waved, high and quick. "That is not the same. You were not there. A recording is not equivalent to real time." Slitted eyes regarded Dev almost contemptuously. "Confronted by a hostile reaction from the Mozehna, or any other species, the resolve of these inexperienced bipeds will wither and die."

"Let's hope not," Tilenyii shot back, "since their hopefully intimidating appearance will be what is backing you up."

The Olone loomed over the supervisor but made no move to attack. Vantolos's hesitation spoke more to the regard in which the A'jeii was held than to any actual concern for a shipmate of a different species. Ignoring the interlocutor, Tilenyii turned back to face the waiting human.

"Speak with your companions. Put forth our offer. There is no compulsion involved."

Of course there isn't, Dev thought sardonically. *Just plenty of room in empty airlocks.* "I will talk with my friends. How soon do you need our decision?"

"If you are amenable," Tilenyii replied, "I would expect such a final determination within a few of your hours. If they refuse, we will proceed as I have indicated. It is required that only one of you need join the landing party."

Airlock, Dev reminded himself unhappily. The A'jeii wanted their humans to help them intimidate an alien species just as the Olone and the Kaijank had previously intimidated humankind.

He looked forward to encountering yet another alien species, but not under the implied circumstances.

———

Jakob Zimmer was appalled. "They want us to help them *steal*? From another intelligent species?" Everything in the hot tea he was presently sipping and trying not to spill, including the cup itself, had been synthesized for him by a couple of pods bracketed side-by-side on what had come to be known as "the food wall." Each of their assigned quarters, including that of the Zimmers, featured a similar facility.

Dev nodded. "That is how I interpret it."

"And if we refuse to participate in this ethically-suspect request?" his wife said.

"Tilenyii made no overt threats," Dev explained. "She didn't have to. The impression I got was that we are expected to contribute to our upkeep. Or else we are likely to find ourselves sleeping in space."

"To put it another way," Pavesi added, "Tilenyii was reaffirming that those who stole this vessel aren't operating a charitable institution." Her brow furrowed as she regarded Dev. "They really think we can help them negotiate with yet another alien species? What about Vantolos and the other Olone on board? Isn't it their mission to handle such things? Why the interest in including us?"

Dev suppressed a smile. "From watching their interaction, I got the distinct feeling that the A'jeii and the Olone cooperate solely out of mutual interest, and that no love is lost between their respective species. Vantolos was present when Tilenyii made the proposal to me. The Olone did not seem happy about it."

From where he was stretched out on the floor staring at the ceiling, Reed emitted a gratified grunt. "Count me in on anything that pisses off the squid. I hate bullies, no matter how many arms they've got."

"Tch." Katou-Zimmer was shaking her head. "Shape prejudice, and from you of all people."

He rolled over to meet her gaze. "I'm not prejudiced against the Olone. I'm prejudiced against anyone who acts like Vantolos did during our encounters back on Earth."

"That simply seems to be the nature of the Olone." Katou-Zimmer continued to chide her colleague. "I don't think Vantolos can interact with other sentients in any other fashion."

"Fine." Reed rolled over onto his side. "So I'm prejudiced against the Olone. File a complaint with the anti-squid discrimination board."

Back on Earth. That was what Reed had said. So casually. So off-handedly. Dev thought of his parents, his occasional girlfriends, and his throat tightened.

"As far as Tilenyii's proposal is concerned, I do not see that we really have much of a choice. We are headed for this Mozehn and the A'jeii expect us to assist them. All they want is for one of us to accompany the landing party, look mysterious, and, I think, appear intimidating."

Katou-Zimmer made a face. "I have been accused of many things, but I cannot recall an instance where someone thought of me as intimidating."

"Apparently it's the 'unknown' factor." Dev shrugged. "I agree with you, but the A'jeii seem to think our mere appearance, as representatives of a species new to the Mozehna, will be enough to give them pause." He looked around at his companions. "I mean, what do we know about how alien species react to such things? Look how humanity reacted to the first appearance of the Olone and the Kaijank. The A'jeii obviously know plenty about the Mozehna." When the silence in the room continued, he added, "All whoever goes with them has to do is stand silently. It's not like they're asking us to shoot somebody."

Pavesi squinted across the room at him. "So you've already made up your mind to cooperate in this, Dev?"

He pursed his lips. "It beats not breathing."

A low sound, half growl, half laugh, emerged from the powerful supine form of Gavin Reed. "At last: comic-book boy and I agree on something."

Dev replied stiffly. "I am a formal consultant for NASA, I have multiple university degrees, and I speak several languages. What in that resumé leads you to believe I read comic books?"

Still prone on the floor, Reed rolled over to gaze up at him. "Don't you?"

Dev looked away. "They are graphic novels. And what does that have to do with anything?"

"Space stuff?" Reed was relentless. "You read comics about space stuff?"

"Some of it, sometimes," Dev admitted. "It all falls within the purview of my specialty."

"Good." Returning his gaze to the ceiling, Reed put both hands behind his head, lifting it slightly off the floor. "Then you can be the one to go down to the surface of this Mozehn. Me, I'm staying here."

"So am I."

Something in Pavesi's tone caused Dev to eye her uncertainly, but Jakob Zimmer was gesturing for attention.

The biologist glanced at his wife, then back at Dev. "Chiara and I would love to go, but neither of us is what even an unknowing alien is likely to regard as 'intimidating.' If Gavin will not go, then you are the one most qualified for this, Devali. We will await your return with interest. Do not waste the opportunity for observation and learning."

"I will try to keep that in mind." Dev was unsure if he was reassuring them, or himself.

"One small item of concern. To keep in mind while you're 'observing and learning.'" Reed sat up. "We know nothing of these Mozehna beyond what Tilenyii has chosen to tell Dev. What if they're not willing to go along with the A'jeii's demands? What if their species' personality is more like the Olone than the A'jeii? What if they show up for negotiations equipped more like the Kaijank?" He was gazing hard at Dev.

"If I had to hazard a guess," Dev replied, "I would say that the A'jeii are not a species willing to reward failure. Tilenyii sounded fairly confident that negotiations will go well. Vantolos was of another opinion."

Reed let out a soft snort. "What would you expect from the squid, when Tilenyii is all but telling him that in this instance he needs backup? From an unarmed human, no less?" A slow smile spread across his face. "What you just said, Dev, about the A'jeii not rewarding failure? What if the opposite eventuates? What if the negotiations, with you present as the 'mystery' alien, go really well? What are you going to do—what are *we* going to do—if the A'jeii subsequently insist that you or one of us are present at any and all future such 'negotiations'? What if the A'jeii, who you indicate don't really get along all that well with the squids, decide to cut them out of further negotiations entirely and just rely on a human presence? That would make the future awkward for us and leave us with a potential real enemy in the form of the Olone on this ship."

Dev's response was emphatic. "I do not think that speculation has any basis in reality, Gavin. From what I have been able to ascertain, the Olone were integral to the theft of this ship. The A'jeii cannot just dispense with them—or disrespect them in the manner you suggest. Besides, there is only one experienced linguist among us." He indicated Zimmer. "We know nothing of other alien species, let alone their languages."

Reed placed a hand over his left side. He was not feeling pain there, nor was he planning to pledge allegiance. It was the location for the handgun that under normal circumstances would have been holstered there.

"I wonder how an Olone would respond to a slug delivered from close range. Would they spill blood like a human? Or go splat like a bug?"

Dev was alarmed. "I have to say that is not a very productive line of thought, Gavin."

"Maybe not." Reed's fingers slid away from his side. "But I can be free to speculate with my mind, if not my body."

Katou-Zimmer eyed him disapprovingly. "On Earth, Vantolos was just doing his job, Gavin. Don't make his actions there into something personal."

"Who, me?" He laid back flat on the floor again. "I'm the quiet, impersonal one, remember?"

"Then we are all in agreement?" One at a time, Dev

exchanged glances with his companions. "We will do what the A'jeii are asking of us?"

"Reluctantly. This time, at least." Reaching up with her right hand, Katou-Zimmer placed it on her husband's. "We will cooperate, but without joy or gladness."

"Don't worry so much, Chiasa." Reed was a font of reassurance today, Dev mused. The big man turned his gaze to him. "If our boy here messes up his strong silent type part in the upcoming local negotiations, you'll be looking for a warm coat before you know it." He cast a grim eye over the others.

"We all will."

—VIII—

Seen from orbit, Mozehn was every bit as beautiful as Earth. So much so that Dev found himself wondering whether or not it might be better to risk abandonment there than to remain on the alien ship with its unpredictable, diverse, morally deficient crew. Oceans, deserts, mountains: viewed from above, it all looked achingly familiar. What would its dominant species be like? Tilenyii had told him they were more advanced than the citizens of Earth. Did they know compassion? Understand the meaning of asylum? Or would they simply eliminate any alien humans stranded on their world as efficiently and ruthlessly as his own kind would eradicate a questionable virus?

When the time came, they assembled as had by now become customary in the Zimmers' cabin. There, an A'jeii named Runoyii regarded them thoughtfully before eventually approaching the waiting Dev. The A'jeii eyed the human without blinking. "If I were to be asked my personal opinion, I would say that this is a dubious notion and that you should not be a member of this landing party."

"But it is not your idea." Since Runoyii was speaking English, Dev responded on the assumption that by now many if not all the highly adaptable and very clever A'jeii understood it reasonably well.

"That is so," the A'jeii acknowledged. "From the time you leave the ship you will be under the command of Vantolos. You will not have a weapon and you are to say nothing unless it is requested of you by him that you say a few words in your own language. You are to follow his lead in all matters, only to contribute if he requests your assistance or in the event that discussions may seem to be veering away from what we regard as successful."

"How do you define this 'success'?" Jakob inquired.

Large eyes swung around to regard the oldest human. "Compliance on the part of the Mozehna with each of our specific requests. Nothing less. A judgment with which you all should be quite familiar." Pausing, the technician looked around the cabin. "I note that one of your number is not present."

A frowning Katou-Zimmer made her own quick search. There was only the single four-walled chamber; no place for someone to hide even had they been inclined to do so. Eyes narrowing, her husband voiced what everyone was suddenly wondering.

"Where's Diana?"

Reed looked up from absently massaging the spot where his holster would normally repose against his chest. "I thought she was with you, Dev."

He shook his head. "I haven't seen her either. Not since earlier. She was not following behind me." He looked accusingly at the A'jeii. "You have done something with her! With our friend!"

One hand described a swift arc in front of the small alien torso. "We have not 'done' anything with your colleague. Could you not surmise my ignorance of her whereabouts from my query? If I knew where the female was, I would not be commenting on her absence."

Moving quickly to the portal area, Reed ran a fingertip along the sensitized section of wall until the expected opening appeared. "Check her cabin first. If she's not there ..." He broke off because he had no idea what they would do if Diana Pavesi was not in her room. Especially in the face of the A'jeii technician's unhesitant and straightforward denial of any involvement in her absence.

Which didn't make any sense no matter how you looked at it, Dev thought. Why arrange for them all to be together only to, for some unknown reason, prevent one of them from attending? He felt a slight chill.

Reed was the first one into Pavesi's cabin, with Dev right behind and the Zimmers arriving more slowly. A puzzled Runoyii trailed behind.

Pavesi was right there, lying on her pod-spawned bed. She was not moving. Going over to her without hesitation, Reed leaned forward to put a moistened palm over her mouth, then bent to listen to her chest. When he straightened, his expression was unchanged. The same could not be said for his voice.

"Dead. She's dead. Still warm, but ..." He stopped speaking, finding no rationale for adding unnecessary adjectives to the obvious.

"Here." At the far side of the cabin, Katou-Zimmer stood looking down at a shelf that emerged from a small pod. As everyone drew near, Dev saw that it was filled with small bits of synthesized vegetable that had been carefully arranged in a pattern. The familiar teacup Pavesi had requested from the appropriate wall pod soon after its workings had been explained to her sat nearby.

"No pen, no paper." Zimmer's voice was muted as he regarded the words Pavesi had laboriously spelled out using slices and shards of synthesized vegetables.

Can't do this.

Can't go home.

Won't do this.

Sorry. Luck to all.

Death before dishonor, a distraught Dev thought. Suicide before scruples. Though they had agreed to assist the crew of the ship that had fled with them aboard, every one of them had experienced second thoughts. Only Pavesi had been disheartened enough to act on them.

"I wouldn't have expected this." Reed was solemn but had been trained to keep his emotions under control. Notwithstanding his training, doing so now clearly required an effort on his part. "Not from Diana. Not from her."

Katou-Zimmer eyed him curiously. "Why not from her?"

The big man looked over at the scientist. "She was CIA. Put on the team not only to help with the original negotiations but to keep an eye on us."

"And you know this how?" Jakob Zimmer's stare was no less intense than that of his wife. "What are *you*, Gavin? More than just our bodyguard, I think."

"Military intelligence. Pavesi's job was to keep an eye on us. Mine was to keep an eye on her while looking after everyone else." He swallowed, only once. "Dammit. I missed the signs. I don't usually miss the signs."

Feeling a sudden surge of sympathy, Dev stepped toward him. "Don't berate yourself. We all missed the signs." Awkwardly, he eyed the body on the bed. "If there were any signs to be missed."

Inserting his diminutive form into the knot of humans, Runoyii glanced at the large, motionless form on the padded platform before turning to Dev.

"What is this? This human has expired?"

Katou-Zimmer looked ineffably sad. "Killed herself. Suicide, if the term translates properly."

"But—why?" The A'jeii was genuinely puzzled. "Like the rest of you, like all of us, she had suitable shelter and ample sustenance. It is not known for one of us, for any of the A'jeii, to voluntarily terminate one's life this way. We fight to sustain life, not to end it."

"Why indeed?" was Katou-Zimmer's reply. "Some people— some humans, anyway—can appear very strong on the outside while no one has any idea what's going on in their inside. In their mind, I mean. Suicide is a human mental issue. It seems our friend was very resilient on the outside but crumbling within."

"So then," the A'jeii technician observed in the characteristically terse fashion of its kind, "there will be three of you to await your companion's return from the surface." Once again, he directed his attention to Dev. "Come; I will lead you." He started for the door panel that held the exit.

"No." His words clipped and unwavering, Jakob Zimmer remained standing by the side of the bed and its unhappy burden. "Neither Dev nor any of us will go with the Olone. Not yet." Seeking the faces of his companions, he found there the reassurance he sought. "Not until our friend receives a proper send-off."

The A'jeii halted. "It is time to try and initiate contact with the Mozehna. Arrangements have been made."

"Tough." Reed stepped forward. "No send-off, no cooperation."

Runoyii regarded the small group of humans. "Negotiations with the Mozehna can proceed without you. This option has already been discussed. However, if you refuse to participate there may be repercussions."

The implied threat was unmistakable. Dev had been expecting it and was certain the same was true of his colleagues. After all, the crew of the purloined ship were not philanthropists. But he held his ground.

"It won't take long," Zimmer told the A'jeii. "Then Dev will assist you without hesitation."

Runoyii pondered a moment. Raising his right arm, he spoke in the direction of his wrist, then paused as if listening to an unseen instrument. There followed a good deal of additional wrist chatter interspersed with listening before he once more eyed the quartet of bipeds.

"Syrenii has acceded to your request, but we must hurry. The Mozehna are assembling their contact team and must be met in a timely fashion." The technician eyed the motionless form on the bed. "May I propose recycling? Among my kind it is the generally accepted method of passing on the physical portion of the …"

Reed interrupted the A'jeii. "No, you may not. Diana's body gets consigned to the void. Intact." He looked over at the Zimmers. "Like Jakob said, it won't take long."

"A waste of time and energy," remarked Runoyii. "But we knew your customs and culture were strange when we studied them in the course of our approach. In the interest of saving time, it will be as you wish." Once more he eyed the weighty corpse. "I will arrange conveyance. Unless you insist on carrying the deceased yourselves."

"No. Help with conveyance would be welcome," Dev admitted. Even with Reed's strength, manhandling the limp, heavy body of their dead colleague would be difficult. Dev was no weightlifter, and the elderly Zimmers could not be counted on to, as it were, hold up their end. Besides, they didn't know how far it was from their living quarters to the nearest airlock.

Not far, as it developed. Nor was there an airlock in the traditional sense. Threading a path through a chamber nearly filled to the ceiling with bulbous containers, Runoyii led the somber procession to a far wall. As Dev and his colleagues looked in vain for a doorway, controls, conduits, and anything halfway familiar that might indicate the location of a lock, the A'jeii technician ran his fingers over a section of curving wall in a complex pattern that was familiar in its execution but alien in its design. Katou-Zimmer was not the only one who gasped when a circular section of wall some twenty feet in diameter suddenly appeared to vanish in front of them.

With the alien craft now holding in orbit above Mozehn, stars were visible, along with a pair of irregularly shaped but surprisingly large moons that gleamed like polished silver nuggets set on black velvet. Instinctively, Dev braced for sudden decompression and a loss of air. But nothing happened. There was no rush of atmosphere out of the chamber, no change in gravity—nothing. It was as if he and his companions were gazing at a projection instead of a hole in the hull. All of them stood in awe at the science behind the opening.

Runoyii did not react at all. As far as the A'jeii was concerned, he had done nothing more than activate an egress.

"Push your companion forward."

Emerging from the shock of the portal's appearance, Reed and Dev stepped behind the floating platform on which they had placed Pavesi's body. The Zimmers stood to one side, holding hands. Dev looked at Reed, who nodded. Together they gave the device a forceful shove. Propelled by the push and suspended above the deck by another miracle of alien science, the platform slid forward. As it impacted the lower portion of the disc portal, a slight golden mist enveloped first the front end, then the portion supporting the body, and finally the end. Once it had passed completely through, it picked up speed. As it did so, Pavesi's form slowly drifted away from the platform itself, until she was floating free and shrinking into the distance. With nothing to restrain her limbs and now under the gravitational influence of the world below, her arms drifted away from where they had been crossed over her stomach.

It looked like she was waving.

With the cold abruptness of indifference, the portal vanished, to be replaced once more by a bland, unornamented section of far more solid-looking hull wall. Runoyii's subsequent remark was devoid of emotion.

"That's done. Please now come with me."

The quartet of somber humans formed up behind the A'jeii to shuffle along behind their guide. "He didn't even give us a chance to say anything," Reed muttered.

"We didn't ask for time." Katou-Zimmer was philosophical. "It's plain that nothing here is surmised. We have to learn to express ourselves and our needs more forcefully, just like we insisted on seeing Diana on her way." Her husband nodded in agreement.

"One less of us now," he murmured. "One more step closer to aloneness."

"The rest of us are still here." Dev looked over at the senior scientist. "'You cannot count all the time on having the physical proximity of someone you love.'"

Reed squinted at him. "Did you just make that up?"

"No." The bulk of his thoughts elsewhere, Dev replied absently. "It is a saying by Valmiki. From the Ramayana." Noting Reed's continued confusion, he added, "It is not a comic book."

The big man nodded solemnly.

As Runoyii led them deeper into the ship they encountered fewer and fewer A'jeii and not a single Olone. Five minutes into the hike they were joined by a pair of suited Kaijank. Dev couldn't tell if they were the same ones who had accompanied Vantolos on his contact visits to Earth, but he recognized the devices they carried. Though these were as intimidating as ever, he had to remind himself that they still did not know if they were weapons.

To think, he mused, that those few devices carried by a couple of Kaijank, plus the sheer size of the alien craft, had been sufficient to bluff an entire technologically developed world like his own into submission. Would the Mozehna react in similar fashion? Would they prove equally acquiescent and comply readily with the demands of their brazen, unexpected visitors? Very soon he would learn the answer to that question. In person.

The hold where a brace of A'jeii technicians were waiting for them was surprisingly small. It took Dev a moment to realize it was the same one via which they had arrived prior to their unforeseen and much-lamented hasty departure from Earth. A swirl of alien automatons were finishing preparations for the landing craft's departure. The fact that no portal for the landing craft was visible in its side did not surprise Dev or any of his companions. By now they were more than familiar with that particular miracle of alien technology.

Surprising Dev, the usually reticent Reed grabbed his hand firmly. "Be careful down there. I'm glad you're wanting to do this."

Dev frowned as the big man released his fingers. "Why?"

Reed's reply was as sincere as it was candid. "Because it means I don't have to." As he stepped back, Chiasa Katou-Zimmer came forward. For a second time she surprised Dev by wrapping her arms around him and hugged tightly before releasing her grip.

"Take care down there, follow instructions, observe, learn, and be ready to tell us everything you see and experience. Most importantly, if you can find out, try to discover why the A'jeii insist that you go at all," she concluded with a reassuring, almost maternal smile.

"Don't worry," he promised her. "All my life I have been dreaming of doing something like this. I never thought it would amount to anything more than idle fantasies." The thought made him smile. "First, we encounter an alien landing party, on Earth, and now I'm part of an alien landing party. As one of the aliens. It will be interesting to see if the Mozehna react to Vantolos the same way our kind did."

Reed glanced over to where the Olone stood conversing with Runoyii. "Maybe you can calm him down a little."

"You know that is not how this gang, if they can be called that, works." Dev followed the other man's gaze. "Anyway, I do not speak Mozehna. Keep quiet, stay in the background, and try to look confident and intimidating. That is what I have been told to do. In other words, just be my alien self. Represent an unknown sentient being. That is all I am supposed to be." When no one offered a comment, he added, "I am sure everything will go smoothly. The A'jeii are very confident."

Reed rolled his eyes but said nothing. Then Dev's view of his companions was partially blocked by a mass of yellow material beneath which crawled still unknown small shapes. That, and a tentacle that waved hypnotically back and forth in front of his face.

"Time to go." Vantolos' attitude and tone were not exactly conciliatory, but they were less pugnacious than usual.

As the expected portal appeared in front of them, Dev followed the Olone into the landing vehicle. Two A'jeii pilots sat forward while the pair of Kaijank settled themselves in back, their domed heads just clearing the ceiling. A last look out the entry portal showed Dev's companions standing and staring back at him: the Zimmers in front, Reed towering behind them. Then the wall of the hull reformed, shutting them off from sight.

A sudden thought spurred him to use a hand to trace an outline in the wall on his left. Sure enough, a viewport appeared. But Reed and the Zimmers were gone. As he looked on, a much larger opening appeared in the side of the alien mothership. There was a very slight lurch. Space subsumed the view as the landing craft silently slid out of the hold. There was no sense of motion as the view rotated crazily, blackness and stars being replaced by the curve of a world below. He caught his breath. Were there any inhabitable worlds that were not beautiful, or was the presence of air, water, and greenery the ultimate expression of magnificence throughout the galaxy?

Nothing could go wrong, he told himself as the landing craft commenced its descent. There might be some tension, as there had been when the landing party headed by Vantolos had first arrived on Earth, but nothing cataclysmic was likely to occur. The A'jeii, Olone, and Kaijank might be thieves, but they were not fools. Being slightly more advanced than human society, the Mozehna might immediately comply with the Olone's demands.

In contrast to the heat and humidity of coastal Texas, the landing party set down in a small valley surrounded by low, rounded hills. A mix of green and purple scrub furred the slopes, occasionally broken by an isolated tall growth that was scarcely a meter wide at the base. The pleasantly cool, ozone-rich air smelled slightly of overcooked asparagus and the sky showed a green tint that was decidedly foreign. Startled by the arrival of the landing craft, several pencil-thin creatures with large membranous wings lifted off the scrub and soared away to the east.

Stepping out of the landing craft behind the last Kaijank, Dev was careful to remain behind the much taller biped. That did not prevent him from seeing that Vantolos was already deep in discussion with the representatives of the Mozehna who had been awaiting the Olone's arrival. Not knowing what to expect and having been instructed to do essentially nothing, he was able to take some time to study their physical appearance.

The solitary Olone loomed over the locals, the tallest of whom might have come up to Dev's shoulders. In height they were thus a little taller on average than the A'jeii, but more slender. So lean, in fact, that it set Dev to wondering if their correspondingly thin bones might contain a higher percentage of metallic elements than his own. Eyes mounted on short, flexible stalks protruded from each side of a head that was only marginally wider than the neck and body on which it was mounted, giving them a very wide range of vision. Stick-like hearing organs emerged from the tops of slightly oval heads. What he could see of skin that was not covered by shining, almost iridescent blue and yellow clothing was the color of aged oak mottled with vertical dark gray stripes. In four-fingered hands they held devices of surprising heft and unspecified purpose. Their size, Dev reflected, might not appropriately reflect their mass. If it did, the reedy Mozehna would not have been able to lift the instruments they carried.

As he looked on from his position behind the two Kaijank, the ongoing discourse between Vantolos and the locals grew steadily in volume, punctuated by occasional louder outbursts from both sides. For such willowy creatures, the Mozehna spoke in voices of surprising resonance. Their speech consisted largely of a rising and falling singsong interrupted by percussive exclamations that sounded like castanets.

Vantolos was now standing on two tentacles while gesticulating wildly with the other pair. Though Dev knew nothing of the Mozehna language or culture, the entire exhibition was highly suggestive of increasing agitation on both sides. The Olone's performance alone was proof enough of that.

Abruptly, the screeching and shouting waned. Turning his body, Vantolos gestured as he spoke to the still concealed Dev.

"Come forward now, human. Let them see you."

Wondering how his mere appearance was supposed to affect the ongoing parley, Dev complied, stepping out from behind the shielding bulk of the two Kaijank.

"It does not look like it is going too well," he observed. "Are the locals not readily acceding to your demands or is this just the way conclusions are arrived at on Mozehn? Speaking from personal experience, might I suggest that a little less bellicosity in your part could be …"

He broke off. The assembled Mozehna, including the two prime negotiators, had immediately switched their focus from the Olone to the new arrival. Though far more massive than the bulkiest of the locals, Dev was bipedal like them, bisymmetrical like them, and even had manipulative digits not wholly dissimilar to theirs. They were all gesturing at him now, murmuring among themselves, clearly surprised by the new arrival. Vantolos resumed declaiming, perhaps reiterating his demands, as Dev halted slightly behind and to one side of the Olone.

"What are they saying?" Forgetting that he had been told not to speak, Dev was unable to repress his curiosity.

The sound of his voice caused the band of Mozehna to redouble their chattering. Thin but strong digits jabbed and fluttered in his direction. Their reaction, thought Dev, gave every indication of them having seen a human before. Which made no sense. Unless they'd had a previous encounter with another sentient species that closely resembled humans. That was a question he intended to put to Tilenyii as soon as he was back on the ship. It was intriguing, even exciting to think that another species that dwelled in this corner of the cosmos might closely resemble humankind, even to the tenor of its speech.

Choosing to ignore everything he had been told, he took a step forward with hands outstretched. "Hello. I know you cannot understand me, but I am called Devali and …"

If he expected Vantolos to reprove him he was surprised. Not only did the Olone not try to silence his human companion, he resumed gesticulating with the pair of tentacles he was not standing on. If anything, his latest gyrations were more rapid and encompassing than any that had preceded them. As rapidly as they could, the principal pair of Mozehna negotiators responded in kind. Dev looked on with interest.

It was one of the Kaijank who interrupted the increasingly animated debate, striding forward to murmur something to Vantolos. As the Olone looked up and past the Mozehna negotiators, Dev followed his gaze.

Coming over the slight rise behind the assembled group of Mozehna delegates and heading down the slope toward them was a trio of machines. Dev could not tell if they moved on wheels, tracks, a cushion of air, or via some means of combined support and propulsion utterly unknown to him. Each mechanism flaunted a webwork of feathery instrumentation on top. While these might have comprised communications devices or been designed to accomplish some other innocuous end, the manner in which Vantolos and the two Kaijank reacted to their approach suggested another, less benign purpose. Raising their weapons, the Kaijank began backing up in the direction of the landing craft. As Dev stood and stared, fascinated by the approach of the Mozehna mechanicals, he felt the end of one tentacle wrapping around his right wrist. Vantolos was likewise retreating and pulling Dev with him. Though he did not resist, a captivated Dev could not take his eyes off the advancing alien machines.

Unexpectedly confirming his earlier suppositions and those of his colleagues, one of the Kaijank triggered the long device he was carrying. A sound like an old-fashioned electric transformer blowing up filled the air, stunning Dev with its volume. The detonation appeared to have no effect on Vantolos. Scrub and soil erupted in front of one of the oncoming Mozehna vehicles. As they came to an abrupt halt, a number of locals scrambled to get on top of them. Vantolos increased the pace of his withdrawal, causing Dev to stumble a couple of times as he struggled to keep up. Meanwhile the second Kaijank also unleashed his weapon. Dirt and rocks erupted skyward in front of the Mozehna machines. Either the Kaijank had terrible aim,

Dev decided, or else they were deliberately aiming not to hit anyone.

By now every member of the Mozehna negotiating party had fled in the direction of their machines. Heedless of the Kaijanks' warning shots, several of their number now stood atop the vehicles, struggling with the feathery apparatus that was mounted on each.

Back on board the shuttle Vantolos did not wait for the human to settle himself into a seating pod: the Olone busied himself with his own liftoff preparations. So did the Kaijank, who were more agitated than Dev had ever seen representatives of their kind. As the landing craft rose, he leaned over to wipe open a port in the hull. Below, he could still see the Mozehna trying to angle their vehicle-mounted instrumentation upward. He never was able to tell if they managed to get off a shot, or deploy a ray of some kind, or unleash a sonic weapon, or threaten the small spacecraft in any way. Smearing the view, he turned in his pod to face Vantolos.

"Correct me if I am wrong, but that negotiation did not appear to proceed as you intended."

Turning his upper body toward the human, Vantolos let loose with a stream of high-pitched babble that even by Olone standards Dev qualified as a rant. Then, realizing that the attentive biped could not understand anything that was being said, the mediator switched to English.

"I knew that bringing you along was a mistake. Your presence did not intimidate or confuse the Mozehna."

"So, you think it would have gone better if I hadn't been there?" The usually stable landing craft rocked slightly, suggesting that they were passing through some heavy atmospheric disturbance or else that the pilots were putting on extra speed.

"Certainly! Of course. But I followed instructions. To show you. You saw the result."

Dev made a face. "Why would seeing me set them off like that if they'd never seen someone like me? What is it about my human appearance that led you and the A'jeii to think my appearance would coerce them?"

"As you say, it was an idea of the A'jeii. Myself—*I* expected your appearance to do nothing. Plainly, that was exactly the case."

"No, it wasn't." Dev leaned toward the Olone. "While they were not intimidated, they *did* react strongly. Why did they have the reaction they did?"

Vantolos looked away from him. "The shock of the unexpected. Unfortunately, the shock did not produce the response for which the captain had hoped."

All the way back to the mothership Dev continued to press the Olone for additional details. If Vantolos had any to dispense, he chose not to do so. Just before they docked, Dev finally gave up. The negotiations had, to say the least, not gone well. As chief negotiator it was likely that the blame for that would fall on the Olone. Dev realized that for the moment it might be prudent for him to stop asking questions that might make the situation worse.

But for the life of him he could not understand how they could do so.

———

In the Zimmers' cabin his colleagues regarded him with a mixture of confusion and curiosity. In that, he reflected, they were all of one accord.

"I have gone over the confrontation again and again in my head." Though addressing all of them, Dev found himself focused on Katou-Zimmer. "I didn't say a word. Just stepped out to show myself when Vantolos asked me to come forward."

"And you say that was when the Mozehna reacted to your appearance?" Jakob Zimmer was stroking his beard, as deep in thought as Dev had ever seen the senior biologist.

Dev nodded. "Immediately." He looked over at Reed. "What I am guessing is that their version of heavy weaponry arrived soon thereafter. Whether it was going to put in an appearance anyway and the timing of its arrival with my exposure was coincidence, or whether my stepping out galvanized the response, I cannot say." He looked back to Katou-Zimmer. "The Mozehna did not just 'react' to my appearance. I would judge their response to have been a mixture of anxiety and aggression. It was almost as if they recognized me."

"You mean your kind, your species," she said quietly. "Not you personally."

The look on Reed's face was memorable as he jumped in. "That's impossible. If anything, they might be familiar with another species that happens to resemble humankind. Based on what Dev has said, another species that the Mozehna regard with some awe. And maybe a little fear. Convergent evolution at work."

"Maybe." Dev was reluctant to agree. But what other possible explanation could there be? "If that is the case it could explain why the A'jeii wanted one of us to accompany the landing party. But if they thought my appearance was going to somehow intimidate the locals, they certainly had that element of the equation badly wrong. If anything, instead of intimidating them, my appearance went some way toward inspiring a hostile response."

"We need to find out what this is all about," Jakob concluded with finality. "I, for one, am tired of being treated like cargo. As if we should fall down on our knees in gratitude for not being killed outright."

Actually, that was a real possibility that had long been on Dev's mind, but he was not about to broach it. Not now that the elderly professor had asserted his defiance.

"We need to understand what happened down there. We need to know why the A'jeii thought your appearance might overawe the locals and why it provoked an entirely different reaction." Katou-Zimmer was of the same mind as her husband. "We may be prisoners of these aliens, but that does not mean we should spend the rest of our lives as uninformed tools. We need to confront Tilenyii about this."

"Or better still, Syrenii," Jakob countered.

"Then we are agreed?" Katou-Zimmer looked at Dev.

"I want answers as badly as you do." He glanced over at Reed. The big man shrugged.

"Gotta admit I'm curious. Maybe not as curious as the rest of you, but curious enough to go along."

———

As they made their way resolutely toward the bridge, they drew curious stares from passing A'jeii. As usual, the numerous automatons they encountered in the corridors ignored them. Leading his colleagues, Dev deliberately did not alter his path to accommodate the machines, forcing several to dodge out of his way.

It was easy enough to locate the captain. As soon as the determined quartet of humans entered the always impressive open space, Dev espied the leader of the multispecies band of thieves seated in her usual location forward.

Noting their arrival, Tilenyii intercepted them as they tried to advance.

"What do you want here?" Wide eyes shifted to meet Dev's own. "I know that your encounter did not go well. That is a pity. A remedial response is being prepared. As it does not involve you or any of your companions, you may return to your cabins."

Not much taller than the A'jeii, Katou-Zimmer leaned toward the supervisor. "We've come to talk to Syrenii. About what happened down the surface. And about our situation. About our ultimate purpose on this ship."

Gesturing forward, Tilenyii sounded irritated as she replied. "The captain is busy. The captain is always busy."

"Then you can answer our questions," Katou-Zimmer persisted.

"I am also busy. If you have questions, ask your cabin information pod."

"We've tried." Jakob took a step forward as a wheeled automaton passed close behind him. "Room pods are great for supplying food and taking care of hygiene; not so much when it comes to answering questions of greater significance."

"I have no time for you. We are preparing a response to the Mozehna and there is much that needs to be considered. Go back to your cabins." She pushed her face closer to Jakob's. "Or would you prefer to observe the forthcoming activities from outside the ship?"

"You know," Reed murmured to no one in particular, "I've had about enough of you wide-eyed runts and your threats. I've been threatened by the best. You're not." Whereupon he stepped forward quickly, put one muscular arm around the A'jeii's neck, reached into a pocket, and placed the edge of the knife he drew against the supervisor's neck. Tilenyii might belong to a technologically advanced species, but she was completely helpless in the big man's grasp.

It was impossible to say who was more startled: the A'jeii on the bridge or Reed's companions.

"Where—where did you get the knife?" A shocked Dev could only stammer.

Reed was dead solemn. "The food pod in my room. No different from asking for any other kind of utensil."

Jakob eyed the big man intently. "Interesting, Gavin. That is very interesting indeed."

Leaving their stations, several A'jeii came running toward the knot of humans. Unseen until now, a pair of Kaijank appeared on the uppermost level and descended toward them as rapidly as their cumbersome suits would allow. They were bigger than Reed, but their arrival didn't faze him. Holding the A'jeii supervisor off the deck with one arm, he retreated until he had the wall against his back.

An alarmed Katou-Zimmer raised her voice. "Gavin! Let her go!" A glance showed that the pair of Kaijank were close now, though she could not tell if they were armed. "This isn't helping!"

"It might: it remains to be seen. You three stay where you are. This is my call, my decision. I'd just as soon die on board a ship as out in space or 'accidentally' suffocated in my cabin." He pressed the blade he was holding tighter against Tilenyii's neck. The supervisor immediately ceased struggling. "What do you think, Jakob, Chiasa? If I cut her throat will she bleed out faster or slower than a human? And will the blood be red?"

—IX—

They had their answer as to whether the Kaijank were armed or not when the pair of domed giants halted, drew what looked like aerodynamic teacups from holders at their waists, and pointed the leading edge of the unfamiliar devices in Reed's direction. When Dev moved to intervene, Katou-Zimmer held him back.

"Running out of people to talk to," she murmured to him. "Whatever happens to Gavin, Jakob and I would like to have at least one other human for company."

Mindful of her request, he held back. Not that he could do much of anything anyway, he told himself. Physically, he would be as helpless against the much bigger Kaijank as he would have been against Gavin Reed. Nor was he likely to dissuade the aliens by pleading for restraint in a language neither of them understood.

Breathing hard, Vantolos chose that moment to arrive. The gathering A'jeii made way for him.

"Now then." Puffing hard, he waved one tentacle while balancing on the tripod formed by the remaining three. "What is going on here?" Slitted eyes shifted to Dev. "Your colleague is threatening the supervisor with a cutting instrument. Do you realize how dangerous this is for all of you!"

Seeing that she wasn't going to dissuade Reed from his chosen course of action, the petite Katou-Zimmer drew herself up to her full height to confront the Olone. "It's been nothing but dangerous moments ever since you forcibly took us away from our homeworld. We need answers to some questions. Syrenii is apparently too busy to talk to us." She gestured toward Reed and his diminutive captive. "Now Tilenyii is too busy to talk to us."

"Whereas I am never too busy to talk." Vantolos' response was welcome if unsurprising. "I will be pleased to attend to whatever questions you wish to ask. But first you must let the supervisor go."

Reed tightened his grip around the A'jeii's chest. "She stays close and warm until we get some answers from you. Also, a promise not to retaliate against me or my companions when I let her go." A thin smile creased his face. "Understand that there's nothing malicious in what I'm doing. I'm just engaging in an old and tried human method of negotiation. Of all the beings on this ship surely you can appreciate that."

"I can be loud, but I am not inclined to employ physical violence as a means of persuasion," the Olone retorted.

"No." Reed's smile widened. "You leave that to the Kaijank."

If the implication behind the big man's reply irritated the Olone, he gave no sign. "What is it you wish to know?"

Careful to maintain his grip on the squirming A'jeii supervisor, Reed met the Olone's slitted gaze. "We know that your negotiations down below didn't go well. We know that something peculiar happened when Dev showed himself to the Mozehna." He glanced over at his uneasy younger colleague. "Dev thinks the Mozehna might have reacted the way they did because they recognized him. Or rather, his species. Our species."

"That is absurd!" Vantolos snapped. "It would imply that the Mozehna had encountered your kind before."

"Yes, that's exactly what it would imply." Reed didn't equivocate. Maybe he didn't possess the Zimmers' rarefied academic background, but he was perfectly capable when it came to applying logic. "It would imply either that some Mozehna had been to Earth, or that Dev isn't the first human they've seen. Which is it, squid-boy?"

"Your appellation is foreign to my knowledge of your language. As to your dual query, the answer is neither. It has to be neither. Ah!"

Scuttling backward several steps, the Olone made room for the arrival of a very imposing automaton. With an outward patina that shaded to dark bronze, it was several heads taller than the Kaijank. The body was composed of half a dozen vertically aligned cylinders mounted atop a circular base that hovered several centimeters above the deck. Emerging from the upper center of the synced cylinders, a flexible metallic neck terminated in a globular head. Glowing softly yellow, two round lenses inclined in Reed's direction. As Dev and the Zimmers backed away, a pair of sharply tapering cones emerged from one of the six cylinders.

"Let the supervisor go now," Vantolos said tersely, "or you will die. It is to be regretted."

A grim-faced Reed pressed the sharp edge of the knife tighter still against Tilenyii's throat and the supervisor let out an anxious wheeze. "What's it going to do? Disintegrate me? Envelop me in a cloud of poison gas? Electrocute? Regardless of the method, I bet I can cut this female's throat before I lose consciousness."

"I do not think you can," Vantolos replied.

Reed stared unblinkingly at the Olone. "Are you willing to sacrifice your supervisor to find out?"

Vantolos paused as if listening to someone unseen. "Yes." The flexible upper body turned toward the automaton. "Kill him."

Startling both Dev and his wife, not to mention the assembled aliens, Jakob Zimmer darted forward in front of the automaton. "No, don't! Cancel that order!"

Twisting on the end of its flexible neck, the machine inclined its lenses toward the elderly human. At once confused and alarmed, Dev held his breath.

Vantolos was beside himself. "Follow through! Kill the human!" Slitted eyes glared at Zimmer. "Kill all of them!"

Oddly emboldened, Zimmer held his ground as his wife came up beside him. "Cancel that. Kill no one. Respond in my language, if you can."

Straightening its neck, the automaton stared straight ahead. "Kill no one. I assent."

Utterly enraged, Vantolos started toward the bulky machine. Zimmer raised a hand in the Olone's direction. "I'd hold my position if I were you."

"Why?" Vantolos glared at the human. "This is only a momentary interruption in the inevitable course of things. A minor malfunction on the part of this particular automaton. As soon as it is corrected, you four will die! I have determined that your presence on the ship is no longer condoned, no longer necessary. I will have your limbs torn off before you are ejected!"

Zimmer replied quietly. "I don't think so."

Bewildered by the chain of events, Dev struggled to understand what was happening. "You stopped it from shooting at Gavin. How ...?"

Zimmer offered a reassuring, almost fatherly smile. "I was thinking how strange it was that Gavin's cabin pod would provide him with an object that could be used as a weapon. It intimated that he, or any of us, could request and have delivered to us more than food and drink. Much more." He shifted his gaze to Reed, still backed up against the wall and holding the A'jeii supervisor tightly in front of him. "I think if you had asked for it, Gavin, one of the pods in your room would have provided you with a gun."

"More absurdity! The pods in your cabins," Vantolos began, "are designed to respond only to sensible requests."

Zimmer turned to him. "Then how was Gavin able to obtain a potentially lethal blade?"

"An error of judgment. It will be corrected." Some of the Olone's prior bluster seemed to have dimmed.

"Was my asking—no, my *ordering* this machine," and Zimmer indicated the automaton standing silently nearby, "not to kill also an error of judgment?"

Dev became aware that nearly all normal activity on the bridge had ceased. Having been apprised of the direction the confrontation with the quartet of humans was taking, nearly all of the A'jeii were staring in their direction. So were a pair of Olone and a lone Kaijank.

This was about much more than Vantolos ordering one of the ship's devices to shoot Reed, Dev realized. Something of much greater significance was at stake, and for the life of him he couldn't understand why it should be so. He continued to be utterly baffled by the automaton's response to Jakob Zimmer's directive to essentially stand down, a response to a verbal command, he told himself worriedly, that could change at any moment, with lethal results.

The confrontation did produce one other immediate response. Leaving her station forward and flanked by a pair of senior A'jeii, Syrenii was hurrying toward them.

Halting beside the simmering Vantolos, the captain surveyed the standoff, peered up at the quiescent automaton, and said sharply, "Kill the human restraining supervisor Tilenyii but be careful not to injure her."

Displaying a preternatural calm, Jakob Zimmer likewise looked up at the massive machine. "Cancel that order. Harm no one. Reply in my language if you …"

The mechanical anticipated with alacrity. "Harm no one. I assent."

Jakob pressed on. "Furthermore, you will harm no one without prior authorization from either me or my three compan- ions, nor will you allow anyone to come to harm." He was staring at Syrenii now. "You, your fellow automatons, and the ship itself will continuously watch over the four of us to see that we come to no harm. If an attempt to harm us is made," and he switched his gaze to the pair of now uncertain Kaijank, "you and one or more of your fellow automatons or the ship will intervene to assure that we come to no harm."

"I assent."

Thoughts churning furiously, Dev presumed that if Zimmer's directives were being followed correctly, then the mechanical was speaking not only for itself but for every other automaton on the ship as well as the ship's own AI. If indeed they were capable of being distinguished from one another and were not in fact all components of the same synthetic mind.

Syrenii's next words ensured that they would find out without having to wait. She turned to yell at the bewildered Kaijank.

"Use your weapons! Kill the four visitors *now*! Do not injure the supervisor!"

Dev tensed while Reed struggled to conceal his bulk behind the much smaller A'jeii he continued to hold captive. One of the Kaijank started to raise the rifle-like weapon it held.

While its body remained motionless, the automaton raised one limb so fast that Dev perceived it only as a wisp of motion. A brief burst of yellow-green light emerged from the tip of the limb to strike the business end of the Kaijank's weapon. This immediately began to glow and then to melt, leading the big biped to drop it with alacrity. As Dev stared, the surprisingly subdued luminescence commenced to crawl up the length of the weapon like a yellow-green worm, only fading away when it reached the far end. It left behind a length of slag the color and shape of burnt pasta surrounded by a halo of dark discoloration on the otherwise pristine deck. Showing admirable discernment, the other Kaijank promptly dropped its own weapon.

Without really thinking through the possible consequences of his action, Dev responded instinctively by walking over and picking up the abandoned device. While he had no idea how to fire it or even what the consequences of doing so might be, he felt more confident with it in his hands than in the Kaijank's. Behind him, Reed let out an exclamation of approval.

Aliens and humans regarded one another in silence until a gratified Zimmer turned toward Reed. "I think you can let her go now, Gavin."

The big man eyed the professor uncertainly. "She's our only hostage." He nodded in the direction of the captain and the several A'jeii who were now gathered behind her. "I let her go, there's no telling what they might do."

"If they could do anything, Gavin, I think they would have done it by now."

Katou-Zimmer spoke up. "What more could they do than try to have us killed?"

Still Reed hesitated, keeping the knife at the supervisor's throat. "I don't know. I'm not an alien." He looked, unexpectedly, at Dev.

"What d'you think, shaggy? What's your take on the situation?"

Dev didn't hesitate. His parents would have been proud.

"If you kill her, it doesn't change anything except that we will have gained the undying enmity of her crewmates." He nodded at Zimmer. "Jakob somehow seems to have gained control over the automaton."

"Not just the automaton." The professor sounded very satisfied with himself. "Over the ship itself."

"That doesn't make any sense." The knife in Reed's right hand moved several centimeters away from the supervisor's throat. "Why the hell would this ship or any part of it take orders from you? Or from any of us?" He lowered the knife to his side. "More importantly, why the hell do your commands override those of the A'jeii, or Vantolos, or anybody else on this ship?"

Spreading his hands, Zimmer shrugged. "I don't know, Gavin. I don't know the answer to that. But for now, I am willing to accept the reality. You should, too."

Reluctantly, the big man released his grip on Tilenyii. Thus freed, she hurried to join her anxious colleagues. Their relief was manifest as they surrounded her. Ignoring the freed supervisor,

Syrenii focused her attention on Zimmer.

"You realize this is only a pause, a temporary reprieve for your continued existence."

"No, I don't think so." Zimmer eyed his wife, who nodded in agreement. "I really do think that, for reasons as yet unexplained, this ship has allowed my colleagues and me to assume control of its higher cognitive functions. Not necessarily to your detriment, mind. As long as you agree to cooperate."

"This is beyond contemptible!" Had he been capable of levitation, Vantolos would have been angrily waving all four limbs. "You overstep your bounds, biped!" He raged at Zimmer. "A moment will come when your attention fades, and in that moment your limbs will be torn from …!"

"Shut up, Vantolos."

Eyeing the captain, the shocked Olone started to respond, reconsidered, and went uncharacteristically silent. Turning back to the Zimmers, Syrenii continued as though the tense confrontation had never taken place. As though nothing had happened. When she next spoke, her tone was almost pleasant.

"What kind of cooperation did you have in mind?"

"You agree that I and my friends are, for whatever reason, now in control of this ship," Zimmer informed her.

"I agree to nothing. But since I can't find a way to kill you—yet—then we will proceed on the understanding that if we can come to some sort of mutually acceptable arrangement, no one will kill anyone."

"Sounds good to me," Reed said. Dev noted that the big man continued to keep a tight grip on his knife. He considered handing over the alien rifle he had picked up but decided against it. For the moment, he would keep it. While the highly trained Reed could undoubtedly make better use of the device, given his temperament it might be a good idea to keep it out of his hands for a while. At least until Zimmer and Syrenii had reached some kind of understanding. The weapon was cool to the touch. Though Dev studied it intently he was unable to locate anything resembling a trigger and so was careful not to let his fingers wander too freely over the relatively smooth surface.

"Our request—our demand—is to be returned to our home. To Earth." Zimmer was quietly insistent.

Syrenii's head bobbed several times to one side. None of the humans could interpret the gesture. "It has already been explained to you on several occasions that that is impossible."

"Why is it impossible?" Katou-Zimmer regarded the captain with a mixture of frustration and curiosity. "You never explained exactly why, never went into any detail."

"There is no need for detail." Syrenii glanced at the supervisor. Tilenyii mumbled something back in the soft A'jeii language before the captain returned her attention to the visitors. "Just accept that it is dangerous. You shall continue onward with us, sharing in whatever gain we may acquire."

Moments ago, Gavin Reed had shown beyond a doubt that he'd had enough. Now it was Dev's turn. "No, we will *not* continue onward with you! We are *going home*. And I do not think we need your approval to do so." Intent on his insistence, he was unaware that he was waving the Kaijank rifle around a bit wildly. So he did not notice how the small cluster of A'jeii as well as Vantolos and the two Kaijank shied or ducked away from its muzzle. He turned to the Zimmers.

"Jakob, if we're somehow now in control of this ship, *just tell it to take us home*! Back to the world it just came from." Getting control of himself, he lowered his voice as he stared hard at the A'jeii. "But first ask it if returning is somehow 'dangerous.'"

A grinning Katou-Zimmer was nodding approvingly. "Well considered, Dev. A bit abrupt, but well considered. Sometimes we become so lost in the moment we overlook the obvious." Duplicating her husband's stance, she turned to the no longer threatening mechanical. "*Ship*. Is there any inherent reason why you should not return myself and my companions to our home-world? To the most recent one you have visited?"

Contorting on its flexible stalk, the head inclined toward her. Unblinking eyes peered down as the mechanical replied. "No.

There is no inherent reason I cannot return to the world most recently visited."

"Then," she took a deep breath, "I and my companions order that you do so."

A collective sigh rose from the assembled A'jeii. Turning, Vantolos let out a long hiss-like moan and ambled away, his attitude (insofar as Dev could tell from the alien's posture and gestures) that of one just shy of contemplating suicide. Chattering softly among themselves, the A'jeii scattered: some returning to their stations forward, others wandering down the other access corridor. A still-shaken Tilenyii went with them.

That left only the captain, Syrenii, to continue to confront the euphoric humans. "I tell you one more time that this is not a good idea."

Dev looked down at her. "We are still waiting for you to tell us why it is not."

Syrenii met his gaze evenly for a moment, then dropped her eyes and replied softly, "I cannot do that."

"Can you tell us why we were able to supersede your command and that of the A'jeii for this vessel?" a curious Katou-Zimmer wanted to know.

The A'jeii captain looked up, meeting each of their stares in turn. "I cannot tell you anything. But I *can* ask *you* a question. What do you intend to do once you have been returned to your homeworld?"

Dev looked at the Zimmers. The Zimmers looked at Reed. "Go back to our lives, I imagine," murmured Katou-Zimmer. "That's all we want."

"And us?" Syrenii gestured in the direction of the bridge. "The A'jeii, the Olone, the Kaijank: my crew?"

A thoughtful Dev had already pondered the matter. If it was up to him, he would have tried to keep control of the ship. The danger in such a course of action lay in the fact that they didn't know how Jakob had acquired that control. Consequently, it might vanish as unexpectedly as it had materialized. That could leave a hostile group of aliens once more in control of it, and in

Earth orbit. Despite the temptation, reason dictated that while they were still in control the prudent course of action would be to see the starship's stern receding as soon as possible beyond the orbit of Pluto. That, of course, was what the aliens desired as well.

"As far as I personally am concerned, you can go on your way, and good riddance. The ship has been ordered not to harm us. We'll extend that command to cover everyone on the planet." He looked over at Zimmer. "Jakob will know how to word it so that once we've been returned, neither you nor this ship will be able to do any us mischief, or it will backfire on you."

Syrenii performed the A'jeii equivalent of a shrug. "There is no reason for us to do so. We will simply want to leave your system as swiftly as possible."

Reed stared hard at her. "No interest in revenge?"

"'Revenge'?" The A'jeii appeared to struggle with the concept. "There is no profit in revenge. Such a notion implies a waste of resources. We do not waste resources." A low whistle emerged from her mouth. "Perhaps it is, after all, for the best. You wish to be rid of us and we wish to be rid of you. One can only hope that the timing proves suitable."

Dev frowned. "The 'timing'?"

"It is nothing," she assured him. "Nothing for you to concern yourself with, anyway."

He started to respond, decided not to. She had essentially agreed that it would be best for all concerned if the four humans were, after all, returned to their homeworld. That made excellent sense, considering that they had taken over the stolen vessel. The humans would go home and the A'jeii and their cohorts would retain control of the stolen ship.

And humankind would have experienced its first contact with other sentient species, Dev mused. "There will be reams of information to keep our specialists busy for decades to come. We might ask you a few questions about the cosmos on the way home. To add to the store of knowledge we will be able to deliver." A wry grin spread across his face. "I imagine we will be anointed instant celebrities whether we wish it or not. There won't be anywhere on the planet where we can hide."

Jakob Zimmer was nodding slowly. "It will be necessary for us to expose ourselves to the media before the government can sequester us away in some underground facility." His smile was thinner than Dev's. "I do not look forward to endless rounds of debriefing. Quickly and freely unburdening ourselves of what we know to the public at large will ensure that countries that did not supply this ship with 'guests' will not have reason to react to our return in paranoid, dangerous fashion." Turning away from both the aliens and his colleagues, he fell into a deep, whispering conversation with his wife.

Syrenii glanced from him to Dev. "So as soon as we see you safely back to the surface of your world, you have no problem returning full control of this ship to us and seeing us depart your solar vicinity?"

"Nope," Reed chimed in. "None. Once we're off the ship we won't be in control of it any longer, though as I mentioned we'll leave orders for it—and for you—to leave us permanently in peace. You'll be free to go on your way. Wherever that is."

Syrenii gestured with a small hand. "Then we will do our best to expedite your return. Even though we think it is not a good idea. It may be that all will go well."

Dev's gaze narrowed. "I am still puzzled by your reluctance, even now, to return us to Earth. It seems such a simple, straight-forward request. As it has been all along. What could possibly be a problem with that?"

But the A'jeii captain had turned and was walking away, murmuring to those A'jeii who flanked him on both sides. A hand on his shoulder momentarily startled Dev.

"Their future isn't our future, Devali. We go our way—home—and they go theirs."

Dev nodded slowly. "What if they decide to come back later? We will put prohibitions on this ship. But what if, despite what Syrenii said, they decide to return with a different vessel? One that is heavily armed?"

Reed removed his hand and stepped back. "I'm pretty good at interpreting human reactions. I don't know how or if that translates to analyzing alien ones. So this is only an opinion, but even disregarding what she said about not wanting any kind of revenge, I get the impression that the A'jeii don't have the slightest interest in returning to Earth once they've repatriated us. For any reason whatsoever. The Olone either, for that matter. It seems to me that at this point, the sooner they see the last of us and our world, the happier they'll be." He looked sharply at his colleague. "Don't tell me you're thinking of an alternative to going home?"

"N—no." Not for the first time, Dev found himself contemplating their astounding, astonishing, utterly impossible surroundings. "No, as much as this all fascinates me and fulfills dreams I have had since childhood, I suppose I want to go home, too."

His response to Reed's query, Dev told himself, did not sound entirely convincing. But there really was no alternative. He was not about to cut himself from the rest of humankind and the company of other human beings to throw in forever with a band of alien thieves.

"Then," Reed concluded, as he toyed with his pod-provided knife, "I am going to celebrate. By taking a shower. Even if it does consist of endlessly recycled water that probably incorporates alien wastes."

———

Much as he wanted to discuss matters with the Zimmers, Dev had to respect the older couple's desire for some private time. So when they declined to respond to his entry request, he reluctantly shifted his attention from their quarters to Reed's. While it unquestionably would have been preferable to lay his confusion before the more academically inclined pair, given the choice between ruminating endlessly in his own mind or discussing it with another human being, the choice was straightforward.

Having been supplied by his room with towels of uncertain provenance but excellent thread count, Reed was still drying his head when he granted Dev entry.

"Y'know," the big man said as he turned and walked toward the rear of his quarters, "as much as I'm looking forward to getting home, I'm going to miss a few aspects of this ship." Lowering his free hand, he gestured at the far wall. "Take these synthesize-on-demand pods we have in each room." There was a glint in his eye. "Ask for food, you get food. Ask for clothing, you get clothing. Or towels. Or a knife." The blade he had held at the throat of the A'jeii supervisor lay unsheathed on a shelf. He favored his visitor with a knowing wink. "Don't tell me you haven't wondered what would happen if you asked for a handful of diamonds."

"I haven't." Dev was nothing if not truthful. "But I may, since you just planted the idea." He took a seat in the chamber's single chair. "I did not come to discuss alien synthesizer technology, fascinating as that might be. I came because I am having difficulty resolving the meaning behind unfathomable alien reactions."

Reed tossed the damp towel on the bed, flopped down, and put his hands behind his head. "I don't give a damn about their reactions as long as I'm back in Langley in time for Christmas. But go ahead; what's on your mind?"

"I do not know how much additional detail to provide. You were not there. With me down on Mozehn."

"No, but the account you've already given us was plenty descriptive. So?"

Dev shook his head slowly. "I have thought and thought about it, and I still cannot understand why the Mozehna reacted to me the way they did. For that matter, to this day I still have no idea why Vantolos and the A'jeii thought the Mozehna might react to me at all."

"Wasn't the idea that your strangeness might somehow intimidate them, or frighten them, or otherwise advance the negotiations?"

Dev nodded. "Yes, that was it. But the bigger question remains. *Why* would they think that? I was not armed, and while I am larger than an A'jeii, I am smaller than a Kaijank. I cannot see anything about myself that a representative of a different species would find threatening." He tapped his chest. "What is there about *me* that would give a member of *any* alien species pause?"

Reed made a face. "Nothing that I can see—no offense intended. That's still a question for the A'jeii or the Olone to answer, and it doesn't seem as if they're willing to do so. Everything happened so fast that the Zimmers never got a chance to ask them. You ask the A'jeii again. Now that we're going our separate ways, see if they'll finally tell you what was the real point of including you in the landing party." He chuckled slightly. "We're looking at it from our own perspective. Maybe there's something about our body type, or our eyes, or our smell, that the A'jeii thought would be particularly menacing to the Mozehna."

While the same thoughts had already occurred to Dev, it was good to have them confirmed by a colleague. "If so, you are right: I'm not seeing it. I mean, it is not like the Mozehna have seen humans previously."

Reed's smile vanished. He was dead earnest as he turned on the bed to scrutinize his associate.

"We don't know that, man."

Dev started to smile; halted as soon as he perceived that his colleague was serious. "Come now, Gavin. Surely I was the first human the Mozehna ever set eyes on."

"I repeat: we don't know that. Maybe some time long ago the A'jeii, or some other species we haven't met yet, kidnapped a human or two and carted them around with them. For show, or for that unknown intimidation factor we were just speculating about. Unless the A'jeii or Vantolos or somebody on this ship is willing to discuss that possibility, we can't know that something like that *didn't* happen. It would sure go a long way toward explaining why the Mozehna reacted to your appearance the way you said they did. Or maybe we're talking an extreme case of convergent evolution here. Maybe there's a humanoid species in this part of the cosmos that closely resembles us but has nothing to do with terrestrial evolution."

Dev considered. "If that was the case, I think Vantolos or Syrenii or someone would have told us as much. Because there was no reason not to. Unless," he frowned, "they have a specific reason for keeping such knowledge from us."

"We can speculate 'til the oratorical cows come home." Reed raised himself up on one elbow. "Forget the A'jeii. Why don't we try asking the ship? It provides food, drink, clothing, small weapons, and you got one of the automatons to answer some of your questions once before."

Dev was embarrassed. "Too obvious, I suppose. I am often overlooking the obvious. Of course, we should ask the ship. Want me to do it?"

"No. It's my cabin. It supplied me with a knife. Let's see if it'll supply me with information."

Climbing off the bed, he walked over to the far wall: the one that was spotted with dark-centered, highly responsive pods. There was no need to address his query to any one of them in particular. Most if not all were designed to synthesize and supply commodities. For all the two men knew, it was not any of the pods that responded to requests but the wall itself.

"Ship. We have just visited the world called Mozehn." Reed glanced over at an eager Dev, then continued. "My friend here accompanied a landing party that traveled down to its surface and returned. He has reason to believe that the Mozehna have previously encountered representatives of our species, or if not humans exactly, then other bipeds that look much like us. Can you confirm or deny this?"

"I can confirm it." As always in response to their requests, the synthetic voice that emerged from somewhere within the wall was devoid of emotional modulation.

Dev exhaled sharply. Reed continued.

"Were the bipeds previously encountered by the Mozehna from Earth?"

"No."

"Were they human, like myself and my friend? If so and they did not come from Earth, what world did they come from?"

"They were human. I do not know the name of the world they were from. They were not from your world."

The two men were silent for a long moment before Dev, unable to restrain himself any longer, spoke up. "This is big stuff. Very big stuff. We need to tell the Zimmers." He shook his head in wonder and disbelief. "Humans, but from another world. Panspermia. Convergent evolution. Or something else we cannot even imagine."

Reed was more cautious. "All this is assuming the ship knows exactly what it's talking about. Its parameters for defining 'humans like us' might be way off. But if they're not—if what it just said is accurate—then yeah, big stuff. Wait 'til the folks back home hear *this* one. Who knows? Maybe someday soon we'll get the opportunity to meet our galactic cousins."

Dev was thinking hard. "Maybe that would not be such a good idea."

The big man frowned. "What are you talking about? First, we find out there are other intelligent species out here, now we find out—if this ship's AI is accurate—that there are others like us. Other humans."

Dev was nodding slowly. "Let us assume that to be the case. These other humans are just that: 'other.' They are not from Earth. If they have visited places like Mozehn, it is reasonable to assume that their level of technology is at least equal to that of the A'jeii and the Olone. History has shown that when one technologically superior group of humans encounters one that is measurably more primitive, the primitive peoples invariably lose out. Badly."

Reed's seriousness returned. "You're imposing terrestrial cultural patterns on aliens who we know nothing about. They may be human body types but if they're not from Earth then they're still aliens. You're making socio-cultural assumptions, just like you're assuming their level of technology. We don't know that they possess the equivalents of A'jeii or Olone tech."

"No, we do not. But I think it is reasonable to assume as much. And I also think I know how to find out."

Telling himself that there was no reason why Reed should have to ask all the relevant questions, Dev moved toward the same wall his host was confronting.

"Ship. The A'jeii have told us that you were stolen from your owners. To which species do you rightfully belong?" Beside him he could hear Reed suck in a breath.

As always, the ship's AI responded without hesitation.

"Humans."

Dev nodded slowly at nothing in particular. Certain mysteries were being resolved. Seemingly unconnected concepts were falling into place.

"Humans like those with whom the Mozehn previously had contact?"

"Yes." Very calm and matter-of-fact was the AI.

Dev turned to his colleague. "That clarifies a great deal. The A'jeii, Olone, and Kaijank stole this ship from alien humans. It explains why Syrenii and the rest thought that my presence on Mozehn might help to fast-track their negotiations with the locals: a human arriving on a human-built—or at least a human-owned—ship. It implies that this vessel isn't entirely devoid of offensive capabilities. Otherwise why would the Mozehna find its presence, and mine, potentially threatening?"

Reed grunted. "I'll grant half of that theory. You still don't look very intimidating to me, Dev."

"That is because you know me as one of your own kind. We know nothing of these alien humans. Maybe they are ferocious warmongers ten feet tall."

"You're not ten feet tall," Reed pointed out. "If that's the case, why would the Mozehna think you are one of those who visited their world previously and who, for whatever reason, *did* intimidate them."

Dev shrugged irritably. "So, they're not all ten feet tall. Only those chosen to be warriors, or invaders. Like the A'jeii utilize the Kaijank." He peered hard at the bigger man. "Do we really want to chance encountering such aliens, even if they are human or humanoid, and thereby risk making them aware of the existence of Earth?"

Reed pondered, then finally nodded slowly. "You make good points, Dev. Some of them more than a little unsettling. But it doesn't matter. Such decisions won't be up to us. We're government employees. When we get home, we'll compile and file our reports and add our individual opinions. Then the powers that be can make whatever ultimate decisions have to be made. Me, I'm going to the beach. At least these alien humans, whether they're warmongers or pacifists or whatever, don't know of our existence. We know of theirs, now. Maybe you're right. Maybe it's better to let it stay that way for a while."

"The Zimmers will have their own thoughts on the matter."

"And they'll compose their own reports." Reed was not dissuaded. "We'll be back home and back to our normal, everyday existence. That suits me just fine. I repeat: whatever happens, it won't be up to us."

Reed was wrong—but not for the reasons he imagined.

—X—

t was quiet in the Zimmers' cabin as the four of them shared a meal. Not for the first time, Dev found himself looking up as if to see Diana Pavesi among them, spooning synthesized cereal along with imitation milk. If only she had succeeded in mastering her internal fears and depression a little longer, he told himself. If only she had, perhaps, asked one of them for help, or consultation, or even a swift kick in the logic center, she would still be among them. On her way back to Earth. On her way home.

"Are you all right, Dev?" Katou-Zimmer was eyeing him with her characteristic maternal mix of detachment and concern.

"Fine, fine. I was just thinking of Diana." He bit down on a piece of bread. It tasted, remarkably, just like bread. And why shouldn't it, he told himself, considering how the aliens had taken on corn and wheat and soy in bulk during their brief sojourn at Earth. It even had tiny black seed-like specks embedded within. In regard to taste and content it certainly was a safer bet than, say, ship-synthesized seafood.

"A shame, that." Seated on the bed near his wife, Jakob sipped black tea. The miraculous synthetization technology of the alien ship could duplicate a wide variety of proteins and carbohydrates, but for unknown reasons it had difficulty with common sweeteners. The tea itself, however, was fine. "She was a steadying force."

Dev nodded, took another bite of his mock roll, and glanced toward Reed. The big man was eating standing up, a habit he had acquired while on various unwholesome assignments around the world that had occasionally required him to vacate his location with unseemly urgency.

"What about you, Gavin? What are you going to do when we get home? Besides go to the beach."

Reed deliberated for a moment before looking back and responding. "I've given it a lot of thought. Initially, it didn't seem like a viable notion. But the more consideration I've given to it, the more doable it seems." He let his gaze rove over his companions. "I thought we might take over the world."

Jakob lowered his cup. Katou-Zimmer just stared. Dev smiled at the joke, quickly perceived that Reed was not joking, and tried not to stutter as he responded.

"Considering that as an actual hypothesis, Gavin, I have to regard it as something of an impossibility for four ordinary people."

The big man eased himself away from the wall he had been leaning against. "Not for four ordinary people—and for what it's worth, I don't consider either myself or any of you as 'ordinary'—but for four people who are backed by a patently superior and enormously powerful alien technology."

Katou-Zimmer spoke gently. "Gavin, the aliens in control of this vessel have no interest in our petty terrestrial politics. They have stated as much. All they want is to be rid of us and to be on their way." She glanced at her husband, who nodded in agreement. "They want to leave. The last thing I would expect them to want to do is linger in the vicinity of our solar system with an eye toward helping the four of us do anything. Our interests, whether ordinary or absurd, are not theirs."

The big man was unmoved. "I completely agree."

"Then how, Mr. Reed," Jakob murmured, "can you propose

utilizing their technology and this ship to 'take over the world'? Something of a traditionally juvenile masculine fantasy, I might add. Or do you simply wish to become king?" The initial shock of Reed's declaration behind him, he once more sipped at his tea.

Reed wasn't fazed. "By utilizing the same method the aliens did during our first contacts. Bluff. And I don't need to be king." He grew more animated, now gesticulating with both hands. "See, if one of us tried to get themselves crowned king of the world, or all of us anointed a commissariat of four, there would inevitably be pushback. Despite the perception of overwhelming alien power, some folks would resist. It wouldn't take much. As you've correctly pointed out, the aliens on this ship intend to depart as soon as they've put us back on the ground. I just said 'take over the world' to get your attention."

"In that you have succeeded." Dev spoke while chewing his mystery roll. "Then if your actual goal and your intent is not as announced, what is it?"

Reed lowered his voice. "The aliens are going away, but what if we tell the folks on the ground that they're leaving open the option to come back one day? To restock their stores, or take in a movie, or whatever. And that in their absence they need some folks to look after their interests here. To travel around the planet and make recordings for them or draw up lists of possible supplies they might need in the future. Local people to act as their representatives. People who would need to be assisted in their work, have their harmless efforts facilitated, on penalty of unspecified retribution if said work is not properly carried out." He paused for impact. "People like us."

Katou-Zimmer found herself beaten to a response by Dev. "Even if we were interested in participating in such a deceit, what would be the point? Speaking for myself, I am looking forward to returning to my work."

"Really?" Reed stared hard at his colleague. "Your 'work'? With all that implies? Meeting schedules, racing to make appointments, living on a set government salary, hoping they don't take away your health care or reduce your retirement?

Having to keep your mouth shut while taking directions from people who you know are dumber than you and who only got their jobs through political appointments or family connections?"

Forced to consider his colleague's challenge, Dev cast a surreptitious glance in the direction of the Zimmers and was surprised to see that they were gazing quietly in his direction waiting for him to respond.

"As opposed to what?" he finally said.

"Not being king." Having clearly thought through his scheme, Reed spoke with confidence. "Not being president. Not being appointed rulers of any kind. Just becoming the aliens' official satraps. Empowered to go anywhere and do most anything while simply observing and taking notes." His hands spread wider than his smile. "Free everything! Food, lodging, use of private planes from any airport in the world. We'd be the official alien ambassadors, and everyone would have to facilitate our work. At minimal cost to assorted governments and no cost to us. We'd essentially spend the rest of our lives doing whatever we desired while living on a blank international check."

"Unless," Katou-Zimmer pointed out, "someone finally decided to call the bluff and stick a knife in our respective backs just to see how the no-longer-here aliens would react."

Reed nodded: he'd thought of that, too. "Not an impossibility. Neither is dying the day we return home from slipping and falling in the shower. But why would terrestrial governments chance calling something that might or might not be a bluff when the upside is so cost-effective? A company providing you or me with a private jet could apply to its local government entity for reimbursement. Same for hotels, car dealerships, you name it. I know how government funding works. Not just in the US, but around the planet. In the overall budgetary scheme of things, funding the jet-set lifestyle of four individuals—" he paused to throw the Zimmers a meaningful glance "—two of whom are already elderly, is a pretty easy decision to make. Especially if the downside of not complying is the risk of planetary destruction." He chuckled and crossed his arms. "I mean, if any of you were in a position to make that call, which would you opt for?"

"What if the aliens were to intercede with the truth?" Katou-Zimmer challenged him.

Reed laughed and shook his head. "The aliens won't be around to comment on the bluff, remember? They're leaving! Even if they weren't leaving, I think Vantolos at least would appreciate the effort." His smile faded somewhat. "Syrenii and the rest of the A'jeii, maybe not so much. But like I said, they won't be here. Why should they care anyway?"

"I commend you for the extent of both your ambition and your imagination." Finishing the last of his tea, Jakob set his empty cup aside before offering the big man a fatherly smile. "But though I say this with the best will in the world, I am afraid Chiasa, and I cannot partake of such a ploy."

Reed's expression fell. "Replying with the best will in the world, why the hell not? Are you two looking forward that much to living out the rest of your lives on your university retirement checks and social security payments?"

"It isn't that." Reaching over, Katou-Zimmer took one of her husband's hands in hers. "We can't do it, Gavin, because it isn't right."

"Oh, man." Reed rolled his eyes. "Look: by appointing ourselves 'representatives' of the aliens we're not hurting anybody. As I've explained, the risk is minimal. We're not hurting anybody. Spread across dozens of companies and governments, the cost to provide the four of us with comfortable lifestyles for the rest of our lives is minimal bordering on the non-existent. So I ask you again: what's the harm?"

"Nothing to companies," Jakob admitted. "Nothing to government. The harm is only to our souls."

"Oh, god," Reed muttered tightly.

Katou-Zimmer smiled back at him. "Exactly."

The big man took a deep breath, started to say something, hesitated, and looked over at Dev, who had been quiet for some time. "What about you, Mukherjee? If I remember my mission prep correctly, your take on souls is somewhat different. You in on this?" He nodded in the direction of the Zimmers. "Or are you gonna go all metaphysical on me too?"

Finding himself pinned between the expectant glare of the big man and the more empathetic expressions of the two senior scientists, Dev had nowhere to hide, either physically or morally. So, he replied honestly. It was easier, anyway.

"I do not know. I must confess that I find myself torn. While I like my job more than well enough, I am not so wholly enamored of it that I find the prospect of a life of complete ease entirely unappealing." In response to Katou-Zimmer's frown he added quickly, "At the same time, I am proud of the fact that I have never done anything deliberately deceptive, much less illegal, in my entire life. So—I don't know. I can only say that I will think about it."

Reed threw up his hands. "Great! Here we have the opportunity of a lifetime, potentially the best thing to come out of this whole cockeyed experience, and for partners I've got three saints!" Noting Dev's hesitation, he concluded, "Two and a half, anyway."

"You should drop this, Gavin." Jakob's tone was wholly disapproving. "It's not worthy of what we have experienced. It's not worthy of you."

"Not 'worthy' of me?" Reed scowled at the older man. "What do you know of what's worthy of me? For that matter, what do you really know of me? You ever been shot at, Jakob?" When the scientist failed to reply, Reed nodded knowingly. "I thought not. I have been, multiple times. I could show you some scars, but this isn't school and we're way past show-and-tell. Ever had someone try to run you off a road in Cyprus? India? That's happened to me. Then there was the time this rat-faced little guy tried to poison me in Yekaterinburg. But I'm still here. I've paid my dues. More than paid them. As a dutiful government employee and as a human being. So, excuse my presumption if I do think this opportunity *is* worthy of me. And speaking frankly, even though none of you have had the kinds of experiences that I have, confrontations that nearly resulted in my death on multiple occasions, whether you believe it or not, as a consequence of this journey, the three of you are worthy as well."

Katou-Zimmer's response was softly voiced. "What will you do, Gavin, if we continue to decline to participate in your proposal?"

"What will I ...?" He stopped, discerning her implication. "Yeah, I could do something, I suppose. None of you could stop me. I've killed before. It's part of my job description." A slight shudder ran through Dev even though the big man was not looking in his direction. "But I wouldn't do anything, Chiasa." The grin that creased his face was twisted. "Because despite what you may think, I have a soul. Bluffing to gain an advantage is one thing. Killing to do so is entirely something else." He paused for a moment to eye each of them in turn.

"You're not just my colleagues: you're my friends. I do have boundaries. I do know when and where to draw the line. You're safe from me. I hope you're as safe with your final decisions." Looking back as he spoke, he headed toward the wall that provided an on-demand egress. "I don't know when we'll reach Earth. None of the pods in my cabin will tell me. Best I can get out of the AI is 'soon.' I don't know if that's referencing alien chronology or ours. So hopefully, you all have some time to ponder my proposal. The choice seems pretty clear-cut to me. We go back to our regular jobs and lives, or we take a chance on enjoying a life of luxury. And respect. Especially respect. And nobody gets hurt." His final glance settled on Katou-Zimmer.

"Metaphysics aside, I don't see that option as placing anybody's soul in jeopardy. One thing I do know, though. Like any bluff, this one will have a hell of a lot better chance of succeeding if at least one of you backs me up."

At a sweep of his hand across the wall, the portal appeared. He stepped through and was gone.

Following the big man's exit it was very quiet in the Zimmers' cabin for some moments, until Jakob Zimmer spoke up. "You do what you wish, Dev. We will not judge you. From a practical standpoint, Gavin makes quite a case. Ethically, however …" He shrugged. "This sort of deception is not for Chiasa and myself."

Dev pursed his lips. "Speaking entirely theoretically, do you think Gavin's proposal would have any chance of success?"

Jakob sighed heavily. "I am ashamed to say that he makes a very good argument. Indulging the whims of a quartet of people, two of whom are unlikely to even be around for much longer, would mean nothing to governments and corporations. Only the four of us would know that the rationale for such indulgence has no basis in fact. Or morality."

"But at the same time, the two of you would not expose the bluff if Gavin decides to go ahead with it?"

"Or if you decided to join with him, no. It would not be worth the time or trouble. And Chiasa and I have no time left to expend on trouble." He nodded in the direction of the now closed portal. "Despite what Gavin may think, the two of us are looking forward to returning to our work, and to our studies."

"I don't need a private plane." Katou-Zimmer smiled at Dev. "Only privacy. Peace and quiet and a place to work."

Dev had to repress a laugh. "As the first humans to travel on an alien ship, and to another world, how much privacy do you think you'll be allowed?"

"We will deal with it as best we are able," Jakob told him. "And we will do so with our ethics intact."

Dev nodded understandingly. The Zimmers' response to Reed's proposal made complete sense.

Just not necessarily to him.

———

'Soon,' as Reed had been told, turned out to be comparatively accurate. Scarcely another week had passed when Tilenyii came to their cabins to announce to each of them individually that they were crossing the orbit of Mars and were already decelerating with an eye to shortly entering Earth orbit.

The A'jeii spoke to Dev as the human dressed. The alien had no interest in the larger biped's naked body, what inquisitiveness she might have felt having long since faded as a matter of curiosity. "You will be put down in the same exact location where you last set foot on your world."

Dev struggled to hasten the donning of his pants. It wouldn't do to return from an alien abduction in his underwear. He intended to prepare as best he could for a homecoming such as the world had never seen. Not to mention that he still had not decided how to respond to Gavin Reed's daunting yet undeniably tempting proposition. If he chose to go along, he accepted that the Zimmers would not interfere but were prepared to judge him. He wasn't sure that mattered.

It would matter if his parents knew, he had told himself repeatedly. But unless the Zimmers backtracked on their insistence that they would not give anything away, no one else would know if he decided to support the big man's global-size bluff. Despite a week of near-constant mental struggle, he had yet to come to a decision.

That indecisiveness didn't make him bad, he told himself. It only made him human.

Reed's proposal had left him deeply conflicted. He knew he couldn't keep postponing a determination. Soon they would be arriving in Earth's orbit. The aliens would put them down right back near Houston, from whence they had been extracted, and proceed to wash their hands of them. Every government, every media outlet on the planet would want to talk to them. They would be whisked away to some secure CIA or NSA hideaway where they would be looked after and formally debriefed. Only at the conclusion of the official questioning would they be allowed back out in public, to appear on talk shows and do interviews and, with luck, perhaps be offered lucrative employment or endorsement contracts.

Of course, he told himself, if he chose to go along with Reed's scheme, the latter would prove entirely unnecessary.

The Zimmers were the key to it all. They didn't have to participate in the big man's plan, only ignore it. If anyone queried them as to the truth of what Reed declaimed, they could simply reply that the authorities should talk to him about any arrangements that had been made with the aliens. They didn't have to lie, only omit. Could they be counted on to do so? Dev didn't know. Would it expedite his decision if he could be sure of their reaction? He didn't know that, either. He told himself that he was a good person. A nine-to-five good person, to be sure, but still a good person. He was more enticed by Reed's proposal than he cared to admit.

As it turned out, he was spared the need to choose between temptation and his conscience because the ship they were on never made it to Earth.

———

The section of wall containing his portal hummed softly for attention. Probably Gavin, he told himself as he rose from his bed. Wanting to know if Dev was on board with his plan. Even as he activated the portal to admit the visitor, Dev still had not decided how he was going to answer.

There was no need. It was Tilenyii who was standing outside, not Reed. Dev was more relieved than he cared to admit, even though the arrival of the A'jeii constituted nothing more than a postponement of the decision he still had to make. Had they entered Earth orbit already? If so, he could have accessed a portal in his quarters to reveal the view.

"Come with me." The A'jeii seemed unusually subdued.

Dev frowned. "Have we arrived?" Leaning through the opening, he peered down the corridor. It was empty. "What about the others? Are they on the shuttle already?"

"They are not on the shuttle. They have gathered forward, with the rest of us." Though the A'jeii's short legs were moving rapidly, Dev had no difficulty keeping pace with the shorter stride.

"Gathered? Why forward? Why not at the shuttle?" A horrible, naked thought crossed his mind. "We're still going home, aren't we? To Earth?"

The A'jeii peered up at him out of wide, dark eyes. "To be quite honest, I don't know where you are going. Or any of your companions. Or for that matter, myself and my own colleagues. Nothing is certain any longer. There are no more assurances. Not for you, not for I, not for anyone on this vessel."

Dev swallowed. Something had gone wrong, but what? "What is going on? Why is everyone gathering forward?"

The A'jeii emitted a surprisingly low-pitched whine. "We tried to tell you there was a reason why it was not a good idea to return to this system. That reason has manifested itself."

"I do not understand." They were heading for the vicinity of the bridge, Dev noted with rising unease. "What reason?"

A deeper whine. "The owners of this craft have arrived here. Their intent was to try and track our departure path from this system. By returning, we have spared them the trouble."

Try as he might, Dev couldn't find it in his heart to be sympathetic. The A'jeii had treated him and his companions with indifference, the Olone had treated them with contempt, and the Kaijank with intimidation. Whatever happened to the ship thieves was none of his or his friends' concern.

What was of concern was how the owners of the stolen vessel would view its quartet of human captives. Though he as yet knew nothing of them, he doubted the adroit Reed would be able to bluff them the way the big man had hoped to bluff the leaders of Earth's governments. Surely, he thought, the rightful owners of the ship would sympathize with the primitive captives and return them to their own world, which was so very nearby. Surely, they would not confuse captives with captors. Surely.

He could not tell if the entirety of the alien crew was present in the bridge area, but there were certainly more A'jeii and

Kaijank than he had previously seen in one place. Vantolos was there as well, along with a pair of other Olone. It was the first time Dev could recall seeing the Kaijank unarmed. They stood off to port, their muscular limbs hanging limp at their sides, looking thoroughly depressed behind their half-dome helmets. Dev gave a slight shiver. Anything dominant enough to unsettle them must be formidable indeed.

As Tilenyii had assured him, Dev's companion was also present.

"Was wondering if you were going to join the party." Reed looked unhappy. His splendid planet-girdling bluff, so meticulously thought out and primed, was now so much brain chaff. Useless in the face of an unknown new menace. Ignoring the disconsolate Reed, Dev focused his attention on Katou-Zimmer.

"Everyone is okay? Do we know anything yet about the ship's owners? Do we know anything at all? Tilenyii was not helpful."

She tried her best to sound encouraging. "Only that Syrenii and the rest were ordered to assemble here—and wait. Being part of 'the rest,' we had to come too. Are you all right, Dev? We were starting to worry about you."

"I am fine. I was half asleep when Tilenyii came for me." Raising his gaze, he surveyed the assembled aliens. In the course of his stay aboard the alien craft he had learned enough about their gestures, posture, and expressions to divine that they were at present a sullen lot. "Our hosts do not seem too happy."

"They don't know what is going to happen to them." Jakob Zimmer made a sweeping gesture. "Is there anything else that strikes you about this less-than-joyful gathering?" When Dev didn't reply, the scientist explained. "There are no automatons here. None of the ship's omnipresent ambulatory robotics are present. Can you recall a time outside your cabin when you did not encounter at least one or two?"

Dev thought. "No. No, I cannot. I imagine the owners have immobilized them. Or at least removed them from the equation."

Moments later, an answer of a sort arrived. But it was not like any of the automatons Dev or his companions had encountered previously when wandering the vessel's corridors. At its appearance, a nervous murmur arose from the assembled A'jeii. Vantolos cursed in several wholly unfamiliar languages. Crouching, the Kaijank looked to conceal themselves behind the A'jeii. They failed.

From out of the main corridor a massive machine came toward them, gliding silently atop an invisible force that raised it no more than half a centimeter above the deck. Dev's breath caught in his throat. Reed's hand drifted toward his concealed knife, though what the big man thought he could do against such a mechanized colossus only he and his trainers knew. The Zimmers looked on in silence, hand in hand, waiting.

Slabs of what might have been gray armor encased a metal body whose flanks barely cleared the walls of the corridor. The curved, rounded base was likewise armored. Clusters of small cones pointed forward from the base while larger ones of more elaborate design jutted from the torso. Atop the cube-shape that constituted the bulk of the machine's mass, a squarish head gazed down at them out of thick, horizontal, narrow lenses. Depressions and projections on the head gave the breathtakingly martial device an aspect of barely repressed ferocity.

It halted, the head swiveling slowly as if to take the measure of each of the assembled in turn. When it started forward again, advancing in preternatural silence, it came not toward the waiting Syrenii or any of the other A'jeii. Tiptoeing on their tentacles, Vantolos and his fellow Olone skittered prudently clear of its path.

Reed took a wary step backward while Dev sidled sideways to place himself between the leviathan and the elderly Zimmers. It was an entirely unconscious and instinctive gesture of which his parents would have been unutterably proud.

Halting, the machine inclined its armored skull toward the trio. In a voice that was as smooth as it was synthetic it uttered a string of sounds. What followed was a response as startling as it was unexpected.

"I—can understand it." There was wonder in Jakob Zimmer's voice.

"So can I." Chiasa Katou-Zimmer was shaking her head slowly in amazement. "Not well. Certainly not as clearly as Jakob. Everything sounds slightly different than it should. But it's still comprehensible."

"That's crazy." Reed's fingers tightened around his useless, concealed knife. "You're both gone crazy." Behind the humans, the sudden chatter of the assembled A'jeii suggested that they agreed with the big man.

A still bemused but increasingly relaxed Jakob looked over at him. "Not at all. Some things do not change much, even over very long stretches of time. One never knows what will and what will not." His gaze returned to the bulky war machine looming over them. "It's speaking ancient Hebrew. A revived speaking language but never an extinct one. It says it's a golem, and that we have nothing to fear from it."

"A what?" Still on edge, Reed was unconvinced they had nothing to fear from the hulking device.

"It's an ancient, very ancient, bit of Jewish folklore." His initial apprehension continuing to fade, Zimmer was now eyeing the machine with admiration. "A golem is a figure fashioned from inorganic matter, typically clay, mud, or some other kind of earth, that is brought to life through magic. It would appear that this one is made of sturdier material, though the technology involved in animating it might very well seem like magic to us." He paused a moment, added, "In Hebrew, 'golem' means 'shapeless mass.'" Deliberately, he took a step toward the colossus.

"Mr. Zimmer, I don't think—" Dev moved to intercept him, only to find Katou-Zimmer blocking his path.

"Leave Jakob be. Let's see what he can do. As you know, his knowledge of languages is exceptional. This is one he is familiar with since childhood."

As Dev, Reed, and the gathering of aliens looked on, Jakob Zimmer proceeded to embark on an increasingly fluent dialogue with the automaton. It was some while before he finally turned back to his wife and companions.

"It's quite a story. I was only able to sample a small portion of it. There are many new words and the machine had to speak simply in order for me to understand. But the gist of it is that we are safe now." He glanced toward Syrenii, who was deep in anxious conversation with Tilenyii and several of her other assistants. "If our original hosts were planning some treachery, they will not now be able to instigate it. We are under the protection of the legitimate owners of this vessel."

Having finally released his grip on the haft of his concealed blade, Reed looked up at the machine and nodded once. "*That* is one of the owners of this ship?"

Zimmer smiled. "No. Like the other automatons we have encountered, who have now been placed firmly back under the control of their owners, this one is merely another device. Another tool."

"I see." Advancing cautiously, Dev put out a hand and tentatively ran it over the polished, curving lower portion of the machine. It did not react to the contact. "So our safety is now ensured thanks to the intervention of a bunch of Jewish robots."

"Something like that." Zimmer put a hand on the younger man's shoulder. "We can all relax now."

"You can relax if you want to." Reed continued to regard the golem-machine warily. "Me, I'll relax—maybe—when I'm back home in Langley." He frowned. "Who engineered and built this thing? Where do they come from? Why do they—or at least their machines—speak ancient Hebrew? Hell, are the builders even human? The ship's AI said the owners are, but nothing about the builders."

"As to the language," Zimmer replied, "what I am hearing is a variant of ancient Hebrew that includes numerous untranslatable words, doubtless of recent invention. Many of which I hope to learn. I am sure they are common enough to the civilization that has given rise to this machine. Many are likely to be scientific or astronomical terms. As to your own questions, you can ask them yourself. According to their device, they are here to retake possession of their property, this vessel."

A thought made Dev turn. The A'jeii were still caucusing uneasily. He gestured in the direction of their former captors. "What happens to them? To the A'jeii, the Olone, and the Kaijank who took this ship?"

"You can inquire as to that as well, if the matter is of interest to you. Meanwhile, why not introduce yourself to the golem, here? Its size and appearance masks a genuine curiosity."

Dev made a face. "I do not speak Hebrew, ancient or otherwise."

"Then it is time you learned a little, because it may soon prove very useful." Zimmer turned back to face the machine, whose slitted, inhuman red eyes peered down at him. "Now repeat after me, Dev.

"Shalom ..."

—XI—

The Hebraic automatons flooded onto the ship. Thankfully for Dev and his companions' peace of mind, the horde of mechanicals that seemed to fill every corridor were far smaller than the behemoth they had initially confronted. Most were no bigger than a toaster while the majority could be held easily in a man's palm. They scurried about determinedly, each one engaged in a mission of its own whose ultimate purpose the four humans could only imagine.

It was left to Dev to think to ask the ship what was happening. All it did was refuse to answer. Katou-Zimmer tried also, as did her husband, with the same negative results. No matter how they phrased a query, the ship that had previously been comparatively voluble now declined to answer anything. Was it under orders to ignore their requests? Or had its AI been completely reprogrammed? Dev thought to ask that, too. The answer to every question was always the same.

"I am unable to respond to that inquiry at the present time."

"When will you be able to respond to it?" an exasperated Reed asked. The ship replied promptly, with, "I am unable to respond to that inquiry at the present time."

When Dev and his companions reached the point where the

ship responded to a query about when it would be able to respond to a query by saying it could not respond to that query —at the present time—they gave up. Nor were the A'jeii or Vantolos or any of their former captors forthcoming. They had all retired—or been forcibly retired—to their own quarters.

Unable to find out what was happening, Dev and his companions had returned to their own rooms. Busy with their own tasks, the horde of mechanicals that had boarded the vessel went about their business indifferent to whatever the humans might choose to do. Presently, he lay on his bed in his quarters looking on as two dozen small robots wandered about; poking, prodding, and connecting themselves to pods and apertures he had not even known existed. Some walked on two legs or four, others traveled on tracks, and a few utilized the same unknown, near magical suspension technology that had been displayed by their far larger and more intimidating counterpart. Each was as beautifully machined as a jewel. None of them appeared to be armed or capable of delivering anything more dangerous than a stern pinch.

This was a great relief, because in their inspection and inscrutable modification of his living quarters one of the intruders would occasionally crawl or climb or drift over his recumbent form. Mostly they ignored him, intent on fulfilling their programming. Occasionally one would pause, coming to a stop on the bed or sometimes on his chest, to examine him out of monocular, dual, or multiple lenses, or perhaps to observe him by means other than ocular. At such moments he would fight to remain as motionless as possible. In the course of each brief confrontation he would smile, not knowing if the meaning behind his expression was recognized but seeing no harm in hoping that it was.

Insofar as he could tell, given his less than rudimentary knowledge of alien robotic engineering, there were no organics among their number. Only a bustling bevy of automatons. He could speak English, Hindi, Bengali, Urdu, and some German and French, but the notion that ancient Hebrew might one day prove useful had remained forever outside his purview. Hopefully the Zimmers were having better luck acquiring information from the ship's new mechanical masters. But as Jakob had told him before he and Chiasa had retired to their own cabin, "Just because I can maybe ask them questions doesn't mean I will get any answers. They very likely will respond as uninformatively as the ship."

Where were the builders? a frustrated Dev wondered as he lay pondering. *What* were the builders? Or was the ship now in the possession and under the control of a civilization composed entirely of intelligent machines? He had read plenty of stories that delved into just such a possibility. None of them had provided a roadmap for coping with the reality. Especially when one had to figure into the situation the fact that he and his friends were confronting a bevy of intelligent machines that had acquired a functional knowledge of an ancient human language.

The answers to some of his questions were provided by Jakob Zimmer when the four of them gathered in the Zimmers' quarters for the second of the day's meals. They could, and did, sometimes eat alone, but the time for that had passed. In order to share means of survival, they now had to share knowledge. Unfortunately, it was only Jakob and to a lesser extent Chiasa who had any to share. Reed made clear right away that he had nothing other than his own irritation to contribute.

"They're turning my quarters upside down." Seated in the single chair in the Zimmers' cabin, the big man looked unhappy despite the size of the synthesized sandwich he was masticating. "Going through everything I've managed to accumulate. Stuff I planned to take home with me. A synthetic alien drinking cup will be worth a fortune on Earth no matter what material it's made out of."

Katou-Zimmer eyed him appraisingly. "So, does that mean, Gavin, you've given up any thoughts of bluffing your way into a position of power and endless free lunch?"

He sighed resignedly and took another massive bite of his food. "Honestly? I haven't decided. The A'jeii were going to put us back on the ground near Houston and then disappear into the firmament. Could be that these machines are going to do likewise. If that's the case, then the opportunity for me—for us—to solidify our standing among our fellow simians is still there. But everything's in abeyance, including what I might try to do, until we see what our new Tinkertoy overlords have in mind for us."

"There is one thing we need not worry about," Jakob said. Dev perked up as the older man delicately nibbled on a fake wheat cracker. "I have spoken to several of the devices."

"So, you can still talk to them." Reed sought confirmation. "And they still understand you? You can have a two-way conversation?"

Jakob nodded. "Somewhat, although it is difficult. As I noted earlier, there are many new words whose meaning I do not know but which I try to infer, and others whose meaning has changed over the centuries. In this, mutual understanding is no different from trying to speak old English. There are words I can recognize that now mean something very different from the original. But despite the barriers, I am managing. And, I would hope, becoming more fluent. Or at least more facile."

"What is it we don't need to worry about?" Dev slipped a rolled-up section of faux cheese naan into his mouth.

Zimmer looked over at him. "The devices understand that we are captives on this stolen vessel. Or rather that we *were* captives. That is no longer the case. We are free to move about the ship as we see fit."

Reed glared over his sandwich. "We've always been pretty free to move around the ship. I'm sick of moving around the ship. I want to move around a mall, and a supermarket, and the Baltimore waterfront. What I want to know is: are they going to take us home?"

"Oh yes," Jakob informed him cheerfully. "As soon as they have fully reintegrated the necessary commands and components into this craft's systems, they will be returning us to Earth. In fact, they are very much looking forward to it, since they trace their origin to Earth as well."

Dev nearly swallowed his naan. "That would explain their knowledge of old Hebrew, but not how and why they choose to utilize it as a means of interspecies communication."

Chiasa was toying with a salad, every leaf of which had been synthesized from an extensive menu of organic components. "That's because, according to Jakob, their originators came from Earth. Those originators are not here themselves because the devices sent out to look for and recover this ship are wholly mechanical. But if the golems—excuse me, if the robots—are being truthful, then those who built the vessel we are on, the ship the mechanicals arrived in, and the mechanicals themselves, all owe their existence to a people who dwell far from here." She glanced over at her husband. "Very far indeed."

"I'm still confused." Reed turned to her spouse. "I don't suppose you got any further clarification from the machines?"

"As a matter of fact, I did. The mechanicals were very forth-coming, although it took several attempts to ensure that I was understanding them correctly." Jakob nibbled down the last of his cracker, plucked another from the bowl resting in his lap. "It turns out that we—our species—has known a number of the details from the beginning. We just haven't had the proper perspective with which to interpret something already recorded."

Dev frowned. "Recorded where?"

"In the Bible." Jakob set aside the bowl of synthetic crackers. "Have you ever heard of the Ten Lost Tribes of Israel?"

Dev shook his head to indicate that he had not, but Reed nodded knowingly. "When I was a kid, my grandmother insisted I go to church. That also meant Bible study. So yeah, I've heard of 'em. What's that got to do with the creators of robot golems? Or golem robots."

Zimmer turned thoughtful. "The ten tribes were exiled from their homes by the Assyrians, circa 722 BCE. According to Isaiah 49:9, 'Say to the prisoners go forth'—these are those exiled beyond the Sambatyon River." He leaned toward his younger companions who, though more than a little bemused, were now listening intently. "That information is then followed by this: 'To them that are in darkness, show yourselves.' According to the pair of responsive mechanicals with whom I spoke, that passage refers to a sizable group of the exiles who were hiding from a descending spacecraft." He waved a hand for emphasis. "Forget about those who speculate that Ezekiel's wheel was a spacecraft. These references are much more specific."

Hard as it was to believe any of what the scientist was saying, Dev found himself caught up in the tale. "Let us say that there is something to what you were told."

Zimmer pursed his lips. "What reason would an alien mechanical have to lie? Much less to invent such a tale for a few humans formerly held captive on one of their own vessels."

For the moment, Dev chose to ignore the riposte. "Okay then. History is not filled in and remains full of large gaps. Unlikely as it sounds, let us say for the moment that the mechanicals you were querying were actually relating historical truth or something resembling truth. According to what you were told, a bunch of displaced Israelites were visited by an alien craft." He spread his hands to indicate their surroundings. "What does that have to do with all this? And with the robots themselves? Other than the use of an ancient language, how does it relate"

Zimmer continued. "Isaiah goes on. 'These are those upon whom the cloud descended and covered.' According to the mechanicals, the writer—or in this instance, the reporter—is talking about a number of the exiles being taken aboard the alien ship. Then we get, from Isaiah, 'They shall feed in the ways and *in all the high places their pastures.*' We're being told that not only is this group of exiles going to receive the aliens' knowledge—that's the 'feed in the ways' part—but that they're being taken to new worlds." He let his companions absorb that before adding, "Right about this time there are two tribes that vanish from history altogether, and from records of the ten lost tribes. The tribes were called Reuben and Gad. And one more thing."

"Good thing my grandmother isn't around to hear this,"

Reed murmured. "Where the Bible was concerned, she was pretty big on inerrancy."

Zimmer grinned at him. "That's just it: there's no contradiction here. It all fits together, both biblically and from the standpoint of secular history. As related by the mechanicals, the aliens who spirited away the two tribes came from a place—a world—called Dahf'fiotica. The Jerusalem Talmud Sanhedrin, 10.5 records this by describing the fate of the members of the two missing tribes by declaring, 'These are those who were exiled to —Daphne of Antiochia.'" He paused. "Daphne of Antiochia is plainly as close as the people of the time could come to making sense of the alien name and transliterating to something with which he would have been familiar."

The hush in the cabin was broken only by a methodical crunching sound as Zimmer resumed munching crackers. Fluid counterpoint was eventually added by the sound of Dev swallowing from the tumbler of tea he had brought with him. The silence was understandable. Katou-Zimmer had nothing to add to what her husband had averred while both Dev and Reed were actively trying to digest what they had just heard. In its detail it was fantastical. In its implications it was profound. It was Dev who finally voiced the obvious next question.

"Assuming—and it's one *Naraka* of an assumption—that everything the machines told you is true, what eventually happened to the two tribes that were abducted from Earth? Or rescued, depending on your point of view."

"Oh, they were definitely rescued." Swinging his legs off the far side of the bed, Zimmer walked over to a waiting open pod and deposited his empty cracker bowl in the dark gap. It vanished as soon as his hand was safely clear, on its way to be reprocessed by the ship's extraordinarily efficient recycling system. "Judging by any historic account, the Assyrian exile was a period of considerable hardship and despair for the ten tribes. The Assyrians were not what one would call benign conquerors.

"In contrast, the tribesfolk who were taken offworld were studied by the Dahf'fioticans in order to add to that benevolent species' vast store of knowledge. In return for allowing themselves to be studied, the Reubenites and Gadians were helped to survive and prosper. They learned the aliens' language and adopted what they could of their culture. Most importantly, when the time was right, they were given access to the aliens' technology and expertise. With the galaxy containing a surplus of habitable worlds, something we ourselves have suspected and only begun to realize, the progeny of the two tribes were given a world of their own on which to expand and develop. Like all humans, when provided with proper medical care and a modicum of prosperity, our kind is not averse to having large families." Zimmer sat back down on the bed.

"The result is that the tribes, who began to refer to themselves as the Gadeu, came to successfully exploit, dominate, and spread out across half a dozen star systems. According to the mechanicals, they remain in close contact not only with their liberators and mentors the Dahf'fiotica but with several other sentient, star-traversing species with whom they have subsequently come in contact." He shook his head at the wonder of it all. "We, as humans, have always speculated if there was other intelligent life in the universe. Well, there not only is, but there is apparently quite a lot of it—and some of it is us."

"Then this is not a Dahf'fiotica ship we are on," Dev remarked.

"No." Katou-Zimmer spoke up. "It's a Gadeu craft. Engineered with Dahf'fiotica technology but built by the Gadeu themselves."

"That certainly explains a lot." Reed was still coming to grips with the fact that at least some portion of his childhood Bible school teaching had not been entirely accurate—or alternatively, forthcoming. "How quickly and easily the cabin pods were able to synthesize human food, how well the furniture that's been made for us fits our human forms, and so much more. But if this ship was built by these Gadeu, then where are they?"

Zimmer had an explanation for that, too. "While their population has grown to substantial proportions over the centuries, there's still no reason or need for them to send out manned vessels to track down this one. It is considered more efficient to send out automated search craft to carry out such a task. We have been privileged to experience the confirmation of that for ourselves."

Dev looked disappointed. "Then we are not going to meet them, these Gadeu, in person? Their mechanical servitors are simply going to return us home and depart our system with their recovered property?"

"That is the plan for now." Zimmer tried to sound hopeful. "News of our presence on this ship is being communicated back to their worlds even as we speak. Personally, I find it hard to believe since contact has been re-established that these ancient people won't want to re-engage with the world from which their ancestors were taken. Or rescued."

"Maybe," Reed pointed out, "they still hold a visceral if unreasonable fear of the Assyrians. Knowing as they must how far they themselves have advanced technologically, it wouldn't be unreasonable for them to assume that those who had vanquished their ancestors had also advanced proportionately, albeit without alien help. I'd think they'd at least be wary, if not downright fearful."

The Zimmers exchanged a glance, whereupon Katou-Zimmer nodded. "A very valid observation, Gavin. We will of course be able to put any such apprehension to rest once we are given the opportunity to engage in direct conversation with the Gadeu. We can assure them that they have nothing to fear from their ancestors' tormentors because the Assyrians are no more and have not been a collective threat to anyone for thousands of years, though their own ancestors still exist in the Middle East."

She focused her attention on Reed. "I imagine, Gavin, that all of this new information will finally put to rest any lingering notions you might have about anointing yourself the aliens' satrap on Earth. Since now that contact has been re-established, they will likely soon be appointing actual representatives of their own."

Letting out a huge sigh, the big man leaned back against the wall behind him. "In addition to making me go to church, my grandmother also kept a bucketful of sayings at hand. As poor as we were, one I heard a lot was 'easy come, easy go,' especially when the lottery tickets she bought every week never won big." He shrugged resignedly. "So, I had free rein of Earth for a day, if only in my mind." Suddenly alarmed, he regarded his colleagues. "None of you are going to bring those foolish speculations up when we're officially debriefed, are you?"

Dev laughed. "Do not worry. I imagine every human has had such a wish, or dream, at least once in their life. No one will ever know that you might have come close to having the means to fulfill it."

"Thanks." Reed looked genuinely relieved as he turned to the older couple. Zimmer looked strangely preoccupied, but his wife responded with a gentle laugh.

"Don't give it another thought, Gavin. Your momentary flirting with megalomania is safe with us. As Dev says, it is a common affliction." She adjusted her posture on the bed. "People will in any case be too overwhelmed with improbable facts to spend time pondering the random conjectures of we three returnees. They will have more aliens to deal with, and the reality of what Jakob and I have come to refer to as the Gadeu diaspora." Her eyes shone.

"Think of it! I wish I were young like you two so that I could see everything that is going to happen. Contact with the Gadeu and their technology will change Earth and human society in ways that we cannot begin to imagine."

Her husband's voice sounded as if he were emerging from a deep sleep. "I can do some imagining. I must confess first, however, that the thoughts I have been having are hardly original with me. They have been around for quite a few centuries."

"Please, share them with us," an eager Dev responded. "I would like to know what an experienced, seasoned scholar like yourself views as a possible future for humanity based on what we have experienced and what we have learned."

Zimmer nodded thoughtfully before replying.

"Salvation."

Reed grimaced. "Now you sound like my grandmother. I can see alien technology such as what this ship represents changing the future, but I can't exactly square that with 'salvation.' Who do you think it's going to save?"

"Not 'who' so much as 'what.'" The scientist was warming to his subject. "You should understand, Gavin. We have something significant in common. Your people have been looked down on and persecuted for centuries. The same is true of mine, only in our case the persecution has been unrelenting for millennia. Your people, whether they chose to live there or not, can rely on not one but two continents as a true homeland, in both of which you can move about in relative freedom. Whereas when it comes to regarding a plot of land as a 'true homeland,' mine are restricted to a smidgen of sand and soil not much larger than New Jersey. You could drop the whole nation of Israel into Lake Michigan and it would sink out of sight."

"That's certainly interesting." The shift in subject matter left Dev confused—and suddenly uneasy. "What does it have to do with alien tech and 'salvation'? Are you saying that you think the Gadeu are going to use their technology to somehow ensure the security of the country of Israel?"

Rising from the bed, Zimmer began to pace the floor. "Of course not. We don't even know where the Gadeu are, or if we'll ever even be able to make contact with them. That's a matter for them to decide, and for the future. What I'm saying is that we might be able to make use of their technology to accomplish such a feat right now. Their instrumentalities have regained control of this vessel. Perhaps they might be persuaded to— intervene—on behalf of their builders' ancestors. There exists an inescapable continuity that might usefully be exploited."

Now it was his own spouse who was eyeing him uncertainly. "Jakob, you are talking crazy. Just because you can communicate with these newly arrived machines doesn't mean they will do anything and everything you tell them. They appear to be entirely capable of independent thought and action. Why should they take orders from anyone, especially from a non-Gadeu?"

He smiled tightly. "Chiasa, my love, one cannot expect to have results without experimenting. You may be quite right. I could ask for something and they might very well ignore me utterly." He paused for emphasis. "On the other hand, they might not. Think of the possibilities!" He looked to his right. "Our friend Gavin has already pondered such options. Of course, he was only thinking of himself."

"Hey now …" the big man started to protest.

Zimmer ignored him. "Whereas I am pondering a course of action that would result in the survival of an entire populace and the securing of their homeland for all eternity."

"That is very admirable." Dev was not immune to rational argument. It was the scientist's increasingly strident tone that was troubling him. "How, exactly, would you propose to do this?"

"Since its founding, Israel has been faced with enemies on all sides. Permanently ensuring its safety would mean inducing those who would do it harm to suspend their threats, for all time."

"A lovely notion," his wife agreed. "How do you propose to employ alien technology to do that?"

He turned to his wife. "A demonstration. One should be sufficient. If not, another might be arranged. Something impressive enough to convince the country's most implacable enemies that they would do well to finally agree to an enduring and unbreakable peace."

She was shaking her head regretfully. "Jakob, I have been married to you long enough to know how your mind works. Your thoughts flow like a river whose direction and current I have learned to recognize. You are contemplating making a threat."

"A threat?" Dev was aghast as he stared at the older man. "Utilizing alien technology? Leaving aside for the moment any considerations of morality and rightness, how, and with what?"

He gestured in the direction of the distant bridge. "Remember what the A'jeii told us? This is a transport vessel. It mounts no weapons. There are no giant death rays on board, no containers full of alien nuclear bombs. Are you going to try and bluff Israel's enemies the same way the A'jeii and the Olone thought to bluff the Mozehna?"

Moving closer to her husband, Katou-Zimmer looked hard into his eyes. "And what does it matter anyway, Jakob? You are not from Israel: you are from Connecticut."

His voice was at once affectionate and calm as he replied gently. "My ancestors are—let us say, not from Connecticut. As to why I care—" turning, he nodded toward the silently watching Reed "—ask Gavin. The situation regarding his own ancestors is analogous even if the historical progression is different."

Dev moved closer. "Didn't you hear me, Jakob? There are no serious weapons on this alien ship. If there were, Syrenii or Tilenyii would have alluded to them. So what then? Are you going to ask for airtime when we get back to Houston? To put forth your bluff on international television? What happens when one or two leaders in the Middle East call it out? Won't that make things worse? Assuming, of course, that our own government—you know, the one that rules Connecticut—doesn't forbid you from embarking on such a folly?"

Turning away from his wife, Jakob smiled at him. "You are right, certainly. Our Earthly superiors, from NASA right on through the CIA and the NSA, would not look kindly on such a course of action. Not to mention what the reaction would be among the stratified paper pushers at the Department of State. Therefore, it cannot be a bluff."

"Then how can any threats you conjure have any basis in reality?" Dev was thoroughly exasperated.

"I don't know." The admission was startling. "I'm going to have to query the golems."

Dev gaped at him. Reed started to chuckle. Only Chiasa Katou-Zimmer had ready words for her husband's response.

"That won't achieve anything, Jakob. Either they'll respond negatively, or they'll ignore you. There's no time, anyway. According to the last information they gave us, we'll be arriving in Earth orbit any moment now."

He started toward the wall that contained the portal leading outside. "Then I had best ask my questions right away, while there is still time."

His companions gaped at him as he waved a hand over the wall, opening the portal to the corridor outside.

Katou-Zimmer lowered her voice. "Jakob, don't do this. It is a waste of time anyway."

He smiled back at her. "If your opinion is correct, my love, then it will indeed be a waste of time. But not much of that, and no harm done."

She turned to Reed. "Gavin, stop him!"

The big man shrugged. "Stop him from doing what? Talking to the robots?" He looked to where the scientist stood framed in the open portal. "Like you said, it's a waste of time. And if it's not …" He paused thoughtfully for a moment. "If Jakob comes up with something, well then, it might have other applications."

Her attention shifted to the cabin's remaining occupant. "Devali, can't you say something to him?"

Dev shook his head slowly. "What can I say that you have not already said? If he will not listen to you, why would he listen to me?"

"Perceptive as always. You are a bright young man, Devali Mukherjee." Zimmer stepped out into the corridor. "I should be back soon. As Chiasa says, not much time to waste." The portal closed behind him.

His wife started after him. For a moment, Dev thought that Reed might block her way. But the big man remained where he was, deep in contemplation of other possible futures. That left only Dev to confront her, with nothing more than words.

"Let him go, Chiasa. He is determined to see his crazy through to its end. He will speak to the mechanicals, if they will even listen to what he has to say. They will tell him the same thing that the A'jeii told us: that there are no large weapons on this ship. He will realize that one cannot make such a grandiose threat as he proposes without the means to back it up, as he has already admitted that bluffing will not work." He stepped back from her. "Then he will rejoin us, we will maybe have something to eat, and afterwards each of us can prepare for our repatriation home in our own way." He smiled reassuringly. "You worry overmuch."

She sniffled slightly. It might be, Dev reflected, the first sign of real vulnerability the redoubtable Katou-Zimmer had exhibited since they had been taken from Earth.

"He's my husband. This isn't like him. He's a gentle, compassionate man."

Reed crossed his arms. "I've known some gentle, compassionate men who, when the circumstances warranted, and the situation was right, fell straight into cold-blooded killer mode."

Dev glared back at him. "You are not helping, Gavin." He looked back at Katou-Zimmer. "There is nothing to worry about, Chiasa. He will get this nonsense out of his system and that will be the end of it."

Looking up, she put a hand on his arm and squeezed gently. "Thank you, Dev. Yet again I see why you were given this assignment. You are wise beyond your years."

No, he thought. *Just flexible as the circumstances require.*

She wasn't finished. "Maybe you can do something about it besides console me." She pointed toward the wall that abutted the corridor. "Go after him. Tell him you've joined him only to keep him company, that you're curious to see what will happen when he talks to the golems."

"I *am* curious to see what will happen when he talks to the golems—the robots. But like I already said: if he will not listen to you, why would he listen to …?"

She interrupted before he could finish. "You're not married, Dev. It's one reason why you were selected for this mission. If you were married, you would understand." She sighed. "Sometimes the closer you are to a person, the less likely you are to listen to what they have to say. I know it sounds contradictory, but often that's how life is." She nodded toward the wall. "Go on, go after him. I imagine he's headed toward the bridge, though I suppose he can speak to any of the machines he encounters no matter where he might find them. I suspect they are all in constant communication with one another."

Uncomfortable with the prospect, he turned toward Reed. "Gavin, why don't you go?"

The big man straightened. "First of all, Dev, Chiasa asked you, not me. Second, there are some folks who claim, for who knows what reason, that on occasion I can be something other than tactful." He shook his head. "Can't imagine why they'd think that. Your temperament is better suited for diplomacy than mine and besides, one of the reasons you were assigned to this mission was because you're supposed to have done the greatest amount of research on theoretical alien contact. You're less inclined than I am to shoot at something like a belligerent golem."

"You do not have a gun," Dev pointed out.

"See? Logic and reason." Moving toward the far wall, Reed stroked it to re-open the portal out to the corridor. A quick glance in both directions revealed no movement, either organic or mechanical.

"You are going after Jakob?" Standing in the center of the Zimmers' chambers, Dev was still hopeful.

"Nope. I'm going back to my quarters. I'm going to take a nap. If we're heading straight back down to the surface, I want to be as rested and mentally sharp as possible." He glanced back at Dev. "And if something else is in the offing—I also want to be as rested and mentally sharp as possible." Stepping through the opening, he turned right up the corridor and disappeared.

As he gazed after the big man, Dev felt a hand on his arm. "Go ahead, Dev. Find my husband and try to persuade him to put aside this foolishness. He is a scholar, a scientist, and a researcher. Not some kind of hoary avenger of ancient wrongs. Or contemporary ones."

Still Dev protested. "It does not matter. The ship is *not armed*."

"True—if the A'jeii were telling us the truth. But we don't know about the golems, and we know nothing about any capabilities of the ship *they* arrived on."

He started. "That is true. I had not thought of that."

"Well then, go, go quickly." She pressed his arm reassuringly. "Jakob and I have been married a long time. I know he'll respond to kind, reasoned argument. Especially if it comes from someone other than me."

He nodded. Then he took her hand, gave it a gentle squeeze in return, and reactivated the wall portal that had already closed following Reed's departure. In one respect Chiasa Katou-Zimmer's confidence in him was not misplaced. He already had a pretty good idea what he was going to say to her husband.

What he was wholly unsure of was how Jakob Zimmer might reply.

—XII—

As he made his way along the by-now-familiar route toward the ship's bridge, he had occasion to avoid other entities, but only mechanicals. Some types he recognized from previous encounters as belonging to the vessel's complement. Others that were unfamiliar to him had doubtless recently arrived on the golem ship. The automatons from both vessels mixed freely and without any visible electronic acrimony. This was to be expected, as they shared the same origin. Only recently had those intrinsic to the craft he and his companions were on been diverted from their original assigned duties. All were once again under the control of their builders.

What he did not see as he increased his pace were any organics. No A'jeii, no Olone, and certainly no Kaijank. Perhaps they had been confined to their own living quarters or sequestered (under guard?) in another area of the ship. Though there was no reason for him to be worried about the fate of his former captors he could not keep from doing so. It was his nature. Compassion had been built into him by his upbringing and he could not simply discard it no matter how outlandish the circumstances and his surroundings.

While the absence of the A'jeii and others from the corridors was disconcerting, the emptiness of the multi-story bridge was even more so. The three levels were deserted except for a few mechanicals that scarcely moved. Each individual device had established itself at a particular station. Silent and intent on their tasks, they did not look up at his entrance.

Jakob Zimmer did. Standing before a trio of automatons, the senior scientist looked in Dev's direction as the younger man arrived. Looked, and smiled.

"Dev! I thought you would rest while waiting for me to return and report."

Slowing as he approached, Dev kept a wary eye on the three mechanicals. Two were identical. Composed of a seamless flow of green and gray metal or ceramic, they stood motionless in place. Leaning slightly down and to one side, he saw that they appeared to rest atop a circle of some thin transparent material. Though this glistened with the luster of clear jelly it was plainly composed of something far stronger though just as flexible. Some kind of frictionless plastic or gel, he decided. About halfway up, the cylindrical body began to taper to a conical shape. At the top, a horizontal disc of gleaming red surveyed and appraised its surroundings. Dev thought the device looked appropriately golem-like.

The third member of the mechanical group was the martial behemoth that had originally greeted them after porting over from the second ship. Though Dev felt that Zimmer was standing a little too close to the three machines that virtually surrounded him, he did not remark on what seemed a proximity bordering on the reckless.

On the other hand, he had to admit, if the automatons suddenly decided to turn hostile, there was nowhere to run from them anyway. As tense as he was, indulging in fatalism was a great way to relax.

"Chiasa asked me to come and check on you. She is worried about you."

Zimmer chuckled softly. "Chiasa always worries about me. Has even before we got married. Whether it's when we're hiking, preparing to give lectures, or making coffee, she's always worried."

"'Coffee'?"

"If I'm hiking, I'm liable to fall and break a leg. If I'm preparing to give a lecture, I might forget my notes or some important component of the subject matter—and if I'm making coffee, I could get burned."

Trying not to be too obvious, Dev indicated the alien machines resting nearby. "This is a little different from taking a hike, and these are not coffee makers. What are you finding out with regard to your—to your notion? Are you even able to communicate what it is that you want from them?"

"Oh yes. It's proven to be surprisingly easy." He regarded the trio of devices that formed a gleaming semicircle in front of him with an admiring gaze. "For one thing, just as the mechanicals assigned to this vessel can communicate and exchange information with one another nearly instantaneously, the same is as true of our rescuers. Which means that they, originating as they do from the same civilization, can likewise acquire information from their recently indentured colleagues. Everything that was known to the robots on this ship is now similarly known to the newcomers. Which means that among much else, they can now understand English." Smiling, he gestured at one of the smaller twinned devices. "Go ahead. Try for yourself."

Facing the machine, Dev found himself suddenly and uncharacteristically tongue-tied. "I—I don't have anything to say."

Once again Zimmer laughed softly. "You mentioned making coffee. Ask it for a cup of coffee."

Once, at university, an assistant professor had asked Dev to find the solution to a common problem in physics. Dev had messed it up badly. That was how Zimmer was making him feel now, and he didn't like it.

"I have got a better idea." Shifting his focus from the smaller machine to the giant looming above the others, he stared evenly at the glistening visual receptors. "If you wished to inflict serious damage on the populated world nearby, what weapons would you employ?" He tensed.

Zimmer did not, but there was a new edge in his voice as he reacted. "Dear me, Devali Mukherjee: you are full of surprises. That is a question I have yet to ask." Turning, he addressed the alien colossus. "My companion has posited a hypothesis. Resolve it."

Though Dev half expected the giant to emit a dramatic metallic squeak as it inclined its head toward him, it did so soundlessly. "We possess no weapons capable of inflicting serious damage to the populated world nearby."

Dev rushed onward. "Then even though you came in pursuit of this stolen ship, your own vessel does not mount large destructive ordnance? Your craft is not a warship?"

"The civilization of which we are a part," the golem rumbled, "does not possess or need 'warships' because it does not suffer war to exist. Accessing those records that are available to me, I comprehend it as an outmoded and ancient concept."

Dev let out an internal sigh of relief. A quick sideways glance showed an expressionless Zimmer. Determined to pursue the question to its end, he said, "The Kaijank on board this ship have weapons."

"The Kaijank belong to a more primitive and socially backward culture," the machine explained. "Furthermore, what weapons they wield are incapable of inflicting damage on the scale to which you refer. The vessel that brought us to this cosmic sector is designed for transporting cargo and sentients. It differs from the one we are on now only in having more sophisticated equipment for carrying out similar functions."

Satisfied, Dev turned to his senior colleague. "There! No warships, no planet-busters, no exterminating death rays. You have already admitted that bluffing is a method insufficient to ensure that you achieve the ends you have in mind." He shifted from chastising his older companion to imploring him. "Now won't you come back with me to your quarters? To your wife, who is anxious and waiting?"

"Shortly," Zimmer told him. Dismissing the younger man, the scientist returned his focus to the attentive, patient mechanicals. This time he spoke in ancient Hebrew—or as close an approximation to it as he could manage. While he could not understand a word of it the choice of language did not trouble Dev. Hadn't the machines just admitted they possessed no advanced weaponry? Despite that confession, the ongoing conversation was beginning to make him apprehensive.

Reaching out, he grabbed Zimmer's right arm. "That is enough alien chitchat for now, Jakob. Your wife is waiting."

Zimmer shook free of the younger man's grasp. "Chiasa has sizable reserves of patience. She can wait while I continue to make progress."

A worried frown crossed Dev's brow. "What progress? I thought you said that bluffing would not guarantee the diplomatic ends you wish to achieve."

"I am not talking about bluff." The older man's tone had grown detached, distant. "I am talking about throwing rocks."

Dev blinked. "I'm sorry—rocks?"

"I shouldn't have to explain it someone as well versed in such futuristic speculative scenarios as yourself, Dev." Zimmer's hands began tracing patterns in the air, as if he was conducting an imaginary orchestra—only in this instance, it was very real physics.

"In my conversation with the golems, I have learned that the vessel in which they arrived is very similar in function to the one on which we have been voyaging. That is hardly surprising. By that I mean to say it is designed for transporting cargo and other non-organic materials. The only difference is that it is notably larger. I have been shown images. To efficiently perform its assigned functions, it is equipped with a number of what we would call 'tractor' beams. Directed energy designed to move objects large and small from orbit into its cargo bays. Sometimes very large objects. Such directed energy is capable of shifting the position of inorganic objects many times larger than what can actually fit inside this or that ship." He indicated their surroundings. "While not as capacious, this craft is equipped with similar devices."

Tired and concerned as he was, Dev failed to grasp fully what Zimmer was trying to tell him. "You are going to have the robots throw cargoes of rocks?"

Irritated now, the older man found himself forced to elaborate. "Not cargoes of rocks. Just rocks. To begin, one very large rock. A small asteroid, to be precise."

The hairs on the back of Dev's neck stood up as the amiable, avuncular scholar continued.

"I can't work the exact math, but the golems can. We'll find something of a size and mass suitable to make, if you will pardon the pun, an impression on those on the receiving end."

Dev stared at his colleague. Or rather, at the aged thing that was presently inhabiting the older man's body. Certainly, Zimmer was not acting like the kindly, reflective professorial type Dev had come to know.

"You are speaking of engineering an extraterrestrial impact. Killing thousands, maybe millions of people."

"Nonsense!" Zimmer was properly irate. "It will be a carefully calibrated demonstration. I'll select an appropriately empty place in the general, wider area of conflict. Perhaps somewhere in the middle of the Rub' al Khali or the Dasht-e Lut. Nothing too overwhelming, but sufficient to convince those in the region who have demonstrated inimical intentions toward the state of Israel that it would be in their best interests to conclude permanent treaties of peace between all affected and interested parties. Otherwise," and he shrugged meaningfully, "the second rock will be larger, and differently targeted."

Dev gazed hard at the older man. "You would not actually countenance something like that."

"Of course not. Call it a bluff with some cards revealed. Those on the ground will have no way of judging the actual intentions of those hovering in orbit."

"Do you not think that some will find it suspicious that aliens would intervene in Earthly politics? Not to mention on the side of one particular political entity in favor of others?"

"What does it matter if some do?" Zimmer spread his hands wide. "A rock from space is a rock from space. No one, no government in the region, will have time to analyze motives. They will all move quickly to ensure they do not face imminent annihilation. The reasons for the aliens' actions they will debate later. What matters are the treaties that will result, and finally settling the mess that the Middle East has become."

Dev took a deep breath. "No matter what guarantees the mechanicals give you, no matter how accurate and efficient the sophisticated cargo-handling capabilities they may claim, there is no way you can be absolutely certain some people on the ground will not be killed. Nomads in the deserts, travelers exploring, scientific teams on site: all those and many more could be in your target area. If you do not at least provide minimal warning, lives could be lost."

Zimmer replied without hesitation. "Lives are already being lost to violence in the Middle East. If nothing changes, lives will continue to be lost. It has been so for thousands of years. Now there is a chance, perhaps, to put a stop to it—hopefully without hurting anything except some politicians' egos. You are correct, Dev, that my proposal carries with it no assurances. No absolutes. But considering what might be achieved I feel it is a risk worth taking." His voice steeled. Suddenly he didn't sound quite so professorial. "I feel it is a risk that *must* be taken. If a few lives need be lost today in return for saving thousands tomorrow, I would gladly volunteer myself to be one of them." Turning, he once again faced the three mechanicals.

I am bigger than him, Dev told himself. *I am younger and stronger than him. I can prevent this.*

Before Zimmer could address the golems, Dev rushed the older man.

And promptly found himself flat on his back. Dazed, he blinked as he saw a sympathetic Zimmer peering down at him.

Looking on impassively, the three robots had made no move to intervene.

"Judo is an ancient method of self-defense, Dev. I hope I didn't hurt you." Still stunned, the younger man supine on the deck did not reply. "If you try to interfere again, I am afraid I will have to ask one of our mechanical acquaintances to restrain you. That would extend to having one of them utilize a limb to cover your mouth so that you cannot interfere with the instructions I am preparing to deliver. That would not be fatal, but it could prove uncomfortable."

Carefully—very carefully—Dev sat up, his palms pressing down against the cool surface beneath. "Why should they listen to you anyway?" he said sullenly. "Why not pay attention equally to me, or Gavin? Or your wife?" He'd landed hard and his back throbbed. "I do not know what you just did or how you did it, but I would not try that with Reed."

Zimmer replied as if he was explaining to a child. "There is no need. Unless I am mistaken, Gavin is in his quarters, unaware of anything that is transpiring here. Chiasa is in ours, hopefully relaxing." He nodded toward the nearest of the three mechanicals. "Everything will be arranged and set in motion before either of them is mindful of what is happening. You are as aware as I of the speed at which these craft can travel. If all goes well and my request is acted upon promptly, the necessary physics will be put in motion and a suitable stone set on course before it becomes necessary for me to explain to the others what is taking place."

"Then what?" Reaching up and behind his head, Dev rubbed a particularly sore spot. "I do not know how Gavin will react, but what are you going to tell your wife?"

"I think Gavin will find the upcoming endeavor of more than casual interest. As to my dear Chiasa ..." He shrugged. "Fait accompli. She may agree with my chosen course of action, or she may disagree. It will not affect events that are in motion." Unafraid but cautious, he took a step back as the younger man stood. "It will all work out for the best, Dev. Please do not try to physically impede me again. I truly do not want to hurt you."

"As opposed to those on the ground?" he shot back. "What happens, Jakob, if despite the destruction wrought by your intended bombardment, one or more of the countries in the area of contention continues to defy your seriously misguided attempt to force a general peace? Are you going to have your conscripted golems hurl another demonstration rock? Maybe nearer to a population center?"

For just a moment, the rigorously self-controlled scholar looked as if he might lose his temper. Then his body untensed, his shoulders relaxed, and he smiled sadly at the younger man who was staring angrily back at him.

"No matter what happens, no matter how this venture works out, every effort will be made to minimize any casualties." Turning, he spoke again in ancient Hebrew to the nearest automaton.

Dev took that moment to rise and charge again.

The giant of the mechanical trio did not move to interfere. It was one of the two smaller automatons, the twin of the robot Zimmer was directly addressing, that slid forward to intercept Dev's rush. It did not strike out at him, did not utilize either of its flexible limbs to flail at the would-be assailant. It simply shifted its position, repeatedly and with inhuman speed, to keep between Dev and his objective.

Frustrated and unable to reach Zimmer, Dev whirled and raced down an opposing corridor. Not back toward his quarters. He would never be able to forgive himself if he simply lay on his bed while the apparently unhinged researcher employed alien technology to rain potential destruction on a blameless corner of the Earth. His parents had not raised him to be an inert spectator. While he ran, he had to repeatedly push out of his thoughts any notion that Zimmer's strategy might actually work. No matter how precise the alien machines, any chance, any chance at all that their aim or control or calculation of velocity might be off by even the slightest amount frightened him more than he cared to admit.

He passed one, two, three automatons. Intent on their programming of the moment, they ignored him. He finally slowed only when he encountered an A'jeii. By chance it was Tilenyii. The diminutive alien looked up at him with what Dev chose to believe was a resigned expression.

"You are running. Why? There is no place to run to. If there were, I and my associates would already have run there."

Dev ignored the implication. It was plain that the Gadeu mechanicals did not have to restrain or lock up those who had stolen their ship for the very reason the supervisor had just stated: there was nowhere to flee and no possibility of the now downcast A'jeii, Olone, and Kaijank regaining control. They were free-roaming prisoners on the very ship they had stolen.

He spoke while striving to catch his breath. It made him seem doubly anxious, though it was unlikely the A'jeii would interpret his respiration as indicative of such. "It is the eldest member of our group, Jakob Zimmer. He is consorting with the machines: he can imitate their vocalizations!"

Tilenyii began to show some interest. "That is interesting. Very interesting indeed. He knows the language of the Gadeu?" Dev nodded vigorously. "You say he is able to interact with the ship's intelligence?" Again, Dev nodded. Tilenyii looked thoughtful. "I wonder if he would be interested in a partnership? Not that it is likely he can divert the mechanicals from their programmed task, which is to return this vessel to its owners, but I feel there is no danger in attempting such an exploit." He started to turn away. "I need to consult with Syrenii and the others on this. The possibilities are ..."

"He is not going to enter into a 'partnership' with the A'jeii or anyone else!" Dev made no effort to hide his frustration or mute his impatience. "That is not the sort of being he is. What he is interested in is trying to bring peace to multiple antagonist parties on our world, on Earth."

Momentary hopes dashed, A'jeii's resignation returned. "I see. And you find this an objectionable aim?"

"It is not that." Dev waved at the air between them. "He

intends to do it, to bring this peace he hopes for, not through discussion or debate but by force! He is going to instruct the golem mind, this vessel's artificial intelligence, to locate a suitable asteroid that can be acquired using the ship's cargo-handling equipment. He plans to transmit directives to the surface ordering the belligerent parties to sign on to a permanent peace or else. Then he will have the ship send the asteroid crashing into a supposedly uninhabited corner of the affected region." He paused for breath. "The implication being that if the parties do not agree to quickly settle all their differences, the next asteroid will strike where it will do some real damage."

Tilenyii gestured understandingly. "It sounds like a well-thought-out plan."

Dev took a step toward the small alien and Tilenyii immediately retreated a proportionate distance. "You have to help me stop him! What he intends is too dangerous. No matter how good the math may seem, there are too many variables. The changing weather above the target zone, the composition of the asteroid that is selected, how its internal mass is distributed, small variations in the Earth's gravity in the area of intended impact—there is no guarantee the drop will not be off just enough to kill hundreds, maybe thousands of people."

"All very true," Tilenyii agreed somberly. "None of which is of any interest to me or my brethren. Jakob Zimmer can bring about this peace of which you speak, or he can slaughter the populations of whole cities." Bright alien eyes meet Dev's own. "We have lost that for which we worked so long and carefully. Our fate is sealed. In case you do not remember, I will repeat again: we have no interest in your primitive tribal disputes."

Dev looked around wildly. "There must be somebody—or something—on this ship that cares! Humans are another intelligent species. The A'jeii are an intelligent species. So are the Olone and the Kaijank. Have you no sympathy for the plight of innocents, of others who are not after all so very different from you?"

"None whatsoever," Tilenyii replied unequivocally. "In fact, it is something of a struggle for me just to stand here and listen to you. Only your bulk prevents me from passing around and past you. If it is sympathy that you seek, try speaking with Vantolos."

Dev was taken aback. "Based on our prior interactions I would not think Vantolos would be sympathetic to anybody or anything that did not directly profit him and his kind."

"You begin to understand." Tilenyii moved to go around the human. "Please let me pass. Even that capacity will be denied to me soon enough."

"But," Dev moved to cut him off, "what am I going to do?"

"You do not speak the language of the Gadeu?"

"No. Only Jakob can speak it, and that with difficulty."

Tilenyii considered. "Then I would try to ensure that when you are returned to the surface of your world you seek a place to live on the opposite side of the planet from the one your colleague has singled out for fractional annihilation." So saying, he feinted to his left, and when Dev shifted yet again to block the A'jeii's path, Tilenyii darted around him and was gone.

If he couldn't persuade Tilenyii to help stop Zimmer, Dev realized, surely there was no chance of convincing Syrenii or any of the Olone or Kaijank. Turning, he raced back in the direction of the bridge, not knowing what he would do when he got there. He had already tried physical intervention only to have Zimmer stop him without even having to call on the automatons for help. He could only try anew, as forcefully and as often as he could, no matter how slim the chance of success.

Accompanied by his retinue of mechanicals, Zimmer had moved to a position farther forward on the bridge. The multi-level platforms on either side were occupied solely by softly whirring and humming mechanicals. They ignored Dev's arrival. The older man did not.

"Dev. Come and watch. It is really quite fascinating what one can do with a little knowledge."

Raising his right hand, he traced shapes in the empty space in front of him. A rotating globe appeared beyond his fingers. It was thrice his height and extraordinarily detailed. Moving his hand again, he zoomed in on the image. Twice he had to pause to query one of the three mechanicals surrounding him. When he had finished, he grunted with satisfaction at his handiwork.

Dev drank in the imagery. "I thought you were going to strike in the Rub' al Khali."

Zimmer made a face. "I decided it was too remote a site for an effective demonstration. Too easy for the Saudi government to explain it away as a natural phenomenon, no matter what kind of preceding broadcast I make. Equally easy for antagonistic governments to declare it a Saudi deception. The location I have chosen is just as safe as the al Khali but more visible. The effects will be noted and recorded by too many terrestrial sensors and relative eyewitnesses to be explained away by a lie."

Dev nodded toward the imagery. "Thousands may die."

"I don't think so." Zimmer was adamant as multiple machines hummed around him.

"You are going to put an asteroid down in the middle of the northern half of the Persian Gulf. Yes, there are no populated areas in the immediate target zone, but the resultant tidal wave will overwhelm coastal communities all the way from Kuwait City to Dubai. Everything from small fishing villages to fancy resorts will be drowned. There are no sea cliffs in that region to hold back the water."

Zimmer shook his head. "You don't understand. Do you think I don't know my basic geography? I've chosen a very small asteroid. The machines have run the calculations. There will be some beach erosion and some harbors swamped, but the wave will be too small to do any real damage. It will be just obvious enough to convince the governments in the region that the action is not the result of natural activity."

"And if there are some *dhows* out in that area of the Gulf itself, fishing in the bull's-eye?" Dev persisted. "Or maybe an oil tanker?"

"A big tanker should have no problem riding out the impact unless it's directly underneath. As for possible fishing boats ..."

For the first time since Dev had challenged his intentions, Zimmer looked slightly uncomfortable. It passed quickly. "The demonstration will be carried out with as much concern for life as is possible given the circumstances."

Sensing a possible advantage, Dev pressed the older man. "That is not a sufficient rationalization, and you know it."

"Nevertheless." Once again, the older man offered Dev a deceptively avuncular smile. "Why not return to your quarters, Dev, and let me deal with this? I will certainly inform you and the others of the consequences as they manifest themselves."

"You can manifest everything right now, Jakob."

A surprised Zimmer looked past Dev, who turned to see a solemn Katou-Zimmer striding purposefully toward the two men and the indifferent mechanicals.

"Stop this right now, Jakob Zimmer. This isn't you. World domination isn't your métier."

"No," he admitted softly. "That option, were it available, belongs more properly to Gavin. I seek only a peace that has eluded my people for millennia."

She halted and glanced knowingly over at Dev, then back at her husband. "This isn't the way to do it."

"Still, my dear, it is what is available to me, and I fully intend to make use of it."

She closed the distance further between them. "I can't let you do it, Jakob."

"You can't stop me, Chiasa."

"I can try." She nodded toward his metallic escort. "What are you going to do? Have them keep me from you? More violence? Is that what you've become thanks to a little knowledge of an ancient language?"

Assailed by his wife's words, Zimmer relented. But only slightly. "Chiasa, darling: I have a chance to do something my ancestors could only dream about. I can secure peace for my people's homeland. No one will die. The intimidation factor will be enough to convince all hostile parties to sign an absolute treaty." A slight smile creased his face. "They will do that willingly, believing that if they do not the 'aliens' will obliterate them."

Katou-Zimmer looked sharply at the hulking automaton standing behind her husband. "Is that true, golem? Would you kill thousands of humans if my husband requested that you do so?"

Dev held his breath. Even Zimmer, confident as he was, eyed the mechanical uncertainly.

"In the absence of our builders we are compelled to follow the directives of those who speak in the old way. It is our programming."

Katou-Zimmer slumped. Dev felt defeated. Until the golem continued.

"However, such directives are no longer applicable, as proper representatives of our builders are here."

Zimmer gaped at the expressionless colossus. "What are you talking about? There is only myself and my companions. The A'jeii and their fellow thieves have been suppressed."

"What you say is now only partially true." The synthetic voice was unchanged. "The Gadeu have arrived."

Looking around excitedly, Dev saw only the methodical mechanicals busy at their work elsewhere on the bridge, the trio surrounding Zimmer, and the scholar's riled spouse. The passageways that led to the bridge remained deserted.

Until Gavin Reed appeared, approaching from the far end of the main corridor. Wearing the biggest smile Dev had ever seen the big man flash, he drew near almost jauntily, waving as he walked. And he was not alone.

The much smaller woman striding along beside him looked pissed.

—XIII—

Her unexpectedly long hair was a lustrous black all the way to below her waist, her figure slim, and her features petite down to the slightly upturned nose. Pulled back into a thick double braid, the jet-black strands were secured with a succession of amethystine rings. The blindingly bright white of the single-piece jumpsuit she wore was broken only by a glistening slash of deep purple that ran from her left shoulder down to her right hip. While entirely functional and populated with a number of unknown devices, the belt that cinched her waist was similarly purple. Like miniature horns, gold-toned devices arched up and over both ears. She might have been thirty, or sixty. At a distance it was impossible to tell. Her stride, for such a small woman, suggested command—though of what, Dev as yet had no idea.

She was accompanied by two men. One, equally dark of hair and countenance, stood scarcely a centimeter taller than her while the other was paler and even more massive than Reed. A natural downturn at the corners of his mouth gave him the look of a perpetual frown. Both the ear and the eye on the right side of his face appeared to be artificial. None of the three were smiling. Both men were clad in attire similar to that of the woman advancing between them except that it was colored a dark brown instead of bright white. The sashes across their chests were narrower and bright red. The feet of all three were clad in half-boots that matched their suits. In the absence of laces, zippers, Velcro, or snaps, Dev wondered what kept the fascinating footwear on the visitors' feet.

Though having not the slightest idea what to expect, Dev was still startled by the vividness of their apparel. For some reason he had expected the shadowy originators of the two starships and the highly sophisticated automatons to favor more subdued attire. All three, Dev decided, would look right at home at a Holi celebration. Trying to ignore their grim expressions, he could only hope that their disposition matched the sunniness of their clothing. Gazing at them in surprise and astonishment, he had almost forgotten about Reed.

"Like you to meet some new friends." If possible, the big man's grin grew even wider as he indicated the diminutive woman standing nearby. "This is Nehorai. She's the chief contact officer for the Gadeu ship that's arrived to supervise the recovery and restaffing of the vessel we're on and see it on its way back to its rightful home." He indicated the two men standing close to her. "These guys are her aides: Maacah and Yoab."

As Dev and the Zimmers looked on, Yoab, the one with the build of a wrestler, came forward to mutter something to the three mechanicals. They immediately turned and trundled off toward another corridor. Impulsively, Zimmer shouted something to them in the ancient Hebrew he had been speaking. Maacah responded with a backward glance, a look of irritation, and silence. As for the machines, they continued on their newly assigned path, utterly ignoring the elderly visitor from Earth. With a sigh and a shrug, Zimmer turned back to his companions.

"Well, it was worth a try. I think my idea would have worked." He was looking at his wife as he spoke. "I'm sorry you wouldn't support me, Chiasa. My people have waited millennia for such an opportunity. Now it's gone." Switching his attention to the newcomers, he addressed them as formally as he could manage in an ancient tongue whose consonants tested his throat.

The woman, Nehorai, gestured almost apathetically. "Your grammar is atrocious, old man."

Though it was a toss-up as to which of the former prisoners was more startled, it was Dev who spoke up. "You can speak English?"

"Is that what it's called?" She peered over at Reed. "It's what this Nubian fed us. A language full of contradictions and confusions. He looks nothing like a reed."

"I am sorry if I seem so startled," Dev told her. "You learned English in a matter of minutes?"

The contact officer turned her attention to him. "Nonsense." Reaching up, she tapped the side of her head "Implant allows it. It's necessary for my work. On this recovery mission I have to speak A'jeii, Olone, and Kaijank in addition to several others. Your own language, while philologically chaotic, is simple enough."

She looked around, studying the bridge. While its complement of mechanicals had ceased functioning, Dev suspected the automatons would be back at work as soon as their ongoing reprogramming was completed. Gadeu mechanicals had arrived to retake possession of the stolen ship. Now the Gadeu themselves had come to complete the repatriation.

"We'll have you back on the old homeworld as soon as we can," Maacah told them reassuringly. Relieved as he was by this pledge, Dev was too tired to let out a shout of approval. A bold, bright "Yeah!" from Reed would have to suffice for the both of them. Katou-Zimmer relaxed. It was, finally, over. They were really going home this time.

Except that Jakob Zimmer would not, could not, leave matters well enough alone.

"We know that you also originated from 'the old homeworld.' From Earth. Yet you haven't visited it. At least, not in a fashion that would convince others of your existence."

As she shifted her gaze to stare back at the scholar, Dev took note of how the indirect light glinted off eyes whose deep purple color matched the chromatic slash across her upper body. Visual implants, he mused. Or at least enhancements.

"Actually, we have revisited this system, but rarely and not recently. We have greater interests elsewhere."

Zimmer challenged her. "Greater than maintaining contact with your homeworld? With your long-forgotten kin?"

"The third planet out from this sun is only our homeworld in ancient stories. Suitable for entertaining children." The officer spoke as if referring to a fairy tale. "Having no fond memories of a time of ancient destruction and captivity, why would we want to revisit its source?"

Zimmer drew himself up to his full height. "Because you still have kindred there. Because we are you and you are us."

"We do not regard that as having been so for some time now." Nehorai was unmoved. "We have built our own civilization, far from the strife and wars that our ancestors had to face." She glanced at her companion. "Correct me if I'm wrong, Maacah, but the last time a remote was sent here to scan this world—some time ago it was—it reported back that nothing much had improved since the time of the Removal."

"That is correct." The short Gadeu with the close-set eyes looked sad. "If I remember my studies correctly, it was unchanged. A world of expansion forever plagued by the usual ongoing strife and wars, ongoing and immutable." He looked over at Zimmer, his expression a mixture of kindness and disgust. "Why would we want to partake of that ever again? Why would we want to intrude and by intruding, soil our souls?"

"Because," Zimmer replied forcefully, "you could put a *stop* to it. More specifically, you could ensure that the ancient land of Israel that gave rise to and was the home of your captive ancestors is finally allowed to exist in peace. You could ensure a safe future for the descendants of the other eight tribes. That's what I was trying to do myself when you arrived and reclaimed control of this ship."

"Jakob ..." his wife began warningly.

He looked sharply back at her. "I don't care if they know! I'm proud of what I tried to do. I'd try to do it again if they'd let me." He stopped cold, a sudden thought taking possession of his senses. "*Would* you let me?" he inquired carefully.

Nehorai had been listening to something distant via her cranial implant. Now she blinked and focused once more on the elderly Earthman. "Would we let you do what?"

Starting forward, Chiasa Katou-Zimmer tried to put her arms around her husband. He shook her off, his countenance suddenly eager, the excitement in his voice indisputable.

"I was going to instruct your golems to use one of this ship's cargo controllers to sling a very small asteroid at an uninhabited portion of the region dominated by Israel's enemies. The idea was to convince them that if they didn't make a permanent peace with—your current kin, then the next big rock aimed their way might do some actual significant damage. It was a threat. A threat in the service of a worthwhile end—but never anything more than a threat. I would never, naturally, do such a thing even if I had the power to carry it out." He hesitated a moment. "Is the meaning of the word 'bluff' clear to you?"

Nehorai gazed evenly back at him. "Very clear. It is fortunate that we arrived in time to prevent you from doing any such thing."

Chiasa looked as relieved as Dev felt. But Zimmer wasn't ready to give up on his idea.

"Why? Why not go ahead and try my strategy? Think about it. In the same part of the world your progenitors came from, our people have been persecuted and enslaved and driven from their ancestral homes since your two tribes were spirited away by the Dahf'fiotica. You've been away for thousands of years, your automated visitants notwithstanding. Now chance and circumstance have brought some of you near. You can rectify the situation. Right an ancient wrong. You can *fix* things!"

Turning, Nehorai murmured to Maacah. Dev, of course, could not understand a word they were saying. It was somewhat comforting to see that, strain as he might to understand the conversation, it did not look as if an eager Zimmer was having much better luck. Eventually the Gadeu pair returned their attention to the terrestrials.

"You are right, Jakob Zimmer. We can fix things."

Dev stood stunned while Zimmer's wife slumped visibly. As it developed, their anguish was premature.

"But not in the manner you propose," Nehorai continued.

Zimmer frowned, then brightened. "Foolish of me. You must have at your disposal even more powerful devices than those designed merely to manipulate cargo. Advanced weapons those on Earth can only imagine. Much more effective for the kind of demonstration I'm proposing."

"We are not going to demonstrate any such thing." Having returned behind them so silently than neither Dev nor any of his companions had noticed his arrival, the massive Yoab strove to utilize correct English, a language which until only recently had been unknown to him. "We long ago forswore the use of physical violence to accomplish goals."

"Well," Zimmer snapped back, "you're not going to intimidate Israel's enemies with any other kind of violence."

"We don't intend to." Nehorai gestured at their surroundings. "We're going to request more ships. Larger than any you have seen. Larger than our own. Though we have access to many, the transfer is still likely to require multiple journeys. And of course, preparations will have to be made at the other end. Suitable reception facilities will need to be arranged."

Zimmer's brows drew together. "What are you talking about? What transfer?"

"I think I know." Both Zimmers looked at Dev in surprise. "I know because my own people, at least as far back as my great-grandparents, underwent something similar when India was broken up by the British. Millions of Muslims were shifted to the new state of Pakistan while millions of Hindus and others moved from what is now Pakistan to present-day India." He eyed the aliens who had turned out to be not so very alien after all.

"You are talking about moving the Israelis, and by extension I would imagine any other Jews, to one of your worlds."

"Purely on a voluntary basis." Yoab looked content with the decision that had been reached. "Anyone who wishes to remain behind on the old world is certainly welcome to do so. But in response to the concerns conveyed by *maskil* Zimmer, we do feel an obligation after all this time to offer refuge to any who would seek it. Those who do will undoubtedly find our contemporary society strange and possibly alien, but they will also find things that are familiar. While it is true that a great deal of time has passed, we feel confident they, and certainly their children, will be able to integrate smoothly with Gadeu civilization."

Zimmer sounded tentative. "That doesn't do anything for those who choose to remain behind, on Earth."

"On the contrary," Nehorai countered, "by demonstrating the ability to move so many individuals offworld, the transfer should plant in the minds of those who would do evil that there are forces in the universe that can also create problems for any who might seek to take advantage of the change in population. It is the best we can do, the most we can offer. A new life for those bold enough to grasp it, and safety from any form of persecution."

"What about the aliens who originally took the two tribes off Earth?" Dev pointed out. "And other aliens? You have never had any problems with them? No hostilities?"

She eyed him pityingly. "Why would intelligent species fight among themselves when there is so much more to be gained by cooperating? The galaxy is vast and dark, and sentients dwell far apart. Contact brings relief that one has friends. Loneliness is invalid as an impetus for conflict. The reverse is true."

Dev turned to the older couple. It seemed that, finally, Jakob Zimmer had given up on any thoughts of threatening Israel's neighbors. Instead of his people leaving their enemies in peace they now had the opportunity to simply leave them, period.

"How do you think the Israelis will respond, Jakob?"

The older man (a *maskil*, Maacah had called him) was still struggling to grasp the import of the Gadeu proposal.

"Certainly, many will jump at the offer. After all, most of their own ancestors came to Israel from elsewhere. Europe after the Second World War, the many countries in the Middle East that have made it impossible for Jews to live there, even the United States. Africa, too." A new thought caused him to glance at his wife before turning back to the Gadeu.

"What about non-Jews who are married to Jews? Or adopted children? What proportion of Jewish ancestry does one have to have to qualify for transfer?"

Nehorai looked to her companions before replying. "I would think a quarter or so would be sufficient. Anything less, including conversions whether recent or ancient, will likely have to be decided on an individual basis. We will take all who can qualify. Ambiguous determinations will be left to the Council machines."

Zimmer stared at her. "You'd leave such important resolutions up to computers?"

"Why not?" She seemed surprised. "Leave it to human rabbis and such determinations would take millennia. You do not let your own machines make such decisions?"

Though Dev felt suddenly embarrassed, he answered without hesitation. "No, we do not. While some of us might recognize and support the viability of such a process, the general population would never stand for it."

All three Gadeu looked sympathetic. "That may be the source of many of the old world's troubles," Maacah observed. "You probably need to improve your machines, or yourselves. Or most likely, both."

"It is not like none of us have been trying," Dev replied.

"Meanwhile," Nehorai told him, "you need to return to explain our offer."

"Better to have my companions do so." He indicated the Zimmers. "I am not Jewish, nor am I in any way related to a member of that ethno-religious grouping." He was suddenly downcast. "That means I surely will not qualify to participate in the transfer."

"I am afraid not." There was a hint of genuine empathy in the contact officer's voice.

It wasn't fair, he told himself. Among everyone he knew, among all his friends, no one would have jumped sooner at the opportunity to move to another world, a new world. He was condemned by his ancestry to be left behind while others who had never given a thought to such a glorious prospect would be freely granted the opportunity.

Unless ...

"I will most certainly join with my companions in explaining your proposal." He felt a renewed urgency. "We will convey your offer first to our own government and to the government of Israel, then to the media at large. It will take scarcely a day for your offer to be known all around the planet. I presume you will provide a timeline for when people can expect to emigrate, details on what they can bring with them and what they must leave behind ..."

"I am afraid they will be allowed to bring very little," she informed him.

"... and how you will ultimately determine who can apply and who cannot. As I mentioned, I of course now have to count myself in the latter group." If he was hoping for her to correct him, he was sorely disappointed.

"Then it is settled." Nehorai stepped back. "Until it is time for you to be returned to the surface, which should be relatively soon, you might as well retire to your living quarters and get some rest. I suspect that when you are deposited back on the old world you will have little enough time to sleep."

Even contemporaneous representatives of ancient civilizations, Dev recognized, could be prone to understatement.

—XIV—

Under the command of Yoab, the recovered Gadeu vessel departed on its long way homeward. With its staff of mechanicals once more fully under Gadeu control a large human crew was not required either to manage the ship or keep watch over the thoroughly disgruntled A'jeii, Olone, and Kaijank detainees on board. Confined to quarters, the eclectic multispecies collection of thieves was left to dwell in their own melancholy, resigned to an unhappy fate once they reached the Gad homeworld.

Standing on the bridge marveling at the spectacular view of Earth, Dev spared a thought for their former captors. "What is going to happen to Syrenii and her crew? They did not mean to abduct us. They were just trying to flee pursuit. To get away from you."

With Nehorai busy ensuring that the Gadeu craft entered a harmless terrestrial orbit it was left to the towering Maacah to reply.

"They will be set before a Sanhedrin, which will determine their fate."

Dev made a face. "What is a Sanhedrin?"

"Justice machine. We turned all of our jurisprudence and

legal matters over to them more than a thousand years ago." He turned thoughtful. "The original Sanhedrins were composed of anywhere from twenty-three to seventy-one rabbis who sat and decided legal matters. Once away from Earth and the shackles of tradition, our ancestors quickly determined that getting twenty-three to seventy-one rabbis to agree promptly on anything, much less complex legal matters, constituted more of a barrier to swift justice than the arguments themselves. So the law was down-loaded into intelligent machines not unlike those you encountered on our recovered ship. These devices are periodically updated and streamlined in accordance with the latest thinking on legal matters. Regarding their future and disposition, the A'jeii and their associates will receive a fair and speedy determination. One devoid of human frailties and foibles."

"They did not hurt us. In fact, they made us as comfortable as they could, given the circumstances."

Maacah looked down at him. "I am surprised to hear you defend them. You were taken away from your homeworld against your will. Had we not located the ship you were on, you would likely have spent the rest of your lives dependent on their supposed benevolence, which could have changed at any time."

Dev did not explain that while his companions would have had difficulty dealing with such a fate, he would not have minded it in the least. "I cannot help it. Now that we have been rescued and are about to be returned to our world, I cannot help but feel a bit sorry for Syrenii and Tilenyii and even Vantolos. As for the Kaijank and their motivations, they always struck me as existing in a state of perpetual bewilderment."

The Gadeu nodded once. "Your compassion for other sentients, even though they did not do right by you, does you credit. I am sorry you cannot be among those offered the opportunity to emigrate to one of our worlds, since you so plainly would like to do so."

Dev replied hesitantly. "There is absolutely no chance?"

"Not unless there is Jewish ancestry in your family of which you are unaware. We can gradually accommodate a few millions of Earth's population only. More than that we cannot do. The resources do not exist."

Dev sighed deeply. "I can trace my family back a couple of hundred years. My ancestors never lived farther west than the area around what is now Nagpur." He brightened a little. "Nehorai said something about conversions being decided on an individual basis."

Maacah considered. "Those would, I am certain, have to have taken place before we announce our offer. A spate of last-minute conversions whose sole aim would be to join the emigration would be denied. I am truly sorry." Maacah turned back to his work, leaving Dev to a string of mournful musings.

These lasted until the Gadeu ship arrived in Earth orbit. The reaction to the appearance of another alien ship, one much larger than its predecessor and not preceded by broadcast announcements of its arrival, led to some panic. This abated as soon as Dev and his companions appeared on the world media to explain themselves.

No tickertape parade followed their repatriation at the landing site outside of Houston. No awards for exploration, or bravery, or determination in the face of never-before-imagined odds came their way. They were spirited off to Washington, away from the eyes of the rest of the world, where anything they had learned of value could be extracted prior to being hidden away in the vaults of the NSA.

No such strictures, however, applied to the Gadeu, who promptly took to all available media to announce their offer. Persons of Jewish descendant, whether living in Israel or London or Tierra del Fuego, would be given the chance to emigrate to one of the Gadeu worlds. Emigrating children would be educated by means unique to their new hosts but perfectly applicable to any human child in preparation for taking their rightful place alongside their Gadeu counterparts. Retirees would receive a chance to extend their useful lives via medical technology that made the best of Earth's hospitals look like abattoirs. Those who wished to continue working would be retrained through methods new and accommodating. Artists of all kinds would be given the opportunity to continue practicing their arts; an infusion of outside influences that would find a hearty welcome on all the Gadeu worlds.

As for those who wished to remain in Israel, their safety would be assured by means that could not be imagined but which that tiny country's immediate enemies would do well not to challenge.

It would take time for transportation vessels to be prepared and for them to travel from Gad to Earth. In the interim, people began to prepare for the great migration. Some who had for their entire lives struggled to deny their actual ancestry now rushed to resurrect it. Others, though eligible, showed no interest in the grand offer, preferring to remain on the homeworld no matter how paradisiacal any offworld opportunities might be. Despite the overt generosity of the Gadeu and the reassurances offered by the four returned humans, there were always the suspicious, the skeptical, and the downright disinterested.

But many—very many—opted to accept the offer.

Not just in Israel but descendants of Abraham and Isaac, Sarah and Rebecca all across the planet were faced with the heart-rendingly permanent decision to stay or leave. Many of those who had formed deep friendships or working relationships with those who were not eligible to migrate opted to remain.

One who did wish to go but who was not qualified manifested itself in the person of Dev as he joined others in a conference room at the Pentagon not long after having been returned. Among those he recognized were Michael Corren, a colleague from NASA; Emilio Natase of the European Space Agency; Wang His of the China Space Division, and the lovely but at present dead serious Maria Amotenada, science advisor to the White House. Outnumbering them were an assortment of colonels, generals, and mostly rear admirals. Though Dev had participated in and contributed to many such meetings, it was the first time he felt truly overwhelmed. Not by the number of participants as much as by the topics to be discussed.

As soon as a Colonel Davis formally opened the meeting, Amotenada turned to Dev.

"How can we be sure these descendants of long-absent offspring of Earth have no inimical designs on our present-day world? How do we know they won't come back still promising help, even if only to a certain segment of the population, as a cover for future conquest?"

"Of course," one admiral murmured, "if they're only interested in taking revenge on certain small portions of the population, in a certain limited part of the world …"

As he mentally assembled an appropriate response, Dev found himself wondering, not for the first time, if he really wished to continue identifying as a member of his species. The A'jeii were more subtle, the Olone more direct. There was nothing for it, however. He was stuck with being a human inhabitant of Earth whether he wished to identify as such or not.

"The Gadeu want only to offer a haven to those descendants of the relatives their own ancestors were forced to leave behind. Nothing more."

Looking around the table he could see that a few of the military representatives did not believe him—but the majority did. In the coming days, the suspicious were likely to be won over, although there would always be some who would continue to believe that something sinister lay behind the visitors' efforts.

Wang pressed him. "To reconfirm: the Gadeuans' offer is only for modern-day descendants of the original ten tribes of Israel?"

Dev nodded. "That is what I have been told. DNA and adjunct methods will be used to determine who qualifies. Converts will be accommodated, where possible, on an individual basis."

"Gonna be a lot of converts over the next months, I reckon." Despite being first and foremost a military officer charged with the defense of his country, General Martens' sense of humor reflected his down-home rural Texas upbringing. "Gonna be some busy rabbis hard at work in some strange places."

"Money will not buy anyone an invite offworld." Dev was straightforward in relaying what Maacah and Nahorai had told him. "I was just told that the Gadeu have ways and means of separating the covetous from the sincere. In any event, spouses and children of descendants will be given first priority."

"We'd do the same if a group of people tried to emigrate here," Amotenada remarked.

Interlocking his fingers on the table, Natase leaned forward for a better view of Dev. "How many are these Gadeuans talking about taking?"

"They did not give a final number. From what I gather, insofar as is feasible they will take whoever qualifies who wants to go. Those chosen will have a chance to start a new life on a new world." He looked around the table. "I suspect there may be some difficulties when the full nature of their program is announced. There will be many who will want to go who will not come near to qualifying." His voice lowered. "Myself, for example."

One of the officers frowned at him. "You're not Jewish, Mukherjee. Yet you'd want to go?"

"It is a new world," he replied immediately. "A chance to see another corner of the galaxy, and maybe more. I have dreamed of such a thing all my life. It informed my maturation and led to my choice of career. But you are correct: I do not qualify." He paused a moment before adding, "The fact that the visitors are the descendants of early Jews does not affect the way I feel. I would just as happily go with one of the many non-human species if they would take me. But if I learned one thing from my recent experience it is this: just because some aliens are intelligent does not mean they are either warlike or philanthropists. Why would they take me or anyone else to settle among them if we have nothing to offer them? The situation with regards to the Gadeu is different. They are making room for distant relatives. Myself, alas, I do not have any relatives among the stars."

He looked over at Colonel Davis. "You can rest assured that the Gadeu have no malicious designs on Earth because we have nothing to offer them. They have everything they need on their own worlds. They do not need our water or any of our resources because they are a part of a galactic civilization." His tone hardened slightly. "'Conquering' backward worlds, whatever that means, would gain them nothing." His attention shifted to an admiral who had earlier given voice to hesitation and uncertainty. "With regards to the ongoing situation in the Middle East, the same can be said for any thought of revenge, which they regard as an antique concept that they left behind when they were taken off Earth. Besides, who would they seek revenge against? The Assyrians? Babylonians?"

Wang spoke up again. "Notions of revenge for ancient wrongs aside, what is to prevent them from taking action against those entities in the Middle East that continue to threaten the nation of Israel? Some of which," she added as diplomatically as possible, "are important suppliers of strategic resources to the US."

Dev spread his hands. "Nothing. Except they insist that interminable conflict has nothing to do with them. Those Israelis who want to stay and sustain their country can continue to do so. Those who would prefer to leave for a new life of guaranteed safety and adventure will do so. My own feeling is that a considerable portion of the population of that very small country will opt to take up the offer to emigrate."

"What happens to those who choose to stay behind?" asked another colonel.

"Their safety will be guaranteed by the Gadeu."

The officer leaned forward, his tone intense. "How? By what means? Did you learn anything of their military capability?"

Dev thought carefully before replying. "The Gadeu are part of a galactic civilization whose technology far exceeds ours. If you were running a country in the Middle East, would you want to find out the extent of their military capabilities by inviting a demonstration on your home soil?" He looked around the table.

"Do any of you think the governments of your own countries would wish to do that?"

The only response was silence.

Amotenada cleared her throat. "When is this grand emigration supposed to commence?"

"I was told it will take time to organize the necessary transportation and, more importantly, prepare adequate facilities on the Gadeu worlds to receive and properly integrate the new arrivals. No exact time frame was provided. At a guess, I would say more than a month and less than a year. Transport will be provided for as long as there are those interested in making the voyage." He smiled slightly. "I believe it is to take less than forty days and forty nights."

"And after that?" Natase asked. "After the emigration is concluded?"

"After that?" Dev shrugged. "I have no idea. I hope contact will continue and expand. I would hate to see several million or more humans given the opportunity to migrate offworld never to be heard from again. I would hate to have learned that there are swathes of inhabited worlds out there whose inhabitants will refuse to have anything further to do with us."

"Except for the occasional ship thieves," Wang commented wryly.

Dev had to smile in return. "One never knows who might show up unannounced at an out-of-the-way world like this one. Perhaps if we grow up enough, quit fighting one another and try to rehabilitate those portions of the Earth that we have defiled, civilized species will seek out our company. If not, we will be relegated to isolation through disinterest and indifference. It is a sad thought."

"We'll work it out." Natase looked around the table. "We have to."

The conference continued for the rest of the day, with lunch being brought in so that they did not have to call a formal break. Much of what was debated comprised little more than a recycling of what had initially been discussed. In a month or so the first descendants of the eight tribes that had remained on Earth would begin their journey to new worlds, leaving behind the world of their birth.

As evening began to settle around Washington and the conference finally broke up, Amotenada approached Dev and drew him aside. "The president would like to talk to you. Strictly off the record. For his own edification and interest. It's been a long day and it's late. I was told that we can schedule it for another time if you're too tired."

He thought about what she had just said. About how his parents would react if they knew that the President of the United States wanted to speak, privately, with their son. There was a touch of bitterness in his reply.

"We might as well do it now. Why not? I have plenty of time."

—XV—

Emigration facilities had been set up in the Mojave Desert on the West Coast of the US and in Alabama in the East. Additional Gadeu transports arrived regularly at designated locations in Britain, France, Italy, and Russia. By far the busiest and most active site was in the Negev Desert as large parts of Tel Aviv, Jerusalem, Haifa, and smaller towns and villages began to empty out.

Among the eligible to emigrate, those who chose to remain behind in Israel were largely Orthodox. With their religious beliefs preventing them from working or fighting in the military, they soon found their situation increasingly untenable. As everyone from engineers, sanitation workers, bus drivers, electricians, plumbers, teachers, and other of the more secular elements of Israeli society availed themselves of the Gadeuans' offer, those left behind began to experience a steady degradation of essential services. Though these were increasingly handled by Israeli citizens of Arab descent, there were not nearly enough trained non-Orthodox technicians to compensate for the departed.

The result was that, gradually but inexorably and despite some inevitable disruption, more and more non-Jews were allowed into the country not just to work but to apply for citizenship, with the result that decades of hostility and mutual suspicion were alleviated by the need to keep buses running and toilets functional. While many of the newcomers did not speak Hebrew and many of those who elected not to accept the offer of the Gadeu spoke no Arabic—or Hindi, or Berber, or Turkish— international English served as a perfectly acceptable and functional bridge among the residents of the newly cosmopolitan country.

Apart from the problems caused by the departure of so many tradesfolk, perhaps the biggest loss involved the majority of teachers.

———

"You have room for books?"

Robert Causeway watched as his old friend lovingly selected tomes from the shelves in his office. For decades they had taught together in the same department at the university. Next week Zimmer was leaving. Turning from the shelves, he smiled at Causeway.

"You've seen pictures of their ships. They're quite capacious." Zimmer's gaze lingered on an omnibus volume of *A Guide to the Gulf Kingdom Dialects*, passing over it to choose instead a slimmer and much older leather-bound volume of *Swahili: A History*. Everything, every bit of knowledge that humanity had digitized, would easily accompany the several million emigrants. Examples of actual antiquity would be scarcer. A leather-bound book certainly qualified as the latter.

"Awe-inspiring would be more like it." Trying to find purpose for his nervous fingers, Causeway ended up hiding his hands behind his back. He hardly knew what to say. "I wish you and Chiasa would stay. You have tenure."

Setting the old book he had selected atop a small but growing pile on his desk, Zimmer made sure the stack was balanced so it would not topple to the floor.

"Tenure. What is that? A whole new world beckons. Just

imagine, Bob: embarking on such an adventure, at my age. I accepted my offer as soon as Chiasa received the standard Gadeu exemption for spouses."

Causeway did not try to hide his melancholy. "We'll miss the two of you at faculty get-togethers, parties. Elaine and I will miss our weekend nights out together."

As he chose another book to add to the pile atop the canvas bag on his desk it struck Zimmer that Causeway was struggling to express emotions that had nothing to do with academics. Pausing in his delving, he walked over to put both hands on his colleague's shoulders and look him in the eye.

"The Gadeu have assured me that communication with Earth will continue. The fact that they are, in a sense, repatriating lost brothers and sisters does not mean they intend to ignore the rest of the species. I am told that *out there*, all intelligences welcome the company and friendship of others. Only occasionally do individuals, not entire species, seek to take unfair advantage of others." He smiled anew as he dropped his hands. "Something I had occasion to experience firsthand."

A mystified Causeway shook his head. While the details were by now well and widely known, he still had trouble trying to visualize what his friend had been through. "Accidentally abducted by aliens, then rescued by descendants of your relatives. It's hard to wrap one's mind around it all."

Zimmer turned thoughtful. "There was nothing else we could do. I and my colleagues simply reacted to the situation in which we found ourselves. It's something humans seem to be good at. It helped that our captors were not inherently evil. Just avaricious. I look forward to encountering less acquisitive representatives of their respective races. As well as entirely new species."

"Some of me envies you, Jakob, but the greater part does not. Giving up everything you've known, from friends to home, the scenery, strikes me as more than a bit frightening. You're not frightened? Even a little bit?"

For a second time Zimmer hesitated in his book sorting. "I

226 ALAN DEAN FOSTER

would be insincere if I didn't admit that I've had some hesitation." He laughed softly. "Interestingly, Chiasa has been relentlessly enthusiastic. She can't wait to leave. That's helped me to overcome any reluctance. All she can talk about is starting a life on a new world, yet one that is inhabited and has been developed by other humans."

"Other humans with a single religious and social history?"

Zimmer returned to his book sorting. "Doesn't bother her. Her own family background is largely secular, as is that of many contemporary Gadeu. It's the culture that's interesting to her. Learning. Knowledge. Exploration. That's what's always been important to her." He tapped the spine of a book too large to be chosen. "You can have this one if you want, Robert." A hand waved at shelves that were largely still full. "In fact, you can have all the rest of these. Anything you don't want, donate to the university library book sale."

Causeway's mouth tightened. "Definitely going to miss the both of you."

"Henderson is going too, you know. Ah." Finding and removing a slender antique tome bound in white vellum, Zimmer used it to top off the pile of books: erudite frosting on his literary cake.

Causeway looked surprised. "Henderson? I didn't know he was Jewish."

Zimmer shrugged. "It's been a long time since we had to wear identification. Also Marklin from History and the Goldwaters over in European Lit. I'm not sure about who's been accepted from the Science departments."

Causeway tried to process the names, ended up shaking his head dolefully. "I don't know them. Or anybody over in Science."

"A shame. You won't have the chance, now. Lost opportunities all around." Having filled the bag, he carefully zipped it shut, straining to lift it with one hand. "Was a time when I could have carried this with two fingers. Now ... I look forward to finding out if the Gadeu have a remedy for arthritis. I'll see if I can get 'Beca to carry it to the car for me. She's going, too."

Once again Causeway looked startled. "Rebecca Stone? Your graduate teaching assistant?"

"Yes." Shifting focus, Zimmer embarked on a final, thorough search through his desk, opening drawers and glancing inside before closing them. "Her whole family is going. And possibly her fiancé."

Causeway frowned. "I thought the Gadeuans were only confirming immediate family members for emigration."

His expression suddenly somber, Zimmer looked up from his search. "That is so. To ensure his acceptance, 'Beca and her young man would have to get married. Quickly." His tone turned sad. "I know she likes him. I'm not sure she loves him. Or if he would go, given the opportunity." When he closed the last desk drawer it shut with a soft *whomp*. "Not my problem. Maybe new problems ahead, but glad to leave the old ones behind."

Causeway made a face. "What problems, Jakob? You have tenure at a major university, your publications are well received, you've had three books published, you make money from speeches, you've been happily married for decades. You have enough income, respect, a happy home life—or so you've always assured me—I'd like to have your 'problems.'"

Zimmer considered, then smiled once more at his old friend: one he might see once a year, every two years, or never again. Such contact would be up to the whims and wherewithal of the Gadeu.

"Thirty-two years ago, before you came to this university and not long after I had started teaching here, Chiasa and I went into the city to see a show. I remember it clearly: it was a touring company of *Cats*. We had a wonderful dinner at Nolen's Steak House, went to the show, stayed out afterward in the park to look for meteors, and got home late. While we were out, someone or several someones had used black spray paint to smear swastikas on our front door, garage door, and living room window. There were also accompanying words that I will not repeat here." He paused a moment, remembering.

"That is all going to go away now. Permanently."

Causeway was visibly shocked. "You never told me about that!"

His friend shrugged. "Why? Why share unpleasantness when the world offers up a fresh dose every day?"

"But—surely nothing like that has happened since?"

"No," Zimmer admitted. "Nothing so blatant. Not to Chiasa and me. But it has happened elsewhere. In other communities, in other countries. After next week I never have to worry about it happening to us again." He gazed evenly at his colleague. "Because even if the reality never repeats itself, Robert, the memory and the worry never goes away." He brightened. "Until next week. It's an old fear, an ancient fear, that I, for one, will be glad to be forever rid of."

———

Reed had his feet up and was lying back on the couch in the upstairs den when Parkhurst came in. Two doors, both capable of being remotely operated, had to be passed before visitors were permitted entry. Reed took his own personal security as seriously as that of the people he was assigned to protect.

Half of the most recent group he had been working with were in the process of packing to leave. Not for Norfolk, not for Baltimore: for another world. Reed wished them well. He had no time for long goodbyes, no matter what adventures he had shared with others. Besides, the Wizards were up 87-78 against the Bulls, and there was still a whole quarter to go.

He did Parkhurst the courtesy of muting the play-by-play from the TV mounted on the wall opposite. "You missed the first three quarters. Jermaine had a four-point play you wouldn't believe."

"Sorry. Beer?"

"Under the couch; where else?" Reed made a face. "You know where the fridge is, man."

Parkhurst returned a couple of moments later, open can in hand. Taking a seat in the big chair that flanked the couch at an angle, he joined his colleague in watching the game. Occasionally he would steal a glance in Reed's direction. By the time of the third glance, he could no longer restrain himself.

"So. You're not going?"

Focused on the game, Reed didn't look over at the other man. "No, I'm not going. First of all, I'm not Jewish. Second, I wouldn't go if I was."

Parkhurst grunted. "Easy to say when you're not."

Reed turned on the couch to look over at his friend. "I mean it. Why would I want to go?"

Parkhurst shrugged and slugged. "I dunno. New world, new opportunities, see something of the galaxy outside this planet, interact with sentient aliens: greatest adventure in the history of mankind. Yeah, why would anyone want to be part of that?"

"Look, Parks: I like my job here. Another six years on and I'll have accumulated enough time to enjoy the maximum thirty years' retirement. I'm not married, I'm not attached, girlfriend is a professional and happy with the arrangement. After I retire, I'll be able to go anywhere I want with anyone I want whenever I want."

"So, this is the best of all possible worlds? How can you say that when you don't know any others?"

"Not true." Reed scooped a handful of cashews from a bowl on the nearby coffee table and began crunching them, one by one to make them last. "I've seen pictures of others. The Gadeu provided them. The ones the Zimmers and the rest of their tribe are migrating to are pretty, sure. Inviting, even. But a life there for someone like me would be a totally unknown quantity, if you know what I mean."

"I know part of what you mean," Parkhurst replied perceptively. "You might not be as much of an outlier as you think. I read that about 40,000 Ethiopian Jews are going. You'd blend right in."

"Not culturally I wouldn't. No barbecue, either. No DC spring cherry blossoms, no visits to Disneyworld, no Bahamas diving, no b-ball."

Parkhurst wasn't ready to concede the argument. "If you go, you could pioneer a lot of that. It would be part of your resumé. Did you know that most of the players in the early days of the NBA were Jewish?"

"Yeah, I read that." Reed chuckled. "That's changed. But I'm not giving up my life to go to another world so I can dominate pickup games."

"Who said you would?" Parkhurst grinned. "I've seen you play, remember?"

Reed took a long breath. "It's just not for me, Parks. Even if I could somehow go, I'm happy right here. If I ever feel the need to experience what life's like on another world, I'll go to a relevant movie or pick up a book. Thousands of other worlds in books."

"In books, yes." His friend turned thoughtful. "Me, I'd give anything to qualify to go."

"You?" Reed was genuinely surprised. "You're closer to retirement than I am. You ready to give all that up? For the unknown?"

Parkhurst finished the last of his beer, set the can down on the table. "Funny thing, the unknown. Some folks are afraid of it, some just ignore it, and some of us are drawn to it." He looked over at his colleague. "You're lucky. You don't feel like you're missing anything."

"That's not quite it," Reed replied. "I *know* I'm not missing anything."

"Then you're a lucky man. I've heard it said that the less a man is afflicted with curiosity, the happier he is." He nodded at the screen. "You see that last rebound? Nobody boxing out."

"That's what happens when you go with a small lineup. Gotta box out."

"Bulls by a basket."

"I got you. Loser buys dinner."

"You're on." There was a pause before Parkhurst added, "I wonder if the Gadeuans have chickens."

"I don't know." Reed considered. "The Bible only mentions *people* being taken, but I suppose the Gadeu could've picked up some other supplies while they were here. Another reason to stick around."

Parkhurst made a *tutting* sound. "I'd even forgo my Aunt Leona's smothered chicken if I could go."

"But you can't." Reed was politely remorseless. "So there's no use beating yourself up over it. Besides, we've got escort duty coming up." He smiled. "Italy exodus, this time. Not an alien world and better wine."

Parkhurst smiled back. But his heart wasn't in it, and his dreams were elsewhere.

———

There were departures everywhere as people sold their homes, most of their belongings, packed their bags, and left aboard the enormous Gadeu ships. Despite that, most of the world paid the emigration little notice because more than 80 percent of the Jewish émigrés came from Israel and the United States. While the majority of the ultra-orthodox opted to remain behind, those Israeli and American Jews possessed of a less extreme and more secular bent rushed to take advantage of the Gadeu offer.

In America alone, nearly 10 percent of the college and university teaching staff departed. Special elections had to be called as almost the same number of Senators left. So did several members of the Supreme Court. Worldwide, they were accompanied by a large number of Nobel Prize winners, something like half of all the winners of the Association for Computing Machinery's A.M. Turing Award for computer science, and a significant number of physicists, chemists, and other scientists. International chess competition took a sizable hit. Representatives in every field from engineering to policing were among the travelers. Surprisingly, only about 10 percent of American doctors left. Unsurprisingly, nobody minded much when they were accompanied by an equivalent number of lawyers.

Not just writers, but painters, sculptors, composers, singers, actors, directors, and many others joined their often less-recognized brethren in taking up the Gadeu offer. Many creative people left. Many funny people left.

Civilization would survive the Gadeuan Emigration, but with parts missing. Many of whose significance would not be properly noted until some time had passed.

———

Television had become a dead issue for Dev. He couldn't bear watching load after load of smiling, happy émigrés leaving aboard the most recently arrived Gadeu craft. Though millions remained to be transported to the Gadeu worlds, he was always sure each ship would be the last. Then all would be silence. Until the Gadeu thought it feasible, or worthwhile, to have contact with their homeworld again. The rest of humankind would be left to sit, and squabble, and deplete the planet's resources and devastate its ecology until such time as it finally reduced itself to ashes or the Gadeu or some other curious galactic race thought to drop by and perhaps lend a helping tentacle.

It was not where he wanted to be.

He supposed he'd been lucky. At least he had, however unwillingly and inadvertently, enjoyed the privilege of spending some time in the company of other sentient species. He, alone of his kind, had stood on the surface of another world, albeit for a less than exalted purpose. He had known something of travel among the stars, and advanced artificial intelligence, and what could be done if minds were applied to the common good (even if sometimes it was an illegal common good). Those memories would always be his, where others of a similar mindset could only dream of experiencing such wonders.

He leaned back in his chair, away from the computer. Ever since his return, and that of his companions, there had been an unending succession of requests for interviews. Huge sums had been dangled in front of him if he would only write a book about his experiences. Having finally accepted one such proposal together with the usual ancillary media rights (if only to stanch the mind-numbing flow of offers), he now no longer had to worry about money. Despite his new financial independence, he had kept his job with NASA. Because that was what had always interested him as a child, had driven him as a student and young adult, and continued to inspire him now. You couldn't buy the cosmos—but you could work with it.

Maybe, he kept telling himself, once the transfer of all those of Jewish descent and their relations who wished to emigrate had been accommodated, the Gadeu would decide to make regular visits. Perhaps one day they might even offer travel to those who were scientifically qualified. That possibility, however remote, was enough to keep him ensconced in his NASA job. The hope that someday, one day, he might once again fulfill his unfulfilled lifelong desire to journey among the stars. To meet other intelligent species, to view the landscapes of alien worlds, to study lifeforms that could only be imagined, to …

Bahkvas, he told himself. The Gadeu had come to Earth for a single purpose. Once that had been realized, they would vanish back into the cosmos. Back to their own sane homeworlds. No reason to linger in the vicinity of a crazy place called Earth, even if it had given birth to their beneficently seized ancestors. Earth would find itself alone once more. *He* would be alone once more. Alone with the internet, and his computer, and his friends who didn't understand.

He wished he could be more like Reed. Reed was his friend. They had been through remarkable things together. But they were different people, with different desires and aspirations and goals. They didn't …

There was someone at the door. Another reporter, or another businessman with a pitch for a joint venture, or another crackpot wanting to know when and where the Gadeu, the aliens, were going to start the real invasion: the one for which the Rothschilds had so plainly prepared the way. Leaning forward, he switched to the feed from the building's new security cameras which he had gladly paid to have installed. As soon as he saw the image on his home screen, he sat up straight and nearly tripped over his own feet in his haste to admit the visitor.

He was sweating when the Gadeu entered his condo. It was not unknown for them to visit parts of Earth that had nothing to do with monitoring or organizing the emigration, but it was unusual. Most likely the visit was all business, and his caller had a question or two to ask about the time Dev had spent on the stolen ship. In particular, he received occasional inquiries relating to the activities of the A'jeii or the Olone. In contrast, the actions of the Kaijank did not seem to inspire as much interest. Such inquiries had always reached him via internet connections. Until now.

The man who entered was clad in a singular one-piece suit of dull gray. He wore no head covering. On his feet were what looked to be indestructible black house slippers. The green insignia on his shoulders and chest marked him as hailing from Reuben IV. Several bits of tech were attached to his waist, though in the absence of a belt Dev could not tell what held them in place. His face was round, almost cherubic, and his lips slightly paler than the rest of his skin. His eyes were very dark brown. Had he been dressed in the everyday clothing of a comparable Washingtonian, the slightly balding middle-aged man would have attracted no attention strolling through the National Mall. Onlookers would have taken him for a visitor from somewhere in the Middle East. Or perhaps Detroit.

He extended a hand, having acquired the terrestrial greeting. A slightly numb Dev shook it absently.

"So, you are the one called Devali?" Though heavily accented, as if newly minted, his English was perfectly comprehensible.

Not knowing what else to do, Dev nodded.

The visitor smiled. "I am Cephas. It has taken some time for note of your desire to pass through the necessary channels. I have something for you."

Reaching down, he brushed his right hand over a rectangular pouch fastened to his waist. The top parted and a single small slip of plastic or some similar material emerged, hovered, and flew toward Dev. When he instinctively swatted at it, it dodged, only to relax into his palm when he opened his fingers. Glistening within the otherwise transparent material were incomprehensible symbols. He looked up.

"I cannot read Hebrew."

"If you press it to your forehead," Cephas told him, "the contents will become known to you. But I will explain. You have been granted an exemption. It is a great honor." He almost bowed.

Dev stood bewildered. "What kind of exemption? What kind of honor? I have already explained that I did nothing except what was necessary to survive. And to help my colleagues do the same."

"Nevertheless, you have been granted an exemption. Because it has become known that you wanted one." Again, the warm, avuncular smile. "It is felt that your exemption is a mitzvah." When Dev still looked blank, Cephas explained further. "Today it would be considered a good deed, but it is really a commandment of sorts. Either way, you have it."

Dev felt he understood now, but hardly dared to do so. "You mean—I can go? With the others?"

Cephas nodded. "A mitzvah." For a moment he seemed uncertain. "You want to go, don't you? That is the overriding desire you have expressed, on multiple occasions, to multiple sources?"

A great rush of appreciation flowed through Dev. His parents would be saddened, his friends would express regrets at his departure, but … "That has been my desire my entire life. Since before it was known that travel between other worlds was possible. Since before it was learned that humans are not the only sentient species in the galaxy. It was a desire I could indulge in only in the writings of others and in my own imagination. That I can—go."

"As soon as you are ready," Cephas assured him. "The communication you hold will allow you to board any emigration shuttle at any transport point. You may bring with you the usual personal effects as they have been described to all émigrés. As has been the case with everyone else, all other necessities will be provided for you when you arrive at Reuben IV or Megiddo. Upon your arrival, a suitable occupation will be found for you based on your Earthly profession or you can choose from among those intrinsic to your new home." He turned to leave.

"Wait!"

Cephas halted, turned back. "You have another question? If so, the device I just gave you will allow you to ..."

"No, no, not that kind of question." Dev had to pause for breath. "I am ready. Can I go with you now?"

The Gadeu looked bemused. "Now?" He gestured, taking in their surroundings, the well-furnished condo, the artwork on the walls, the books on the shelves. "Don't you wish to take anything with you? Anything of your past life, of this world?"

Dev smiled. "I have everything I need. I have my dreams."

They left the building together. Devali did not look back.

ABOUT THE AUTHOR

Alan Dean Foster is the author of 140 books, hundreds of pieces of short fiction, essays, columns, reviews, the occasional op-ed for the *New York Times,* and the story for the first *Star Trek* movie. Having visited more than one hundred countries, he is still bemused by the human condition.  He lives with his wife JoAnn and numerous dogs, cats, coyotes, hawks, and a resident family of bobcats in Prescott, Arizona.

IF YOU LIKED ...

IF YOU LIKED *PRODIGALS*, YOU MIGHT ALSO ENJOY:

Typhoon Time
by Ron S. Friedman

The Race for God
by Brian Herbert

Triploidy
by Bill DeSmedt

Caverns
by Kevin O'Donnell, Jr.

OTHER WORDFIRE PRESS TITLES BY ALAN DEAN FOSTER

Mad Amos Malone: The Complete Stories

Madrenga

Oshenerth

The Flavor of Other Worlds

The Taste of Different Dimensions

Our list of other WordFire Press authors and titles is always growing. To find out more and to shop our selection of titles, visit us at:
wordfirepress.com

facebook.com/WordfireIncWordfirePress

twitter.com/WordFirePress

instagram.com/WordFirePress

bookbub.com/profile/4109784512

Printed in Great Britain
by Amazon